LUMILICOS

LUCID SERIES: BOOK 2

Kristy Fairlamb

wool
street
press

For my husband, Joe.

You'll always be my reason.

—1—

M Y DREAMS BROUGHT ME love, and then they stole that love
away. Yet the hope of seeing him once more surfaced in all
its heartbreaking vibrancy.

I drew in a sharp breath; every one of my six hundred and fifty
muscles tensing in unison. He was so beautiful. He always had
been, not that I ever expected that to change. In all the days, weeks,
and months since I'd lost Tyler, I never truly imagined what it
might be like to see him again. But there I stood, diagonally across
the road, a mere twenty metres from the boy who meant the world
to me yet didn't know I existed.

A confusion of emotions – ecstasy, satisfaction, sorrow – raced
through my veins at the sight of him. His hair flicked down his
forehead, shadowing eyes I knew were as dark as night. A lump
formed in my throat; an accumulation of all the things I wanted to
say but couldn't, and all the things we'd been but in truth hadn't.
Not since the moment I'd been ripped from his arms.

He walked on the footpath beside his friends – friends he hadn't
lost to the awkwardness that followed death like a bad scent. His
laughter filled the air, the kind of easy laughter you find so effort-
lessly when you don't have a care in the world. His stride was light,
his load unburdened from loss and responsibility.

School was out for the day, and as the group paused and kids
continued to drift around them, his gaze lifted to mine.

I resisted the urge to smile and wave, to acknowledge how familiar he was to me. So familiar that I knew if I stood in front of him, I'd see the small dimple on his chin and above that the most perfect lips – lips that no longer knew mine. Mine hadn't forgotten his though, they never would.

His eyes bored into mine, reminding me of the first time I'd seen him in the dream at the airport. I'd like to assume the curiosity in his eyes was recognition, but I think it was just a reflection of the glimmer of hope in mine. Something I'd held so tightly to for so long; it was the life raft that had kept me afloat in my sea of pain, too afraid to let go, because if I did I'd sink slowly and heavily to the bottom of the ocean.

*****

SEVEN WEEKS EARLIER...

THE FRONT YARD OF school sat still and empty. A blue hatchback cruised along the road beyond the school's low iron fence. A growing hum of teenagers in the rooms behind me indicated class was almost over. I sat alone at the table, normally occupied by my four friends, but for a few more minutes would be mine, alone.

I slid the crumpled paper from my uniform pocket and unfolded the page to read the words for the thousandth time. The corner fluttered in the gentle breeze, I held my palm flat across the sheet, holding it in place.

Even in my dreams I never imagined that I should find so much love on earth. How that moment shines for me still when I was close to you, with your hand in mine! Those days flew by so quickly, but our separation will fly equally so.

The scrawl underlining the last line had smudged a little since I drew it two days ago, but the meaning remained clear. As vivid as some of Tyler's final words to me. *'You're going to be great.'* Words that carried me through the constant doubt of whether I'd done the right thing.

How do you know if you've made the right choice? I'd battled with the question for two long days. I lost the one person who meant the world to me when I'd brought back to life all those people who didn't. My head knew it was right, but my heart screamed wrong.

I'd never known pain so agonising. How could something unseen feel so physical? I reeled from a beating as if I'd been kicked repeatedly in the guts with a metal-toed boot and stabbed in the heart by a serrated knife; the only thing missing was the blood. He'd been gone for two days and I still couldn't fill my lungs, not with the permanent vice tightened around my chest, making it near impossible to get enough air in.

I grabbed my sketchbook from my bag, immediately desperate to see him. I wouldn't normally bring it to school, but today I couldn't bear to leave it at home. I flipped to the page where the lines of Tyler's face peered up at me, and I wished with more than the stars that I hadn't had to make that decision. I closed my eyes, hesitated, and turned the page reminding me why I had.

Satisfaction seeped through me as I peered at the old lady who'd sat beside me and the man from across the aisle. She'd made it safely home to the people who needed her, and the man, with his weird grin, went on to fulfil the plans he'd been so eager to the last time I saw him. He still gave me the creeps, but even he deserved life. Like each of the three hundred and twenty-seven souls on board, including Tyler's dad.

Tyler might not be here, and I might be missing what felt like half a lung, but I knew what I needed to keep doing. What I was always meant to do. Help others. Bring people back from an early grave when they still had life to live.

I'd had my mope, now I needed to get back to business, to fly.

'Hey, you're better,' Max called as she limped across the grass and plonked herself onto the bench.

I slammed the book shut, sliding the letter between the pages. 'Not really.'

'Why you here then?'

Because I can't sleep anymore. I've tried to find him in my dreams, but he's not there, he's not anywhere, and I'm all alone. Resisting the urge to scream, I shrugged, lowered my gaze, and dropped the book into my bag.

I nodded to her foot. 'You hurt yourself again? What was it this time, landing or run up?'

Max frowned. 'Landing. You were there, remember.' She hesitated, peering at me closely. 'Has your cold affected your memory?'

Blood rushed to my head, the panic at the reminder of all my lost memories inflicting a sudden surge of fear. When did this happen? I hadn't seen much of Max lately, certainly not been to any of her gymnastics comps. I'd been spending all my time with Tyler.

Or at least that's what I remember doing. Without him ever moving to Antil, the reality had clearly been a little different and left me completely in the dark.

I cleared my throat. 'Oh, um, yeah, sorry. I've been a bit vague lately.'

'When are you not vague?' Max huffed and patted the back of my hand.

Three more bodies landed at the table with us.

'Here she is. Sleeping beauty,' Sean said, before peering closer at my face, namely the dark shade of misery under my eyes. 'You look like crap.' Max whacked him on the arm, and I raised my middle finger with anything but a genuine rise of my lips.

'Thanks, jerk.'

'Everything all right?' Amber placed her hand on the table between us.

'Perfectly fine. Just a cold.' *Oh, and my boyfriend, who we all loved, but you don't know anymore, now has no memory of his life with us, and I feel like I'm living on the moon.*

Amber gathered her wayward golden hair into a messy bun. 'Will you still be good to work on Sunday?'

'Sunday?' I hardly ever worked on Sundays.

'The Harvey event, remember.'

'Right, no, yeah. I'll be fine by then.' What choice did I have? If I didn't swim, I'd sink. I'd have to summon up a few smiles between now and then though, because if there was one thing Laurie liked more than anything else when we served her canapes, it was lashings of smiles.

Cal rested his forearm on the table. 'Dad said the bits he's waiting on will definitely be here next week, so make sure you're free the weekend of the eighteenth.'

'Already done.' Amber bit into her biscuit. 'Luce, have you asked Mum?'

I darted my eyes to her, grappling for understanding, as if her eyes would explain the significance of why we needed to keep that weekend free.

My hesitation prompted her to throw me an anchor. 'For the weekend off work so we can go to the lake house.'

In the middle of winter, and miss time on the snow – it was unheard of. I had no idea why, but I had to give an answer.

'I'm not sure. I think so, but I'll double check on Sunday.' 'Cause *apparently* I was working.

'Sorry I said you looked like crap.' Sean spoke softly, and I stared at the genuine apology in his eyes. Sean always did do a good puppy dog impersonation. His light brown skin and dark hair and eyes all added to the effect. 'I just didn't expect you to still look so sick.' Digging a nice hole, too. 'I mean, you weren't answering my texts, and your mum said you were pretty much sleeping twenty-four seven...I figured you were getting good rest.'

'I was, but I need more than rest to cure me from this illness.'

'Are you sure it's an illness and not a cover up?' he asked, lifting the side of his lip.

'What? No, of course not.' My sluggish heart accelerated faster than it had for days. What did he know? How could he know anything?

'Really? I thought 'cause of the last time we talked and since you hadn't answered me yet, well...' *Huh?* I scrunched my brow as he hesitated with his next words. 'I just wondered if this was about me.'

Him? How could anything be about him? Confusion blurred my vision; this was exactly what I'd been expecting. Black voids of unknown. I clenched my hands into fists, directing the fury for my turbulent life at him. 'Sean, this has nothing to do with you,' I seethed. 'Nothing.' Shifting in my seat, I tried to make my way back into the group conversation instead of the cornered one with Sean, where I had no clue what he was talking about.

It didn't work.

'Have you thought about it...at all?' he asked tentatively.

'Yes,' I snapped.

'And?'

Crap. 'And...I need a bit more time.' *To figure out what the hell you're talking about.* I offered him a half-hearted, pathetic excuse for a smile, which must have appeased him because he nodded and moved his attention back to the group.

I wanted to lower my head onto the table, or better yet, run away to Greece. If this was any indication of what I'd missed and what it would take to work out the last four months' worth of new memories, I had my work cut out. Because in order to move forward without tripping, I needed a clear path ahead, and right now I couldn't see for shit.

—2—

DESPERATION HAD ME CLUTCHING onto the only life rope I could think of – social media. My friend's accounts had to have some answers to my blanks from the last four months.

Starting with Max, I scrolled back through all my missing days, but she spent more time talking and sharing about her gymnastics than anything else.

Cal and Sean, too busy with their soccer to care about sharing anything mundane on their social accounts, were about as bad as me. I had a Facebook and Instagram account but rarely used them. I avoided Facebook as much as possible for the danger of coming across news stories I had no desire to see. But, it'd become a seriously useful tool all of a sudden.

Even though Amber's photos needed no filter, she'd filtered the crap out of them on Instagram. I had no idea she shared so many photos; I had hundreds to go through. Her and Cal, Laurie's cupcakes, snow-capped mountains. I scrolled through sunset after sunset, until my thumb paused mid-scroll – the lake house – the photo she'd taken of us from the deck. Cal with an armload of wood for the campfire, his dad strolling up from the shed, and me, Max, and Sean smiling and waving from the grass below. Tyler, who'd been standing beside me in my memory of that moment, had vanished. I squeezed my eyes closed.

But he wasn't gone completely, simply erased from our lives, from my friend's memories – and his – and replaced with a version where his dad's plane hadn't crashed and he'd never moved to Antil Springs.

He was out there though, and if he was like almost every other teenager in the world, he'd have an account somewhere online. Blood rushed to my head as I clicked on the search bar in Facebook and slowly tapped the keys on my laptop.

Tyler Sims.

Enter.

Ignoring all other Tylers on the long line of Tyler Sims in Facebookland, I zeroed in on the fourth face down the list. Tears prickled behind my lids, the mouse trembling below my fingers as I hovered over an image I feared I'd never see again.

It was an old photo, his hair longer than I knew, wet too. With the ocean as his backdrop and a mate on either side of him, happiness seeped from the picture, his smile reaching out and caressing my sadness. This was the life I'd returned him to, the one he deserved. I remembered telling him I'd be okay knowing he'd be going back to something great, but I lied. It hurt like hell. I clicked on the next image, smiling at an even older picture of Tyler on his skateboard, too far away for me to see his face closely, but enough to know he was putting everything into that jump.

I searched his page for more of anything, but he had it locked down more than Alcatraz. I hit the mouse against the tabletop, disappointment trickling through me. I heaved out a groan. Damn it, how many brick walls could one person come up against in a day?

I landed back on my own feed, a place I normally avoided, but since my dreams no longer crippled me with fear, since Tyler gave me the confidence and ability to save people's lives, I had nothing to hold me back.

I scrolled past selfies of girls from school and amusing memes. A silly photo of Jake that his girlfriend Sarah had tagged him in. I paused, scrolled back up. Abby from P.E. had commented on a news article her older sister had shared: *Recent kidnappings linked.* I clicked on the comments.

Abby: *Think you might need to buy a pack of hair dye.*
Liza: *No way. No serial killer gonna make me lose my blond locks*
Nora: *Looks like the media's trying to scare us again.*

I couldn't remember any kidnappings. But that didn't surprise me. And if they're not linked, then Nora could be on to something: a news outlet clutching at the meagre pickings and turning it into a story for clicks.

But if it was right? I shivered. A serial kidnapper. I couldn't think of much worse to dream about, that was the sort of thing nightmares were made of – especially mine. And what else happened to those girls? I didn't want to see that. But I never had a choice in what I saw. If someone needed me, I would always try my best to help. I stopped myself from clicking on the news story for more details though and let out a sigh, exhaustion from the pressure and all that I'd been through in the last few days wearing me out.

I slumped low in my seat, a heavy weight pushing me down. Throwing my head back, I groaned at the ceiling. I turned and caught sight of the golden spine of *Queen Victoria*, the book Tyler had cleverly used to get a message to me after I'd removed him from my life. The vice tightened around my chest. I tried to take a deep breath but came up short.

Was this how Queen Victoria felt when she'd lost Albert, the love of her life? Had the wind been sucked out of her too? But she was Queen; she'd have had to keep her shoulders held high, her grief intact and hidden behind closed doors. I was no queen, and yet I felt the same, unable to share my grief with anyone but the four walls of my room.

I'd never felt so lonely in my life. Not only had I gone back to having no one to share my dreams with, but my loss, unlike the death of a loved one, couldn't be seen by any of my friends. I couldn't tell them I grieved someone I loved more than anything else, that I'd lost the part of me that knew me more than I knew myself.

Queen Victoria expressed her grief by cloaking herself in thick black, reminding herself daily of the death and sadness of her loss. I twisted the dull jet beads around my wrist. The black bracelet I used, just like Queen Victoria, as a reminder of my grief.

But could she really forget even if she wore a spot of colour? Maybe it was so others were reminded of her loss, and it prompted some empathy on their part. *That* I could understand.

Tyler had shown me something wonderful and now I needed to act as if it'd never happened, because he'd never existed to the people in my life. Not a single person would be able to share in my loss. For that to happen, first they had to believe.

I cursed my dreams and my ability to turn them into reality. Why me? I'd saved all those lives, Tyler's dad's in particular, but damn it if I wasn't annoyed that as a result, it had ruined mine. But it wasn't about me, it never had been. I'd been reminded of that brutal fact far too many times.

I turned back to the laptop, straightening in my seat, finally ready to see what I'd done, see the dead hard truth of my ability. I searched for the news story of the plane crash from last year, and with a few clicks everything I'd dreamt laid itself out in blatant summary; the failing equipment due to pilot error, the crash landing at Kona International Airport in Hawaii, the injuries sustained to fifteen of the passengers, and the investigation which ended in the dismissal of Charles Sims, Tyler's dad. I sighed, the heaviness of what I'd put into place three nights ago coming to rest once again on my shoulders.

This meant Tyler's dad hadn't flown since June twelfth last year. Fourteen months ago. He always wanted to move to the snow – would this prompt him into action? I scanned the library, almost as if I might see Tyler waltz in. Could he have already moved here? Maybe he'd been here for months and I had no idea. A smile tugged on my lips, suddenly glad I'd climbed out of bed this morning.

I'd have to keep my eyes peeled. But surely it couldn't be that easy; the idea seemed impossible. I stuck my earphones in, pressed play on 'Hotel' by Kita Alexander, and packed up my gear.

*****

I SAT AMONGST THE rowdy, craziness that comes with any conversation with my friends, a little on edge for any details that'd draw blanks for me. I laughed at one of Cal's jokes, even though inside I screamed. I wished my friends were enough, but like coffee, once you'd savoured the taste you couldn't go back to a coffee-less life without it feeling flat. I desperately wanted to tell them about this wonderful person they'd grown so fond of, what he'd meant to us all – I couldn't.

I could *ask* them about him though. Suss out if he'd moved to Antil. I placed my elbow on the table and leaned forward. 'So uh, I was trying to remember that new kid's name last night?' I stilled, waiting.

'Who?'

I shrugged. 'The brown-haired one?' God, I hoped there actually *was* a new boy with brown-hair or I'd really look like an idiot.

'Cooper?'

'God, that guy's so annoying,' Sean said. 'Thinks he's God's gift to Antil.'

'Nah, that's not him.'

'Who else then? Wasn't he the only new kid this year?' Max glanced around the table to a chorus of agreed murmurs, and my hope untangled from my grip and flew away with a gust of wind.

'Must've been thinking of someone else.'

Amber's blonde hair brushed my shoulder as she turned to me. 'Is everything okay?'

'Huh, oh yeah, perfectly fine.' I dragged the smile to my eyes. Always fine, no other option. 'I'm being paired with someone in Geography, and I couldn't remember his name. I thought he only started this year.'

Amber tilted her head. 'If you're being paired with him, wouldn't the teacher have said his name at some point?'

Crap. Trust Amber to pick up on that. I shook my head. 'Mr Beck just pointed.' I demonstrated with a wave of my arm, fully working my lie. '"Back row, you two", and I'm sitting there thinking great, I don't even know his name.'

'I'm sure it'll come to you,' she said, returning her attention to the group while the expectation clinging to me fell away and crumpled to the ground at my feet.

—3—

I SAT AT THE kitchen bench with a cut-up apple and a mug of peppermint tea. I needed something to help calm me down. My body hummed in agitation from all I'd come up against in the day, especially with what Sean had said. What the hell had he meant? I took a sip of tea, but it wasn't close to strong enough for what I needed.

Jake waltzed into the kitchen, flicked on the kettle and threw the fridge door open. Slammed it shut and spun, glancing around.

He glared at my mug. 'You finish the milk off?'

'It's black. What's got into you?'

'Shit tonne of homework. I'm gonna need a heap of coffee tonight. Think you can shoot a text to Mum?' he said over his shoulder as he rummaged in the pantry for the emergency milk.

'Where's your phone?' I asked, sliding mine from my pocket.

'Upstairs.'

I typed out a quick message and hit send.

'Done.'

'Thanks. You're a champ,' he said, stirring his coffee before grabbing a handful of grapes and leaving the room.

My fingers clenched my phone, heart pounding. *That's it.* How many text messages had I exchanged with my friends in the last few months? My palms grew sweaty, and I opened my messages. Sean. I scrolled all the way back to April, when this all began, when

Tyler entered our lives, but now never had.

Normal. Nothing. Richie's birthday weekend. Wait, what? I read Sean's words again.

Sean: *Can't stop thinking about the weekend*

Why? What did we do? My pulse resonated behind my temple. I swallowed and kept reading.

Me: *Please Sean*
Sean: *Please what? It was great*
Me: *It was, but it shouldn't have happened*
Sean: *Disagree*
Me: *Fine. Agree to disagree*
Sean: *No way. Best part of the weekend, hands down*

Oh God, what was it?! I tightened my jaw.

Me: *That's not the bit I'm arguing*
Sean: *Right then. Good*

I scrolled further down, past Cal's not-so-big accident, which I must've discovered and managed all by myself without Tyler. The thought made me both sad and proud that I had to do it without him, and that I could.

Me: *You ready for tomorrow morning? We leave at 10*
Sean: *All set. Canberra here we come*

Canberra, not Sydney? I checked the dates, eighth of June, same as my memory. And this time he'd agreed to come. So it had been Tyler that kept him from going the first time round? But why didn't we go to Sydney? I scrunched my face up. Because I didn't have Tyler to push me. He'd encouraged me to do it, reassured me I'd be fine if we stuck to a tight schedule, had it all worked out, got the details of Dreadlock Lady from the number plate. If I never went to see them, what had I used to catapult my acceptance of my gift? Maybe it'd only been Cal's accident, or Granny Tess, maybe both. I'd probably never know.

I slid my thumb up the screen, to texts about winter and the usual, *'going up, coming with?'* Nothing out of the ordinary, nothing to give me insight into my missed days. I reached the end and Sean's last message from three days ago, unanswered because I'd been MIA.

Sean: *So about last night, what I said. You don't have to give me an answer right away, if you need more time. I mean, I know you've been taking time since we kissed at the lake, but I can be patient*

What!
We kissed?
I shook my head. I never thought that would happen again. Confusion seeped through me. Without the option of Tyler, would I always be drawn to Sean? That sounded horrible. That without a better alternative, I'd settle? I loved Sean, I always had, always would, but he wasn't the one for me, with or without Tyler as an option. I wanted to shake my other self and shout, 'You know this, you know this'. Although, stalling for nearly five months suggested my other self *did* know this. Sean really had been patient.

I typed out a long, overdue reply. I didn't think I could do it face to face, not when I couldn't remember all our other face-to-face conversations.

Me: *It's a no Sean. A resounding no. You know I love you, but we can't, I can't. Don't try to convince me otherwise, please*

I swallowed hard, hit send, my pulse racing with the fear and panic. It was too harsh, but he did need a clear message; I couldn't have him lingering, hoping. Not when every part of my heart belonged to someone else. But all that aside, I never wanted to hurt Sean – I typed out two important forgotten words.

Me: *I'm sorry*

I really was. I didn't want to think of how painful those few words, to someone who'd been holding out for something else, would feel. I finished the last piece of my apple, placed my plate in the dishwasher, and trampled upstairs to my room as my phone dinged with his reply.

Sean: *Me too*

*****

THE FOLLOWING DAY WENT by in a blur. *I* was the blur. Clueless black spaces of time, no trace of Tyler, and students wearing thoughtless grins as if my heart hadn't been smashed with a sledgehammer.

Sean sat quietly at lunch. I wanted to feel bad for the overwhelming sadness in his eyes, but my own sorrow left little room for his. I lowered my eyes and turned away. At least today no one would question my morbidity; they had an answer, because based on everyone else's sombre mood, they knew about my text to Sean. He would've told Cal, who would've told Amber, who no doubt told Max...and so we all sat in a state of mutual despair. Satisfied with the blues that kept everyone off my case, I put my earphones in my ears and retreated to my place of solace, 'Supercut' by Lorde the only company I needed.

*****

I HADN'T BEEN ABLE to summon the strength for a run since Tyler left. But more than the inability to find the energy, I'd also been afraid of how it would make me feel, how it always made me feel – alive. I knew Tyler wasn't dead, but I didn't want to feel the one thing that reminded me I remained here without him. But with all my pent-up tension fuelling me on, I powered up the hill from home after school.

I ran past the house that Tyler had – but hadn't – lived in while he was here. I pushed my feet up the steep road to the dirt track on the edge of town, the one no one used but me. Fiery rage pulsed within me as I reached the end of the path and climbed through the fence. The cows moo'd their hellos, and I groaned one back of my own. The sodden grass squished under my feet, a usual occurrence in our alpine wonderland during the middle of winter. I dropped myself amongst the thick, moist blades. I didn't give a crap how wet I might end up.

I stared out over the empty hilly farmland, at the tall mountains poking skyward toward the clouds. It felt like an insult sitting here without Tyler, but life continued to slap me in the face with its normality. Here, have your life, the same as always, but not him – no you can't have him – but carry on, all's good. I squeezed my eyes closed. All was *not* fucking good. We'd sat in this spot together so many times, kissing, holding hands and staring up at the mountains, sharing our dreams. Me, my actual night-time ones; he, his life dreams. They had felt so important at the time; but even they'd gone – turned to dust and floated away with the breeze, like everything else around me.

I missed him so much.

'I told you I couldn't do this, Tyler,' I said to the wind, hoping my words might take themselves to him. 'I need you. What made you think I could live without you? Come back to me, my Robin.' The tears that'd threatened since I slammed the door at home fell onto my cheeks. My cries clawed at the back of my throat, searing me from the inside. But the relief of letting them out into the cold despairing air diminished some of the pain.

I stood on wobbly legs and strode down the hill, not an ounce of care for traipsing onto private property. I continued through the tall grass until I'd wandered so far down the other side of the hill, I could no longer see the fence. A big metal sign poked out of the green grass, facing the winding road to the mountains, although if you were driving and saw it you'd probably need binoculars to read it. Why did they bother?

The sign towered a meter over me. I trudged around to its front and gaped at the massive red 'For Sale' plastered across the top. The words 'Prime real estate opportunity', and smaller but equally significant words, 'subdivide' and 'housing market', obscured in front of me. No, no. I couldn't lose this too. This was my land.

I ran around the sign and started back up the hill, desperation in my feet and heartache in my chest. I tripped over a log hidden in the grass and landed with a thud on my hands and feet. My fingers gripped around a rock in the dirt, and I spun to propel it into the back of the sign. I dug at another one and, screaming out a cry of frustration and pain, threw that too. It hit the back of the metal with a satisfying whack.

*****

We relaxed in the grass with our backs against a tree, our feet outstretched in front of us, one ankle over the other. Her hand rested in mine; skin so soft, it made me a different boy just for holding it. I glanced down at her delicate fingers entwined in mine and then up into her eyes – stunning.

—4—

MARIE GREETED US THE same way she did every time we arrived at the lake house, as if she'd been keenly awaiting our arrival for days. My mouth watered at the smell of baking bread as we entered the open plan living area and dumped our bags by the sideboard.

I eventually found out why we had a weekend planned here at this time of year. Harry needed to do repairs and an extension on the back deck; we were the free labour.

Marie gathered me into a one-armed embrace, her other crumb-covered hand high in the air. 'I've been ordered to take extra special care of you, Miss Lucy.'

Damn it, I thought I'd nailed my perfectly fine impression. What did I need to do to make everyone ignore me and carry on? I screwed up my nose. 'By who?'

'Cal, and your mum of course.' She squeezed my shoulder with a wink. Yes, my mum, of course. Anything short of perfectly healthy always got her attention. I thought I'd hid it well, but maybe no one had brought my 'cold' story as easily as I'd hoped. Perhaps Ollie, but who could tell; his disinterest was more likely fourteen-year-old indifference. But the rest of them, my friends? And Mum; her scrutinizing eyes, watching, waiting for me to trip up.

'Right. Thanks.'

Marie disappeared into the kitchen and left me standing in

the corner of the room as the merriment of our arrival continued around me. Cal jumped on Sean's back and they giddy-upped out to the rear deck, Amber's laughter trailing them. Billy Bob scurried in through the opened doors and I squatted, scratching him behind his ears.

'Hey boy, I'm happy to see you too.' His waggling tail whacked me in the leg, and I grinned, appreciation flooding through me at the reprieve from my sadness, because since Tyler had gone, the moments I didn't feel it were fleeting. Would I ever feel normal again? How could I, when he'd taken half my soul when he left? But I mustn't forget what he left behind, what he'd given me.

Love.

The power to save people's lives.

And he gave me wings.

I might've been struggling to breathe, but I'd been so ready to fly, prepared to take what he'd given me and do my goddamn best without him.

But how do you fly when you're trying not to drown?

Still, in the nine days gone, I'd managed to save more lives gone too soon: a young father in a motorbike accident, and a middle-aged man on a fishing trip gone wrong. If one thing helped me forget my own problems, it was investing everything into someone else's.

And Billy Bob, he helped too. He stayed for one last scratch before trotting away with his tail in the air.

An hour later I sat sideways on the couch, my feet propped on a cushion being elbowed by Sean as he played FIFA with Cal. Amber had curled up in the armchair by the back windows reading, a creamy peach cardigan flowing over her knees. I couldn't see Max. I stared out the tall glass doors to the lake, my eyes drawn toward the still waters and the memories they held.

The background noises filtered away and my attention shifted to the image coming to life on my page – Tyler. I was drawing his arms today – his solid, sculpted forearms. Arms that'd caught me totally off guard that first day, over five months ago, casually and perfectly resting on the lunch table. It'd be the first of many times he'd do that to me.

'Who you drawing?' Max threw herself onto the couch beside me and plopped her head on my shoulder. I froze, I hadn't meant for anyone to see the drawing. What had I been thinking? That I could keep him a secret and then absently sketch him with everyone around?

Steadying the rise and fall of my chest, I slipped my fingers under the cover to gently close the book. 'It's no one.'

Max slammed her hand across the page and jerked her gaze up to mine. 'This isn't *no one*. You look weird.'

My cheeks flamed, from irritation or embarrassment I couldn't tell. 'Thanks.'

Max ignored my sarcasm and continued to probe. 'Who is it? I haven't seen this book before. Can I see?'

See my book of faces I'd drawn from my dreams? I gripped my pencil. Not a chance. My heart lodged in my throat; I swallowed it back down. But if seeing the other faces detracted her from prying into who *this* face was, maybe I ought to hand it over. Still, all those deaths, all those lives. 'Once you see this, you can't un-see it.'

Max's dark eyes fixed to mine, my fingers loosened, and the book slid away.

She flipped through the pages. My pulse raged in my temple as I attempted to ignore the rustling paper and silent pauses with each new picture. I glanced up and caught Amber's silent interrogation from across the room. Her caring eyes studied me, taking in the scene. There was no way she didn't see the fear all over my face. It drifted from my pores like steam from a kettle.

'Luce,' Max whispered, and I lowered my eyes to the opened page on her lap. A fair-haired teenage boy who I'd saved from a car accident a few months ago. I'd drawn his mischievous face, the laughter in his eyes, and scribbled words down the left side of the page; *three teenagers, country road, May 20*. 'Who are all these people? Are they from your dreams?' Her voice wobbled with unease.

I was cornered. Literally jammed into the edge of the couch, with Max pressed into my side. Would she believe me if I told her? What choice did I have, the truth was etched on every page in her hands.

Holding my breath, I nodded.

'For real? How do you remember them so well?'

'After what I see, there's no way I can forget their faces. That's why I draw them.'

'But they're just dreams.' It sounded like a question.

'But they're not.'

Max let out an uneasy sigh and lowered her eyes. 'All these years I've tried to downplay your dreams. I thought it would help, that it might become less of an issue for you.'

'I'm not a three-year-old.' My heart raced in defence. Could this really be happening again?

She sighed. 'I know.'

'Is that why you told me I was imagining things? You were downplaying it, hoping that's all it was?'

'You've seen me watch horror movies. It felt a bit like that.' She mimicked the way she talked out loud while we watched scary movies. 'She's *not* going to open the door. He's *not* chasing her, they're only playing. She's not actually seeing real people in her dreams.' She paused, spoke slowly. 'Except you are, aren't you? It never become less of an issue.'

'It's become more of one.'

'I'm sorry.' Max brushed her fingers across the paper, her soft brown skin striking against the white paper. 'I'm sorry I was so uncomfortable I couldn't handle the truth.'

Her words reached over and squeezed at my heart. I'd been waiting years for my best friend to acknowledge my hurt. My eyes were damp with emotion, and I blinked as I glanced around the room. Amber now sat with Cal in the beanbag, the Xbox controller at his side. Sean, no longer focused on the game, eyed the book in Max's hands.

'What's that?'

Max looked at me, and I closed my eyes, giving my consent. She passed the book to Sean.

'Can someone explain what's going on?' Cal said, glancing from me to Sean, to the book. 'Is this about your dreams? I thought I knew all about them, but I feel like I'm missing something.'

'Me too.' Amber's words were clipped with a questioning tone, hesitating to say even those two words. I understood the feeling.

'She dreams real life events.' Max helped me out.

'No shit, Sherlock, I worked that out years ago,' Cal said. Amber shushed him, but he continued, his voice lower. 'What's the problem with that?'

I tapped my pencil against my thigh.

Max answered for me. 'She relives them in her dreams, like she's actually there. At least I think that's how it works?' She had it spot on. Had she really believed me all this time?

I raised my head, nodded.

'That explains a few things,' Cal said, and I lifted half my mouth in acknowledgement.

'Why haven't you ever shown me this before?' Sean still had my book. He turned a page.

'Maybe because the last time I tried talking to you about them you called me delusional.'

'I've explained that. C'mon, Luce, we've already had this conversation.'

'No, we haven't. We haven't spoken a word of it since we broke up.' *Had we?* My head spun, I closed my eyes.

'What are you talking about?' Sean swivelled on the couch. 'We talked for hours last time we were here, before...you know.' I didn't know. The last time I was here, Tyler had been here, and I'd spent most of my time in and out of my dreams with him. But there was no way I could tell Sean I had no memory of the conversation. One thing at a time.

'Oh, right, yeah.'

Sean returned to the book in his lap. 'So, these are all people from your dreams, from real life?'

I nodded. 'Yeah.' I puffed out the word. The admission, the whole conversation left me desperate for air. I wanted to stagger outside and gasp on the fresh lake breeze – but I couldn't leave. I needed this even more.

'But that's not all.' Amber's words were barely audible, even in the stillness of the room. 'There's more. I can tell.' I caught her expression. The soft understanding in her eyes, an assurance prompting me to speak.

They waited. For an explanation of something I would liken to the Big Bang. Easy to describe, hard to fathom. Could I form the words to draw light on my darkness? But just as sure as science was about the Big Bang, so was I that I had to try. The lonely hole I'd found myself in had become too deep to climb from alone.

I stared up from the depths, into their faces. Cal's eyes were slightly confused, worried too. Max and Sean, identical in almost every way, tonight held different views as they shared a look that only came from their bottomless love for me, and Amber, only ever full of concern for others, leaned forward and grabbed my hand. I clutched the life rope they'd thrown down and didn't let go.

—5—

'IT'S TRUE. THERE'S MORE,' I started, twisting my fingers together, taking a moment. *Here goes nothing.* 'I dream of horrific real-life events as clear as if I were there. I watch people die, sometimes twice a week, and I know far more details than any news reports share.' I paused, staring at the high ceiling and wall of glass across the back of the house.

'That's way more lucid than I ever thought your dreams were,' Cal said. I hesitated with a timid smile. He was only just beginning to find out how lucid those dreams had been.

Ignoring the pounding in my chest, I blinked, and continued while I still had courage. 'But then I dream it again, but a little differently, so the person doesn't die. I always thought this was to help me cope with what I saw, until one day...' I paused and stared at Cal. 'I watched a friend collide with another player during a game of soccer. His head injury was so bad the doctors needed to do urgent surgery. I lived through the second worst day of our lives watching another friend die. I went to sleep that night and dreamt it all away. I dreamt that Eric *did* sleep in, that the bet you made wasn't enough to get him to the game on time, and that small detail did enough to change the course of events. The following day I woke and discovered the true power of my dreams, because... well, you only broke a bone, didn't you.' I waved my hand at Cal indicating his leg.

He glanced down to where it'd once been covered in plaster and back up to me. 'What?'

'Hang on. What do you mean you came to the game? You never come to the game.' Sean's brows drew together.

I didn't mind questions. Questions meant grasping for understanding.

'I did that day.'

'Shit. You did.' Cal, wide eyed, whipped his head round to Sean. 'How else would she know about that bet we made with Eric?'

'Because she heard about it at school?' Okay, maybe Sean wasn't grasping to understand anything.

'Why would I make something like this up?'

'To be honest that's the one thing that makes me want to believe you, because if it's not true then, I dunno...' Sean shrugged.

'I'm insane?' I quirked a brow, daring him to say it.

'No. But I'm insane if I believe you with no evidence. I mean how stupid will we look if we just go along with it. What, then in a few weeks you're like, "Gotcha".'

'My God, you don't know me at all, do you? That's the sort of thing Cal'd pull, not me.'

Cal leaned forward. 'I'm not that much of a prick.'

'Neither am I.'

Max placed her hand on my knee. 'We don't think you're a prick or joking.' She glared at Sean and continued, 'Or insane. It's just hard to comprehend, that's all. You get that, right?'

I did. It'd taken me days to understand, and I'd lived through it *and* with my dreams for years. 'Yeah, I do.'

'You've saved all these people?' Amber skimmed through my book; it was being passed around like a pack of Pokémon cards in a classroom. She examined me, admiration lighting her eyes.

Finding my own dose of pride, I said, 'Yeah.'

'This one was four days ago. How do you come to school and act normal?'

'Practice.'

'Could you do it again?' Sean twisted round and threw an arm over the back of the couch. 'Like tonight?'

'Course I could. I do it all the time. If there's something in the news, someone to save, I can't help but dream it.'

Sean lunged for his phone on the side of the couch. He tapped at the screen. He was going to test me. My fingernails pressed into my palms, and anger swirled in my stomach. I scanned the room, at the eager faces of my friends, keen to understand, wanting to even. Relief settled beside the anger, and I sighed, because if this helped, if this meant my friends knew what I battled with, I wouldn't be so alone.

'You know who's being a prick?' Max said, glaring at her brother.

This time I patted her on the knee. 'It's fine. Let's do this. Then you'll all know for sure, with no doubt in your mind.'

'There's no doubt in my mind now. Because I know you wouldn't lie about something like this.'

'I know. But this won't hurt. Come on, whatcha got for me, Sean?'

'How horrible do you wanna go?'

'I've seen everything.'

He arched an eyebrow as if to suggest I hadn't seen anything as bad as what he'd found. As if.

'First of all, have you heard anything about that kidnapping that happened a couple weeks ago?'

I tilted my head. 'Is that anything to do with what Abby posted on Facebook last week? About there being some kidnappings that've been linked?'

'So, you know about this one then.' He started scrolling,

searching for something new.

'No. I mean...that's all I know. I saw her joking about it with her sister, but I didn't click on the link. I haven't heard the story. I actually try not to hear everything if I can help it.' It was the reason I avoided the news and Facebook in the first place. Otherwise I'd be constantly slapped in the face with news stories, and I'd be drowning under the weight of my dreams.

'Okay, so I'm only going to give you enough –'

'Just give me the headline, Sean.'

He hesitated, the semblance of an apology shadowing his face. But it wasn't his fault. This was my life; I knew the drill. I closed my eyes, letting him know it'd be okay. He studied his phone. 'The body of missing...' He stopped. 'I'll leave the age and name out, then you're not getting too many details.'

'Sean.' Max hurled a cushion in his direction, and he dived out of the way.

'The body of...' He paused and omitted the age and name of the victim with a grunt. '...missing for sixteen days, has been found washed up in Towra Point on the Georges River south of Sydney early this morning. Police suspect foul play and are urging anyone with any information to come forward.'

My shoulders slumped as a familiar sadness crept over me. That poor person. Guilt pressed into me. I didn't even know they'd been missing. I closed my eyes briefly and opened them to the concerned faces of my friends.

'What?'

'You all right, hon?' Max asked.

'I'm used to it.'

'What now?' Cal asked.

'Now when I go to sleep, I'll find out how she, or he, was taken, maybe see what they were doing at the time, who took them, what they did to them. I will feel all their fear, and depending on what they endure, perhaps even some of their pain.'

No one said a word. Expressions were grim, contemplative, remorseful. Sean hid the T.V. remote and took away everyone's phones, removing any chance of finding more details before morning. And when we climbed into bed, on the mattresses lining the floor of the living room, there was no chit chat about the day, or trivial teen issues, or jokes from Cal. Because this time my friends had staggered to the edge of the pit with me and now saw the mammoth depth of the hole. A hole only I would have to fall into it while they stayed safely on the ground above.

*****

THE STREET TO THE *left of me, a short distance away, hummed with sounds of the city; honking cars, people shouting. The busy city life activity only heightened the quietness of the little side street. Tall grey buildings loomed, pointing toward the fading blue sky above. Parallel parked cars sat bumper to bumper all along the curb, and a couple strolled hand in hand toward the action of the main road. Daylight was fading, and instead of the dead calm you get in the waking stillness of the morning, the world was alive and bustling. If I were to guess, the couple over the road were dressed to go out for dinner.*

They waltzed past a set of red double doors moments before two young women, maybe in their early twenties, stepped out. The sign on the building above them said 'Feel Great Fitness – All day, every day personal training'.

The girls were laughing and chatting, bags strung over their shoulders and freshly washed hair tied back in almost identical ponytails, one a whitewashed surfer blonde, the other a deep burgundy brown. Their smiles were large and genuine, a small sign of a great friendship. It made me think of me and Max, or for a correct hair colour comparison, me and Amber. Us in five years – or not; the thought of living in the city didn't fill me with much excitement.

I took a few steps closer, so I could hear them properly.

'C'mon, I'll give you lift,' Brown Ponytail said.

'No it's fine, I love walking, you know that,' Blonde Ponytail replied.

'I know, but ya know, white vans and all.' She jerked her head.

I cast my eyes down the street, at the still and silent van that appeared no more ominous than any of the other parked cars. I frowned and staggered back, because today it was. I shook my head. No, no, no.

'You're such a dork.' Blonde Ponytail laughed. 'I'll probably pass like ten of them on my way home.'

'Yeah, but this one's been here for the last few nights.'

'All the more reason not to worry about it.' She brushed her arm through the air. 'You're such a worry wart, Grace, I'll be fine.'

Grace hesitated. 'You're sure?'

'Yes, I'm sure. Now go home and make yourself something healthy for dinner.'

'Yeah right, what're you having, a toastie?'

'Probably.' Laughing, Blonde Ponytail waltzed away.

'See ya tomorrow.' Grace waved and stepped off the curb to cross the road to her car.

My heart picked up pace, anticipation fuelling my fear for what was unfolding.

Grace arrived at her car, fumbled in her bag for her keys, dropped the gym bag on the ground, and with head lowered, continued rummaging.

I shifted my attention to the blonde strolling along the footpath, my stomach lurching with dread. The door of the van slid open, and I pitched forward as an arm grabbed her from the side, the other hand clasped over her mouth, and yanked her in.

I darted my eyes back to Grace, as if by sheer will I'd be able to direct her attention back to her friend. She found her keys, opened her car and climbed in. Only then did she glance back up the road. Her head tilted, searching her friend out. She slowed as she drove past the van. I followed on foot, the low rumble of the van's engine sending a shiver up my spine. A piece of black fabric hung loosely over the back bumper, jammed in the back door, blocking the number plate.

Grace turned left onto the main road and, unable to spot her friend, steered the car to the curb and plucked her phone from her bag. With her head bent over her phone she missed the van turning right in the opposite direction.

Damn it. I clenched my jaw.

The black fabric flapped in the tail breeze and revealed the last three digits of the number plate – 49A.

Grace glanced up from her phone to the rear-view mirror. Seeing the retreating van, she jumped from the car, worry etched all over her face. She pressed a hand to the back of her neck as she paced the footpath with the phone to her ear. 'Megan, where are you?'

The safety of the road fell away, and I found myself in the back of the van with Megan. She slumped on the floor, bound at hands and feet with black cable ties. Her muffled cries, dulled by a cloth gag knotted around her face, filled the stuffy space. Tears ran from her widened eyes.

The van jolted and I fell backward, landing on my side. I scrambled over to Megan and placed my hand on her cheek, hoping I could convey, through a touch she couldn't feel, some small sense of calm.

'Don't be afraid,' I said. Except she really should be – I was.

We drove for what felt like an eternity before coming to an abrupt stop. The engine fell silent.

'I'll be right back,' a husky voice said from the front of the van. 'Don't go anywhere.' And he laughed. Sick bastard.

My body, propelled by the dream, now stood outside, in front of a two-storey building that was clearly a house, but also a business, with the signs in the windows advertising computer repair services. A home with a business tacked to the front. We were in a mostly residential area, but with the odd business every few houses down the street. *The front door stepped straight onto the footpath, and the second storey had no balcony, only two small windows with blinds down.*

The man ran up the side of the house and dashed through a back gate, disappearing from sight. I shifted my attention back to the front door, grey with an old wrought iron knocker below a black and white sign that read 'Salander Computer Repairs'. The man returned, jumped behind the wheel and started the engine, a crooked grin on his face. A small gasp escaped, and I stepped back, stumbling on the curb.

I shook my head. No, it couldn't be. Could it?

Regaining my balance, I took a step forward. I needed to see his face before the van drove away. My breathing came fast. Please be wrong. I shot another glance through the front windscreen and my heart plummeted straight to my toes – I knew that face. That crooked grin, small nose, and curly black hair shaved at the sides. The face of the man on the plane. The man whose life I'd saved when I saved Tyler's dad.

My world spun, pinpricks of dread filled my vision. I was inside my worst nightmare, and worse than that, I'd created it.

I put a hand to my mouth, the other tightened around my stomach. Oh my God, what had I done?

The van backed out the driveway and my dream shifted. It warped around me and I no longer stood on the curb in a suburban landscape, but in the middle of the bush as the man carried Megan over his shoulder into a kind of shed built into the side of a hill and butted up against a massive tree. It reminded me of the scene in A Princess Bride *where the torture chamber hid inside the tree. Where the hell were we?*

I followed them through the large double door, into a rectangular room the size of a single garage. Galvanized iron walls, clad on one side by what could only be described as a torture wall, with tools that resembled what you'd use in an operating theatre but wouldn't appear out of place if found in a work shed either. I shuddered, swallowing the bile forming in the back of my throat.

Opposite the torture wall, pressed up against the iron, rested a large wooden office desk, the sort you might find in an old high school; two drawers on the left side and plenty of nicks and scratches over its surface. A black stool sat where a teacher's seat might once have lived, ready to be dragged out and used to do some innocent paperwork. But the bed, fitted with crisp white linen at the end of the room, made it anything but innocent. God, what did he have planned? I shook my head in denial of what might be coming. He flipped Megan from his shoulder, and she landed heavily on the bed, her moist eyes held tightly shut.

'Open your eyes, let me see you,' he said, brushing a stray lock of blonde hair from her face. She kept them closed. Good, keep them that way. 'Don't be afraid. I brought you here for a bit of fun that's all. I bought fresh sheets just for you.'

My vision dimmed and my pulse thundered in my ears, the thought of what I'd soon see filling me with more terror than any dream I'd had before. Accidents were one thing, people died from them all the time. Not a pleasant part of life, but it happened – it was normal. This was not, this was sick. I put a hand to my stomach, holding back the nausea crawling inside me.

I clenched my eyes shut, tears pooling at their edges.

Please no.

Wake up. Wake up. Wake up.

—6—

I SHOT UP IN bed, sweat soaked and choking on a gasp. My whole body trembled, the horror still pouring through me.

I shook my head. 'No, no, no, no, no.' I couldn't shake it. Her terror was mine and she'd died with no relief from it. I'd woken up from my fear; she'd been left alone with hers.

My eyes burst open. Oh my God. I'd made myself wake up.

'Luce?' Max stirred from next to me and cracked open an eye. 'You okay?'

I put my head in my hands. 'I killed her,' I whispered into my knees. 'I killed her.' Tears ran down my cheeks.

Max shuffled to my side. 'What're you talking about?'

It was all my fault. My chest heaved, struggling to grasp the fullness of what I'd done. I'd saved him. I'd spared the life of a killer. I lifted my head and wiped my eyes. 'I've done something really bad.'

Sean groaned from the other side of the room, and Amber and Cal stirred. A faint orange glow lit up the lake outside, but on this side of the glass I could only make out the shape and faces of my friends. They huddled around, dragged their blankets closer, reminding me of the mornings when my brothers eagerly waited for me to share my dreams over breakfast.

Part of me wished I didn't have to recount this dream and my responsibility for this death, another part craved for them to know everything.

Clutching a handful of my blanket, I relayed it all.

'Her name was Megan.' I paused as faces turned to Sean for confirmation. His mouth fell open and I continued. 'She was with her friend, Grace when she was taken. Grace had dark brown hair, but Megan's was blonde. I think they were in their early twenties, I couldn't really tell. They were older than us, but not by heaps.'

The shuffling on the beds completely disappeared, the reality closing in with the details of what I'd seen.

'They were just leaving the gym at the end of the day and chatting about what they were having for tea, something about toasties, and then Grace went to her car and Megan walked away. She got yanked into a van.'

Amber gasped and placed a hand over her mouth.

'He took her to some kind of hut or shed in the middle of nowhere. I have no idea where it was.' I shared what I'd seen inside the room and that I'd been able to wake myself up. I inhaled and let out a puff. 'Sean, can you pass me my book and pencil.'

He reached behind him and handed it across the mattress. With the dim morning light, I drew her face: round and full of innocence. The scrape of the pencil on the paper intruded on the stillness of the room as I drew her smile, the one that vanished the second his hand went over her mouth. Amber draped her arm around me and laid her head against my arm as the face of my latest victim took form. And for the first time ever, this one belonged to me. Her death rested on my shoulders.

I scribbled the date in the top right corner, August eighteenth, along with the date from Sean of the actual abduction, August first, followed by the few details I recalled: the gym name, the sign on the front of his door, the last three digits of the van's number plate: 49A.

'I read nearly every article on it,' Sean said, shaking his head.

The air had settled. The reality sinking in as tensions relaxed a little, as if my drawing had done for my friends what it always did for me: helped deal with it.

'So, I passed the test?' My voice was flat, dry.

'With flying colours. I mean, I trusted you hadn't seen the articles, but –'

'You still doubted.'

'I didn't,' Max said. 'You had me at "her name was Megan" and as well as the facts, for the first time, you didn't try to hide the fear in your eyes.'

'And I've never felt so lost for words. Dude, all I'm thinking is, you saved my life. I died and you bought me back and I'm well, I... shit...see.' Cal rubbed the side of his temple.

Sean sat up taller. 'I didn't doubt you –'

'But,' Max interrupted with a glare aimed at her brother.

'But most of that *was* on the internet, except one thing. And now there's not even a sliver of doubt. Not that there was.' He waved his hand, deflecting the bites. He held his phone in the palm of his hand. 'Listen to this article. It only went online this morning. It's an interview with her friend, Grace. They went to the gym three times a week, and Megan always walked home alone. This is what she said: "We went out on Friday nights; that was our thing, but never on the other nights. Instead, we'd joke about the crap we'd eat once we got home. That night it was going to be toasties." Toasties, they were having toasties.'

'But then one of them died,' I spat. 'It's not a celebration.'

'Yeah, right, sorry.'

'It's so far from a celebration.' I dragged my sketchbook toward me and opened it at the front. 'You know how I said I change things, save people's lives, like I did with Cal. Well a couple of weeks ago I changed the events of a big commercial plane crash that'd happened over a year ago. I brought hundreds of people back to life.' I flattened out the pages with the faces of the lady I'd sat beside and the man across the aisle. 'I saved this man.' My stomach recoiled as I pointed to him. 'He's the man who killed Megan.'

'Is that what you meant when you said you did something bad?' Max asked.

I nodded, swallowing down the bile.

Max grabbed hold of my trembling fingers. 'But that's not your fault – you didn't kill her. No matter what it feels like, you didn't do this.'

'And you can save her,' Cal said. 'Like you did me. So, it'll all work out, right?'

As hard as I found it to swallow the part I'd played and accept it easily like Cal, he was right; I might be to blame for her death, but I'd also be responsible for bringing her back to life.

*****

BREAKFAST WAS GRIM, THE coffee a welcome addition to my morning. Harry got everyone working on the deck extension and repairs, which allowed us a distraction from talking about Megan and her death and all it meant, not only to me, but to all of us.

I stole moments through the day to read everything available on the internet, but found it hard to learn more than I'd already seen in the dream. The only thing half useful was the mention of routine and that Megan liked everything to a tee.

If something happened before he got the chance to take her, so her routine was not so predictable, that might be enough to save her. A little something different to shake things up a bit, throw him off their scent perhaps.

In between my investigations I helped outside on the deck. I appreciated the interruption, but it all felt so pointless when someone's life hung in the balance. Technically she was already dead, had been for weeks, but it didn't have to stay that way. I didn't want to imagine someone so young having their life cut so brutally short, not in that way, and not by that man. *That* man. I'd sat beside him on the plane. I saved his life. A sickening, guilty, overwhelming lump sat in the pit of my stomach all day.

'GIMME THE MARSHMALLOWS,' SEAN said as we strolled from the house to the fire, the familiar lakeside scent of smoke and gum hanging in the air. The heat from the billowing mass of copper and pink flames grew with every step.

'No way, the last time you had charge of the bag you ate half of them.' I clutched them tighter to my chest, tossing him a threatening glare.

'So, Luce, you never did tell us why you were watching a game. It's been years since you came to see us play.' Cal deposited his arm full of drinks on the cut log table by the fire pit. 'Did Amber drag you along?'

'I reckon it was our fine physiques that lured her in,' Sean said.

'You wish.' I relaxed momentarily, my grip on the marshmallows loosening. Sean yanked the bag from my hands. 'Hey!' I shot my arm out, lunging to retrieve them. Sean stepped back with a chuckle and dropped himself on the wooden bench.

Laughter rumbled from my friends while I swallowed the lump of nerves converging in my throat. Sean grinned, plopping a pink blob in his mouth. I sank to the bench and tucked my knees into my chest. *How do I explain this next part?* More than being even less believable – if that were possible – I was also acutely aware of how awkward, hurtful even, this could be for Sean.

Frowning, I plucked up a twig from the dirt at my feet.

'You guys ready for the biggest *fact or fallacy* you've ever heard?'

'After the day we've had, we're ready for anything.' Max flung her arm around me with a squeeze and a teasing jiggle. I wrestled out of her grasp.

'So, you know how I mentioned the plane crash earlier? I only saved those people a couple of weeks ago. Once I learned what went wrong, I was able to alter it. But before that, for like a year, the plane had gone down, those people had died. I remember it. I lived while that was the reality for the world, for me. The pilot had a family he left behind, and they moved to Antil about six months ago.'

'Who?' Amber turned to me for a reminder of who this family was. I said nothing. Her eyes widened and she gasped. 'Oh.'

'Someone moved to town and we knew them and then you stopped the plane from crashing.' Cal's face scrunched as he tried to turn his confusion into understanding. 'You changed the past and affected the future? Holy shit.' Cal slapped a hand on his leg and shook his head, his blond hair flopping onto his forehead. He opened a can of Coke and gulped down a swig.

'Anyway, I went to the match because, six months ago the team got a new player. The pilot's son. His name was Tyler.' Tears prickled from the feel of his name on my lips.

'He was the one you were drawing yesterday,' Max said.

Nodding, I picked up a twig and tossed it into the fire. 'He and I –'

'Hang on...I lost you to a guy who doesn't exist?' Disbelief and pain unravelled behind Sean's aching expression.

'He does exist.' I twisted my hands in my lap. 'He moved here with his mum and sister after his dad died. Tyler was wonderful. All of you loved him and so did I.' The tears sprang free. 'But then I saved his dad, and he never moved here, we...you never met him. I still have every single memory of those four months, but anything that changed in that time because of his not being here...I have no memory of.' I exhaled.

The realisation dawning on Sean's face turned into a silent question. I shook my head. 'Nothing up until about two weeks ago. Remember when I stayed home sick for a couple of days? It wasn't a cold. I was just dealing with the fact I'd dreamt the boy I love out of my life.'

The crackle of the flames broke through the silence, and Sean choked out a single word. 'Nothing?'

'Not nothing, but if it happened in the new reality without him here, then, yeah. I can still remember Cal's accident, because that happened with or without Tyler being here. I know we came here for Richie's birthday, but the weekend I remember is different to what you're all describing.'

'That's why you can't remember the conversation?' Sean asked. I couldn't pick if he was hurt, surprised or in awe, maybe all three. 'When we talked for hours, I told you I was sorry, and we kissed?'

'I'm sorry, Sean. Really, I am. I didn't mean to hurt you in the process of all this mess.'

'I know,' he said. 'And you haven't hurt me, Luce. I mean, it hurts, but you didn't do it. It hurt when you texted me your resounding no, but that was my hurt to carry, never yours. I've come to accept we will never be. I think I always knew it, but damn, that was some kiss.'

Everyone laughed, and I leaned my head onto Sean's shoulder. He slid his arm around me and I whispered, 'I'm sorry,' again.

'Would you like me to show you what you missed?' he said with a smirk.

'No!' I slapped his arm and his laughter grew.

The chuckles subsided into a sombre contemplative silence. They had a lot to take in, a concept even I'd taken days to grasp. I sucked in the crisp-scented eucalyptus, reached over Sean's lap for another marshmallow, and anticipated more questions.

'Fact.' Amber's delicate voice held firm, and I cast my eyes to her.

'Fact,' Sean said. I blinked back the tears welling under my lids and he bumped his shoulder against mine.

'Fact.' Cal hoisted his leg in the air. 'Cheers for this by the way.' I huffed out a small laugh, wiping the tears off my cheeks.

I hadn't meant to turn to Max, like I waited for her answer, but I did. She had on her competition face – it gave nothing away. Then her lips turned up and her eyes softened. 'Fact,' she said, and I let out the breath I didn't realise I'd been holding.

One word, that's all it took. One small, four letter word, from the people most important in my life, and I became a sobbing mess. Maybe losing Tyler had all been leading to this. My loss gave me more of my friends. It had felt so one-sided, that I lost him and everything else in the process. But I'd gained more support and belief from my friends than I ever had before. I no longer stood alone in the bottom of the pit; they'd jumped down into the mud with me and suddenly the hole didn't seem so deep.

We spent the next hour sharing stories from each of our parallel lives. What I missed, what they missed, and I told them everything about Tyler.

Sean put a hand on his knee and leaned forward. 'He replaced me on our trip to Canberra?'

'No. You replaced him.'

'Right, course.'

It was weirdly fun, and being able to talk about Tyler, letting go of the secret I'd held so tightly, felt like trading a load of bricks for a bunch of balloons.

'Do you think he remembers you?' Max bunched up her long

legs beside her.

'He went back to a life before he met me. I don't think it's even remotely possible.'

'But you shared dreams with him, right?' Amber said.

'Yeah.' *Wonderful, magical dreams.* I missed those dreams more than anything.

'Wouldn't he still be able to do that?'

'Maybe, but the reason he had those was because he met me. Now I'm nothing to him.' It hurt to say the words aloud.

'Well go and meet him.' Max shrugged.

'Ooh, yes, go to Sydney and introduce yourself.' Amber wriggled on the spot. 'You can wield your magical Lucy powers on him and he won't be able to stop dreaming about you.'

'What comic books have you been reading?' I laughed. 'I don't think it'll work like that. It'd just frighten him away.' I'd already had this conversation with myself so many times. Each scenario I thought of had me looking more like a fruit loop than I already did. 'Plus, I don't actually know what school he went to. He never told me.'

'How did, uh, Tyler, share the dreams anyway?' Sean asked. 'I mean you can do it because you were born –'

'Weird?' I tilted my head on the side, goading him.

'No,' Sean said, scrunching up his mouth. 'I was going to say born into it.'

'We're not really sure, but one of the things we think played a part...hang on, he told me never to tell you guys.'

'What, because it might ruin his reputation?'

'Yeah.'

'But he doesn't have one. All we know is he's a surfer dude from Sydney who managed to charm his way into your heart,' Sean said.

'You mean dream his way in.' Amber giggled.

'Whatever.' Sean shook his head dismissively. 'But seriously, it can't ruin something that doesn't exist, although my preconceived ideas of him aren't that great, so there is that.'

'Oh, c'mon, just tell us already. What does it matter?' Cal grabbed up a log behind him and threw it on the dwindling fire. Orange sparks flew into the air.

'He meditates. The school he goes to does it, and he liked it, so he kept doing it when he moved here.'

'Yep, shouldn't have told us.' Sean slapped his palms on his knees. 'Now I think he's a tool.'

I rolled my eyes and groaned. 'Give me a marshmallow, will you.'

*****

I flew down the mountain, the wind whipping me in the face as my speed increased. She came up beside me and I turned to take her in. Gorgeous dark hair cascaded behind her in thick waves, billowing like a cape. Her smile grew wide and her eyes moved to meet mine – wow.

—7—

B Y THE TIME EVENING came around, I eagerly awaited returning to my dreams so I could save Megan from that horrible man.

'You guys aren't going to remember this in the morning,' I
said, climbing into bed. 'I'm going to change it and it'll never have
happened.'

Amber shuffled closer to pat me reassuringly on the leg. 'But we'll
remember everything else. We'll still believe you.'

'I hope so.'

I didn't really know what would come of the morning. Only one
thing remained certain, I had to save Megan, whatever the cost. I put
her in the grave – but I wouldn't leave her there.

THE GIRLS STEPPED OUT *of the gym, moments earlier than the last
time. They were so caught up in their laughter, they didn't see the couple
strolling past, and stumbled right into their path.*

'I'm so sorry,' Grace said, righting herself against the lady's arm.

*'No, that's okay,' she replied. A smile formed in response to the dying
laughter of the young women, who stepped flush against the wall so the
couple could ease past.*

'Hey, we should go out for dinner too.' Grace squeezed Megan's arm.

*'What, tonight?' Megan slanted her eyes at her friend. 'It's only
Wednesday.'*

'I know, but it'll be nice to eat something decent after all the work we

just did. What do ya say?'

'What, toastie not good enough for you?'

She squared her shoulders, determined. 'Not right now, no.'

Megan hesitated. 'I dunno, Grace.'

'C'mon.' She flicked her head in the direction of the couple ambling away from them. 'If it's good enough for them, it's good enough for us.'

'What? They're dressed up, we're not.'

'Sure we are.' The girls inspected their casual sweatpants and sneakers, and burst into laughter once again.

'Let's do it.' Grace beamed and tugged on Megan's arm, leading her over the road to her waiting car.

Still huffing, Megan climbed into the car, but I didn't need her to be happy, simply alive.

MY EYES OPENED TO a dark room, the stillness of the night hovering around me. Smiling to myself, I rolled over to return to the deep void of sleep. When I woke hours later, light streamed in from the tall wall of windows at the back of the room. A kookaburra laughed somewhere outside, and I wanted to laugh with him, because I'd done it again. I'd saved a life.

Max bolted up in her bed, startling everyone from their sleep. 'I remember,' she panted.

I sighed, I'd been so afraid they'd forget everything I'd told them or even that it'd only been a wonderful dream.

'Me too,' Amber said, rubbing her eyes, and brushing her blonde hair off her face. 'But like, the girl, Megan, you said we wouldn't remember her. I can. She was kidnapped.'

What? I spun my head in her direction.

'What happened to her? Have they found her yet?' Sean said, sitting up.

A frown creased my brow. 'But I changed it, I saved her.' I

scrambled out of my blankets and lunged for my phone on the T.V. cabinet in search of the story – a story that shouldn't be there because it never happened. But appearing on the small screen was a news article I never expected to see. My hands shook as I read the altered details. Megan had been kidnapped, on a Monday, not a Wednesday, and they still hadn't found her body.

'What's up, Luce?' Cal rested a hand on my back.

Ignoring him, I grabbed my bag at the end of the bed, rummaging for my sketchbook. I flipped to the picture I'd drawn the day before, checked the date scribbled at the corner of the page, *Aug 1st*, the day she'd been abducted. I glanced at my phone where the article said she'd been taken on August sixth, five days later.

'He tried again,' I whispered to no one in particular, a buzz forming in my ears. My eyes glazed over. 'I stopped him, but he went after her again.'

'What do you mean? You're freaking me out.' Amber dragged the book from my fingers.

'Have a look at the date.' I jabbed at the page in Amber's hands and shoved my phone in their faces. 'But see, it's changed. You watched me write that date. And now he's gone for her again and in a few days' time they're going to drag her body from the Georges River.'

'Could you save her again?' Sean asked, peering over my shoulder at the book.

He'd been watching her. Had her lined up ready to take down. It wouldn't matter what I did. I could save her over and over in my dreams, but he'd be waiting to pounce again as soon as I woke.

'I could, but how many times will I need to? He had his eye on her, he'll keep trying.'

*****

I PACED THE LIVING room, biting my thumbnail.

I had to stop him.

Clenching my teeth, I grabbed my laptop and sat at the deserted dining room table. The crew were outside, back at work, helping Harry with the deck. Marie, after working all morning on her usual breakfast smorgasbord, had gone to take a shower.

I twisted the jet around my wrist as I waited for my laptop to fire up, mentally adding her name to the many. Guilt stabbed at my heart for giving up on her so easily. But it wasn't easy, it hurt like hell.

I pulled up the news articles again, the ones about suspected serial killer patterns. Another girl six months earlier had gone missing, never found. Similar facial appearance, long blonde hair, tall, pretty. She'd also been leaving the gym when it was suspected she was taken.

It'd never been a random attack, and the likelihood he'd strike again was possible, imminent even.

I ran my hands through my hair. *What do I do?* I wished I had Tyler here to work it out with, but one: he didn't know me, and two: he lived four-hundred kilometres away in Sydney.

Sydney...where did *this* guy live?

I typed in his name, or at least the business name, Salander. Was that *his* name? The face of Lisbeth Salander – *The Girl with the Dragon Tattoo* – appeared on the screen. I hadn't read the book, but I'd seen the movie; the relevance hadn't occurred to me until now. A computer wiz, hacker, a victim of abuse who helped uncover a series of attacks on women. Now that was messed up.

I typed in the full name of his business, Salander Computer Repairs, and clicked on the website. I found the address, popped it into Google maps, and brought up the street view. The house from my dream flickered to life on the screen, complete with grey door and two small upstairs windows.

I checked the contacts page, trying to work out the name of this man. It couldn't be Salander, could it? The only details listed were the street address, phone number and email:

webb@salandercomputerrepairs.com

No name.

I tapped on the table, stood, and paced the length of the room again.

*****

I SAT, CURLED UP with my bare feet under my bum, on the couch, Billy Bob tucked beside me. I stroked his light brown fur with one hand and held my pencil in the other. My book rested on my lap, its pages open with Tyler's face staring up at me.

All we'd done since arriving at the lake house was help with the deck, and talk about me, my dreams, and Tyler. My life had never been so transparent.

'Hey, watcha doin'?' The couch sagged as Amber dropped beside me and took over scratching Billy Bob's ears. He lifted his head to take her in, wriggled closer, and placed his head on her lap.

'Who's that?' She peered at the book. 'Oh, it's him.' Her face filled with stunned admiration.

'Yeah.'

'He's cute.' I mumbled my agreement. 'Have you thought about going to see him, to try to find him?' She dragged her golden hair over a shoulder.

'I don't know where he lives or even what school he went to.'

Even if I did, what would I say to him? 'Hi, you don't know me, but I know you.' Creepy much? No, I simply couldn't come to terms with how something like that could possibly work in my favour.

'Hmm.'

'And part of me wonders if I should just leave him be. I gave him his life back, that was always the plan. And now I need to move on with mine.'

'And yet you're sitting here drawing him. How is that moving on with your life?'

'Moving on with my life doesn't mean I can't remember him.' I brushed my fingers over the lines of his face in the book. 'Besides I needed a break from thinking about how to stop that jerk from killing more girls. I was getting nowhere.'

'What've you found out?'

'Not much. The contact details of the business he's connected to in Sydney. I don't know if he owns the place or not though. I don't even have a name.' If only I could go knock on that big grey door for real, I'd be able to find out. I lurched forward on the couch, shoved my book aside, and marched to the back doors.

'Lucy? What's the matter?' Amber's footsteps followed me outside.

The top of the deck had all been laid, and Cal and Sean were to the side, measuring the smaller edge pieces.

'Hey, Cal, you know how much I love you, right?' I said, digging at the grass with my toes.

He peered up from his kneeled position on the ground. 'Uh oh, what do you want?'

'A ride to Sydney.' I shrugged a single shoulder.

'What? When?' He put a hand to his forehead, squinting up at me.

'Not sure. A weekend, sometime soon?'

'I play soccer every weekend, remember? There's no more byes until the end of the season now.'

'Oh right.' My shoulders sagged. The thought hadn't occurred to me that he wouldn't be able to take me. He'd been my one and only option the second the idea came. I wouldn't even contemplate going on my own. The mere fact I was interested in another trip to Sydney in the space of three months surprised me enough, but I couldn't do it without the security of one of these guys.

Amber batted her lashes at Cal. 'You know, if I could get hold of a car, even a little blue bora v dub, I could drive her.'

Sean stifled a laugh. Asking to *borrow* Cal's car was like asking him to quit soccer. Still, I crossed my fingers.

Cal put the measuring tape down and stood to wrap an arm around Amber's waist. He nuzzled into her neck. 'As much as I love you girls, I'm afraid I would sooner lose my legs than part with my baby for that long. Sorry. Can you borrow your mum or dad's car?'

She pouted. 'I can try. Oh my God, you're going to see Tyler.' She clapped her hands in front of her face.

'No I'm not,' I said, choking back the shock.

Amber's eyebrows bunched in confusion. 'Why you going to Sydney then?'

'To catch a serial killer.'

It was a collective 'What!' from everyone and a firm whack on the arm from Max who'd stepped up behind me.

I swung to face her. 'Look, I know where he lives, or where he works, I'm not sure. I have the address anyway. I need to make sure he's the same man. That the person who owns that business is the man who killed Megan. Then when I call the police, I'll know I'm getting the right guy arrested.'

Max pressed her hands to the sides of her head. 'Are you totally insane?'

'Well...yes,' I said, talking about my dreams.

'No, really, if he sees you, you could become his next victim.' The desperation on Max's face terrified me, but what scared me more was fear for the girls already in his sight. I had to stop him, or at least try. I couldn't live with myself if I didn't.

'He *will* see me, that's the point, because I need to see him. But it'll be fine, he won't care about me, he only goes for blondes.'

'And you want to take Amber with you?' Cal's voice rose, drawing her closer into his side. 'She may as well have a target on her back.'

'She won't be going with me, I'm not that stupid. I just need a ride to Sydney, the rest I'll be doing on my own.' Their unconvinced faces gaped at me. 'If I don't do this, he's going to kill again.'

'Can't you call the police from here, give 'em what you've already got?' Sean suggested.

'And when they ask me how I got my scrap of useless information? I've hardly got anything anyway. I don't even have his name. Or the full number plate of the van. See, I can get the rest of that too when I go there. Then if I've got that I can at least lie and say I saw it sitting outside the gym, say I even saw him take her.'

'They'll want to know why it took you so long to come forward.'

'I'll tell them I was scared. And it won't matter, with info like that, they'll have to respond.'

Amber stepped out of Cal's embrace. 'So, you just need someone to drive you to Sydney.'

I nodded.

'Amber,' Cal warned, his eyes pleading with hers.

She squared her shoulders. 'She's right. We have to do something.' She turned to me. 'But you have to do something for me.'

'Anything,' I whispered, a little uncertain, but desperate for her assistance.

'If we're in Sydney, you have to go and see Tyler as well.'

The air rushed out of my lungs. 'What? No, I can't. I told you that.' Her eagerness held firm. He didn't know me. It would be a disaster – that's if we even found him. But if agreeing to this got me a ride, and the chance to save more girls, then what choice did I have?

I folded my arms and stared out across the lake and into the pastel blue sky. It'd been two weeks since I'd been in this lake with Tyler in our dream, said I loved him, and slipped from the grip of his arms. What would he think about all of this? Would he be as resistant as my friends about me being in danger? No, he was my Robin. He'd be suggesting ways to help. He'd be aiding me in my plan. Like Amber.

I shifted my gaze back to hers. 'Fine.'

—8—

CAL DROPPED ME OFF in front of my house later that afternoon. It felt weird to be back here after all that'd gone down while I was away. I waved as he sped away and retrieved my bag from the ground.

Shouting escaped from the house as I crossed the front lawn, my shoes squelching in the moist soil. Mum and Dad never fought, theirs was a silent disagreement type of relationship, Dad often the retreating opponent in most battles. From the sounds of their voices, he wasn't backing down today. *Do I go in?* I cracked open the door.

'She needs them,' Mum spoke sternly.

'That's what you said last time, but it's you who needs her to have them,' Dad responded. 'If she agrees it'll only be to keep *you* happy.'

'She's miserable, Tom. Surely you've seen her this last couple of weeks.'

'Of course I have.'

They were talking about *me*. I eased the door closed and edged further into the entrance, toward the shouts flying from the kitchen. I held my bag to my chest.

'I hadn't even realised the dreams were bothering her again, but that must –'

'No, because you'd rather believe she had a cold. That's

something that'll go away in time, this won't.' Dad's voice seeped with venom.

'I can't do nothing. They'll destroy her again. If she goes on the tablets, it'll make them go away, that's what we want, isn't it?'

'It's what *you* want, because if she's not having them you don't need to know about them.' I'd never heard Dad be so blatantly honest with anyone in his life. My heart raced, afraid to move, afraid of what they might say next, afraid Mum would burst into tears. I had no idea my parents held so much hostility toward one another.

'I *don't* know about them, she doesn't talk about –'

'Because you won't allow it. She stopped talking about them when she saw you worry.' *How did Dad know all this?* 'Lucy knows, like we all do, that you can't bear the possibility your family isn't as perfect as you'd like it to be.' *Woah, way to go, Dad, keep going, you'll be on the curb in no time.*

'I don't want perfection, just happiness.'

'It's the same thing. Happiness is just another version of perfection, it doesn't exist.'

'Yes, it does.' Mum's words trembled with emotion.

'No. It doesn't.' Dad's voice softened, pleading almost, as if this wasn't a new argument they were having. 'And just because we're not your version of perfect, doesn't mean you have to fix us. I've been imperfect for years, but I know it's not a problem for you if I don't talk about it. If you don't see my imperfections, they don't exist.' What was he talking about? 'I can live like that, but Lucy is sixteen, she should *not* have to hide or live a lie. She's just like me, and that's what you're afraid of more than anything else, isn't it?' I inhaled the shock, clutching my bag tighter.

I imagined Mum on the other side of the wall, eyes brimming with tears. I stepped forward, not wanting to miss a single syllable of their exchange.

Mum didn't answer him. Did that mean she agreed with him – she was afraid I was like him? In what way?

'The tablets won't work, not long term,' Dad said. 'Nothing will. This is who she's meant to be. Nothing she does, or you do, will ever change that. Surely you know this by now, heaven knows how much you tried on me.'

I staggered back, crashing into the hallway table, my bag falling from my grasp and landing heavily on the floor by my feet. I glanced down and back up into the eyes of both my parents. I'd been right. Mum's glistened with tears, exactly like mine. I glowered at the small box in her hands. She'd already decided that was the best option for me – for her. Dad's eyes were dry, but wide open, full of regret...and guilt.

'Lucy.' He lifted his arm, reaching for me, before letting it fall to his side. 'This isn't how I wanted you to find out,' Dad said softly, like he spoke to a startled horse.

'Find out what?' I *was* a startled horse, backed up in the corner, afraid of what they'd do, or say, next.

'That I'm the same as you; I dream too.'

'What do you mean, Dad? Everyone can dream.' A strangled laugh escaped my throat, brushing away his words. Hoping he'd stop talking, hoping he wouldn't.

'Not like us...they don't do what we do.'

'Which is?' I needed him to say the words.

'Manipulate reality.' I caught Mum's ever-so-slight exasperated breath, the quick flutter of her eyes, and the gentle, barely present shake of the head – she didn't believe him. She never believed me, but he had the whole time.

'You knew,' I whispered, edging against the wall away from them. How could he let me think I was alone and going crazy? I blinked back the tears and spoke louder. 'All this time, you knew.' Granny Tess had known for a while before saying anything – but she didn't live with me and she wasn't my father. I snatched the box from Mum's fingers, grabbed my bag, and ran from the house.

I wished Tyler were up the road for me to talk to – he wasn't. Only one other person might understand, someone who admitted she'd had the same ability in her younger years – Granny Tess. I trudged down the road to the centre of town.

*****

GRANNY TESS STOOD WAITING when the bus arrived at the terminal in Canberra. Red hair spun into a bun on top of her head, frizzy tendrils falling around her face. She gathered me into her warm embrace when I stepped off the bus, and for a fraction of a millisecond, my shoulders relaxed. She took me back to her place where Pop waited with more open arms.

'Hey, my darling girl. Everything's going to be all right, you'll see.'

Tears trailed down my cheeks as his words caressed my broken spirit. I tightened my arms around his thick waist, and he held my head to his chest, stroking the hair from my eyes. I wanted to believe him, believe that things would be all right, but it was hard to imagine the calm when you were being tossed and turned in a sea of waves, and all you saw were more storm clouds rolling in.

*****

I WOKE TO THE sound of my phone beeping on the bedside table. It was after nine, school had already started; a message was inevitable.

Max: *Where are you? Everything ok hon?*

I rubbed at my eyes and dimmed the phone to tap out my reply.

Me: *Staying with Granny Tess & Pop for a bit. Had a massive fight with Mum and Dad*

Found out they've been lying to me as much as I'd been lying to everyone else. My eyes grew murky as the realisation dawned on me again.

Max: *OMG are you ok?*
Me: *Not really. But I'll be fine. Xx*

When I returned to my room after a shower, my phone flashed with another message.

Amber: *Max told me. You all right?*
Me: *I will be. Just needed to get away.*
Amber: *Ok take care. And when you're back and ready we can get started on our search. xx*
Me: *I haven't forgotten. X*

AFTER I'D BEEN FED an enormous breakfast, we settled ourselves at the dining table to solve a one-thousand-piece puzzle of a cartoon world map. Scattered across the continents were animals, miniature-sized people in national costume, and anything synonymous to where they were placed in the world: a red bus for London, a kiwi in New Zealand, a lady in a kimono in Japan. We shared a magnifying glass, and every now and then we'd giggle when we realised the couple in Paris weren't dancing, they were having a good ol' Parisian smooch, and the boy in Scandinavia was going cross country skiing, not doing the splits.

I paused on a piece with what appeared to be the Canadian Mounted Police – two rigid men in red coats and brown pointy hats – my thoughts drifted to Tyler's declaration to go snowboarding with me in Canada one day. The memory snagged around my heart.

Granny Tess didn't push me to talk, but her gentle squeeze on my shoulder, each time she passed me a fresh cup of coffee, reminded me she'd be there when I was ready.

That afternoon Pop went out and Granny Tess put on *Rebel without a Cause*, one from her James Dean movie collection. Why she loved those movies I'd never know, but seeing the face of James Dean, with the deep-set dark eyes and chiselled cheek bones, startlingly similar to Tyler's, twisted my heart into painful knots. Tears fell quietly down my face. I brushed them away, but the dam had broken and I could no longer hold them back. My shoulders shook, the sobs ruining any self-control. Warm arms wrapped around me, and I buried my head in Granny Tess's shirt.

'It's so unfair. He's gone and I can't do anything about it. I want to change it back, but I can't, and now he's gone and I don't know if I'll be able to save any more girls. And Dad, he's been lying this whole time.'

'Shh, slow down, sweetie, one thing at a time.' She clasped my hands, her wrinkled fingers smoothing as they squeezed mine. 'What do you want to talk about first?'

'Dad, Tyler.' I choked back a sob. 'No, Dad. Why didn't you tell me he was like us?'

Her words were composed, as if she'd had them prepared. 'It wasn't my story to tell.'

'Why didn't he then? I don't understand why he'd keep that to himself.'

'I don't know.' Her shoulders slumped. 'No, I do. I tried to get him to talk to you. He was going to, it's hard for him to share what he can do.'

I frowned. 'Because of Mum?'

'Yes. Be kind to him when you get the chance to talk, it's not always been easy for him.'

'It's not always been easy for me,' I said. 'But he's my dad.'

'I know.' Granny Tess released a big sigh, turned off the T.V., and returned her gaze to my blotched face. 'So, who's this Tyler you're talking about?'

My chest constricted at hearing his name said out loud by anyone other than myself. 'James Dean,' I said, waving my hand at the T.V. screen. Her brow crinkled with questions. '*My* James Dean, his name was...is, Tyler.' I told her everything then; how he'd come into my life and how I changed his dad's death and the past, and because of that he'd gone. We slouched side by side on the couch, in identical positions with our feet curled underneath us.

'You met him. You really liked him.' My mouth turned up at the fond but painful memory. Granny Tess returned a weak smile, sympathy for my loss or my derangement, I couldn't tell. 'You believe me, don't you?'

'Of course I do.' She didn't even hesitate and patted my knee for extra reassurance. 'No doubt in my mind.'

'How? I mean I know you had a similar ability once, but you said you could never do what I do, so how can you comprehend this so easily?'

'Well for one, you're my Lucy Lou. And two, I might not have had your power, but I've had to live with my own repercussions. I know what it's like to live without someone as a result of a dream.'

'You do?' Could this be something to do with why she didn't dream anymore? Hopeful she'd continue with the details, I pressed my mouth closed.

'Pop isn't the only man I've ever loved.' She stared off into the space over my shoulder. 'His name was Thomas.'

—9—

'THOMAS? DID YOU NAME Dad after him?'

'Yes.' Her eyes turned wistful.

'He's not the father, is he?'

A short chuckle burst free. 'No, he's not. He was my high school sweetheart. He was tall and dark, everything Pop isn't. He rode a motorcycle, that's where I grew my own love of bikes.' A pained smile creased her lips. I couldn't believe what I heard. I thought it'd only ever been Granny Tess and Pop. The thought of Thomas and Tess threw me.

'Does Pop know Dad's named after your high school sweetheart?'

'Yes, he does, and if you don't stop interrupting, you'll never hear why,' she scolded.

'Sorry.' I lifted my hand to cover the small upward turn of my mouth and the words wanting to escape.

'We were so happy. After we graduated, we travelled and then rented a house together, which was quite improper for the time. We were going to get married one day, but we were still so young and wanted to travel more. Everything was, in so many ways, ordinary and perfect, but my dreams had changed me. I'd grown cocky with the power they'd given me, and I didn't even do anything great like you.

'I started to meditate when I was in my late teens. I read that it improved dream control and figured if I could already do things, maybe I could do more, help more, if I had more control.'

'And did it?' I was keen to know if it'd helped her, like it did for me. It had been what helped Tyler and me have shared dreaming while we weren't near each other.

'Yes, it did. Not a great deal, but enough to notice a heightened awareness. And made me more determined to do more. Thomas didn't like my obsession, he changed toward me. I don't know how to put it...' She paused, stared glassy eyed beyond me, before returning her focus to me. 'Nineteen-sixty-two. Fifty-four years ago. I was twenty-one when we decided to have a break. I thought it would do us good. I stupidly had this idea it would help us see what we loved about each other again. Well, it worked for me. Thomas on the other hand realised he could live without me and found someone else.'

'Oh, Granny Tess, I'm so sorry.'

She patted my leg. 'It gets worse than that, my dear. Should we make a cup of tea?' She rose and scuffed into the kitchen to fuel us for what only she knew came next. I jumped up to help, the anticipation almost killing me, but I suspected Granny Tess might be needing the breather far more than I did. She passed me my cup, and we returned to our cocoon on the sofa in the corner of the living room. Granny Tess placed a plate of biscuits on the coffee table. Gees, how long was this story?

'Thomas' new girlfriend lived in Melbourne. I knew he was seeing someone, but I didn't think it was serious, it couldn't be, we'd only broken up six weeks earlier. Anyhow, I'd made the decision to go round and see him, to try to patch things up. I planned on telling him how much I loved him, bear my soul and show him, remind him we were meant to be together.

'It was a Sunday afternoon, no, Saturday, yes, I'd finished my shift at the grocery store where I worked and headed straight to his place; he'd moved back in with his parents. I was too late. His girlfriend, Marlene, had arrived by bus from Melbourne the hour before, and I couldn't say any of the things I'd rehearsed. Instead, he introduced me to her, calling me an old friend. An old friend. Five years together and I'd become an old friend?' Granny Tess paused to sip on her tea, focusing on the delicate rim before speaking again. 'Lucy, do you remember what I said about being selfish?'

'Yeah.'

'Well, there's something far more dangerous...jealousy. It's a lot like selfishness really; you're only thinking about one person when that emotion crops up...you. He'd found someone else and instead of being happy for him, I only thought about what it meant for me. That my life had ended. I'd changed my mind. I wanted him back. My selfishness was fuelled by the jealousy.

'I went to sleep that night and dreamt his girlfriend never came home, I needed more time you see. If I'd had the opportunity to talk to him before she arrived, then I might've had a chance. I'd dreamt up a bit of rain before, so I did it again. This time I imagined a lot, which turned into flooding, which turned into her bus being delayed.' Granny Tess held her eyes closed for a moment, when she opened them, they brimmed with tears.

'I know how you're feeling, to wake and not remember what's happened. I only remembered the original event; my humiliation, my failed attempt to talk to him, and when I fell asleep the weather had been fine, but I woke to news of some of the worst flooding we'd seen in years. It turned out exactly as I dreamt it and her bus never arrived.' Granny Tess pressed her mouth together. My fingers clenched the teacup in my hands. I didn't dare speak.

'I learnt I never got to talk to him the second time around either. Thomas had heard Marlene's bus wouldn't be getting in until late and went for a hike...he always loved to go out in the rain.' Granny Tess's teacup chinked in its saucer; her trembling hand lifted to wipe at a tear gliding down her cheek. 'The floods that I selfishly conjured up in my mind ended up killing two people...a man driving home from work to his family, and the person he hit – Thomas. I wanted him back, but I lost him forever, I killed him.'

I let out a small, shock-like gasp. Jolted, even after everything I knew and experienced. She hadn't been lying, the story did get worse and this time I slid my arms around her shoulders as her silent weeping faded away.

'That's only the second time I've told that story to anyone.' She slipped a tissue from her shirt sleeve and dabbed at her nose.

'Who was the first?'

Her eyes softened. 'Pop.'

'And he believed you?'

'Oh yes. We've always had something special, he and I.'

'Why won't Mum believe Dad?'

'I don't know.' She shook her head. 'I think she wants to, but I think it's part of her makeup as a nurse: to see the facts, the evidence, and then find a solution to the problem. This has neither...evidence nor solution.'

'They had a big fight before I left.'

'I know. Your father called me.'

'I had no idea they had such a fake relationship.'

'It's not fake, they love each other.'

'But how can they if they don't trust each other? Trust, and belief in one another, is more important than anything else. Without that they're just two people trying to live together.'

'Are you sure you're only sixteen?' She laughed.

I smiled with her. 'Something Tyler taught me. He believed me, Granny Tess. I couldn't imagine being with someone who didn't.'

'I know. It took me finding your pop for me to realise that. I've never gotten over Thomas, or what part I played in his death, but I don't think we ever had what I've got with Pop. Could we have been happy? Absolutely, and we were for a time, and I think that's what your Mum and Dad have. It's not as good as it could be, but only we know how much better it can be. For them, it's all they know and they do pretty good considering, don't you think?'

I shrugged. 'I guess.'

'And you're pretty lucky in a sense, your perfect match is still out there.' She patted my leg.

'Yeah, with no idea who I am.'

'For now. If there's one thing I've learnt in my years, it's that the universe has a way of figuring it all out in the end.'

'Then why does it need us to change anything?'

'Maybe for the times it gets it wrong.'

I knotted my fingers together in my lap. 'Do you think it got Thomas wrong?'

'No, that's when I got it wrong. My selfishness blindsided me.' The sadness in her eyes twisted around my heart.

'Did you try to change it, bring him back?'

'I did. I thought of everything, tried everything. But from that day on the only dreams I had were of the floods, and then eventually even they stopped. I still don't like the rain.'

I'll bet.

'So, you never dream? Like ever?' I struggled to imagine it, the thought as foreign as dark, winter streets at midday in Northern Norway.

'Nothing, zilch, only a big lot of darkness up here I'm afraid.' She pressed her fingers to her temple. 'The world rests on your shoulders now,' she said with a grin.

'Thanks, but I'm wondering if Mum might be right.'

'About what?'

'That I should go on the tablets. I mean, look at the mess my dreams have got me into. It feels like I'm drowning, what with Dad and Tyler.' Not to mention my inability to save Megan. 'I brought them with me, I think I'll just take them until I feel on top of things again.'

'So, you've decided then?'

'Not really.'

She creased her brow. 'You're stalling. Why?'

I bit the inside of my lip. The seconds on the clock matched the thud of my heart as I tried to put into words a reason I didn't even know myself.

'People need me.'

Her lips twitched and her eyes lit up ever so slightly. 'They do. And I think you need this too.'

'But how do I manage that when everything else is crumbling around me?'

'Same way you always do. One thing at a time. Once you're home, things will settle with Dad.' She grabbed hold of my fingers and squeezed. 'And you know how to handle your dreams, you've been weaving them seamlessly into your life for years, you can do it again.' She found my eyes and dismissed my doubt. 'Even without Tyler.'

'So, you don't think I should take the tablets?'

'Do you?'

I shook my head.

'And don't you want to try to find him again?'

'In my dreams? He doesn't know I exist, it's impossible.'

'Nothing's impossible,' she said, smiling as Pop hobbled into the room.

'Hey, that's my line,' he said. 'What's she convincing you to do now? Don't do it, Lucy.' It was a playful warning, and he leaned to kiss the top of my head. He turned and did the same for Granny Tess, except she tilted her head and he kissed her on the lips.

'I'm simply suggesting she go find the boy of her dreams, *in* her dreams.'

'Oh, is that all?' His eyes widened with a chuckle.

'Yeah, you know, the usual, because as you always say –'

'Nothing's impossible.' He gave me a wink and strolled from the room.

And it really wasn't. Although, I didn't have a chance to go and find Tyler, because when the news came on the T.V. later that night I was as usual, drawn to it. A teenage girl had been killed in a hit-and-run. My stomach dropped, heart clenching around the all-consuming desire to change the senseless disaster. And when I caught Granny Tess's nod of approval, any remaining desire to run away from my dreams vanished.

—10—

A FAINT MOON HUNG low in the dark sky. I stepped to the edge of the small country bridge and peered over to the train tracks below, a distant hum rumbling through them. I lifted my eyes: no train yet.

A set of lights appeared to my right, and I turned as a car approached, its tyres crunching on the dirt track leading to the single-lane bridge. It crawled slowly and stopped before reaching the bridge, parking off to the side in the tall unkempt grass.

Four teenagers, three girls and a boy, jumped out and ran toward me.

'We made it.' A girl with long brown hair hopped up to the side of the bridge, her excitement spreading across her face.

They were all around the same age, baring no resemblance to one another, so I pinned them as friends rather than siblings. They stood in a row, the bridge barely coming above their waists as they clutched the stone barricade. The single light of the train's front engine loomed larger as it neared.

A woman climbed from the car. She leaned against the bonnet, satisfaction creeping onto her face, content to watch the action from a distance.

We were in the middle of farmland, the still air adding to the eeriness of standing on a tiny one-lane rickety bridge so late at night. But the teens showed no fear as they stood on tiptoe to experience the thrill of the train brushing closely underneath them.

The blast of the horn pierced the silent night, and the silver light gained on us, growing, blinding me. The freight train flew under us, the rush of wind throwing my hair behind me. Adrenaline pulsed through me, a grin taking over my face, fully understanding the desire to come out for this.

The four teens whooped and squealed with laughter. I shifted my attention to the woman behind us, her shoulders shaking as she joined in the merriment.

My hair blew in front of me and as I collected it up to return my face to the blowing wind, I caught sight of a car stopped in the middle of the road a short distance away, its headlights lighting the road in front of it. I stepped away from the side of the bridge to get a better view. It hadn't parked, it'd just stopped. How weird. What was it doing?

The last of the train rumbled under the bridge and the wind died down, the laughter still spilling into the night. The group turned and spread out as they lazily made their way across the bridge back to the car. I balled my hands into fists, planted to the spot. Everyone else too high on adrenaline to detect any imminent danger.

The stopped car sped forward, gravel spinning as the accelerator hit the floor, the car aiming straight for the group. The mother turned toward the light and back to the kids. 'Look out!'

They scattered all over, and the car veered left, toward the edge of the bridge, where the long-haired girl had darted for her escape. She widened her eyes and tried to jump away, but she had nowhere to go. I lurched forward, sprinting to reach her as the car slammed into her body, flung it onto the bonnet and, threw her over the crumbling edge of the barricade. I rammed my chest into the stone wall as she landed with a thwack onto the tracks below.

I shook my head, anguish twisting in my guts. 'Oh God, no.'

The car sat immobile as wails sounded around me, but I couldn't take my eyes off her disjointed and unmoving body. The car groaned to life again, and I spun as it kicked up the dirt and reversed away, as if removing itself from the guilt of what it'd done. Two black shadows sat in the front seats, and before anyone had a chance to stop them, they drove away.

WHEN I WOKE, HEART pulsing with the same adrenalin I'd experienced in my dream, I went into autopilot. I reached for my jet bracelet and slid it onto my wrist, acknowledging the loss in the same way I did for every life I watched pass. I dragged my pencils and sketchbook from my bag and drew the thick lines of her long hair as it trailed over her shoulders. Doing what I needed to come to terms with the loss I'd witnessed. But then came the fun part. Where I investigated why this had happened and what I could do to prevent it and change the outcome, to bring her back to life.

Carrying my laptop, I plodded out to the loungeroom where Granny Tess sat with a cup of tea.

'Good morning, dear. Sleep all right?' She lifted the cup to cover the sly smile edging onto her lips.

'You know I didn't.'

Her shoulders dropped. 'Sorry. Was it horrible?'

I raised my eyebrows. She should know the answer to that.

'I am *not* helping. I'll go and make you a coffee.' She shifted to the edge of her chair, about to stand.

I laughed at her nervousness and waved my hand. 'No, it's fine. Although, I won't say no to that coffee.'

When she returned from the kitchen with a steaming hot mug, she perched on the edge of the seat, twisting the teacup in her hands. She gazed down and back up, failing in her attempt to appear disinterested. I doubted she'd been this close to any dreams in a very long time.

'I need to figure out why they drove into her.' I opened my internet browser and brought up the newest article, scanning the details. 'They've found the driver.' Drunk and high as a kite apparently, which explained the erratic behaviour.

'And she was only seventeen,' Granny Tess said. 'How old was the victim?'

'Kayla was fourteen.' Two years younger than me. Way too young to die.

'Did they know each other?'

Scrolling down the page, I read more. 'Doesn't seem like it. Sounds pretty random. Just another couple kids from her high-school out getting drunk.' And with no reason behind it, like most of the deaths I saw, it meant evaluating every moment leading up to the accident to work out the split second where things could change.

By the time I closed my eyes that night I had it all figured out. The mum.

Nothing could change the course of the car, but the mum could change the course of the kids. She'd alerted them to the speeding car, prior to that they were all euphoric and in their own little world. Without the few seconds of warning and head start, Kayla wouldn't have been standing in the way.

If the mum didn't climb out to watch the kids with as much interest, she wouldn't have been in the position to call out to them. Unaware until the last few moments, the car would've crashed into the side of the bridge right next to her, but not into her. If it played out as I imagined, she'd remain safe and alive.

And she did.

The major incident that'd been shared all over the news became a minor incident only the four kids shared with each other, so the following morning, when I told Granny Tess about it over break-fast, she had no idea what I was talking about.

AFTER BREAKFAST, WHEN I should've been at school, again, we sat cross legged on a cushion on the cement floor of Granny Tess's art room for the second time since my arrival. Rain pelted the roof and huge gusts of wind blew the trees into a frenzy. I silently reached my hand over to Granny Tess's, because although I loved the sound, I now knew how much she didn't.

We closed our eyes.

Meditating with her beside me had been weird at first, but even if I didn't say it, I liked being forced into the practice. Each time grew easier, and eventually my mind, with its vast wilderness of death, loss and betrayal, became a wonderland with only one thing on the horizon – Tyler. It was heaven. All thoughts of sadness vanished, and all I saw and felt in those long minutes of silence was him – his belief, his trust, his love.

*****

I MARCHED STRAIGHT TO my room when I returned home later that afternoon, getting straight to work methodically unpacking my bag: shoes back on the bookcase, clothes thrown into my wardrobe, tablets in my bedside draw. I paused at a noise on the other side of the house, stilling my breath. Letting it out, I grabbed my sketchbook from my bag and dropped it onto my bed. I'd shifted from the anger phase of Dad's secret, and now with every sudden burst of sound in the house my heart skipped a beat, and I found myself smack bang in the middle of 'get it over with already'.

Twenty minutes later, I rested sideways on my bed, back against the wall, book and pencil in hand. A light tap on my bedroom door sounded. It wasn't Mum, her knocks said 'I'm coming in'. Dad's were more a question.

'Come in,' I said, and Dad stepped tentatively into the room.

'Can we talk?'

I closed my book and placed it on the bed. 'Don't think we really have a choice, do we?'

The mattress sunk as Dad sat on the edge of the bed. He plucked up my pencil and tapped it against his leg.

Wanting the pain over fast, I ripped the band-aid straight off and asked the first question. 'Why didn't you ever tell me?'

'I couldn't.' He lowered his head, fingers fidgeting in his lap like an eight-year-old. I'd never seen Dad so unsure of himself. Lifting his head, he stared straight into my eyes, a nervous frown on his face. 'I didn't want to scare you.'

I frowned back. 'Scare me? Do you know how frightened and alone I've been?'

'Yeah.' It came out as a whisper. 'I've felt it myself.'

'Then why wouldn't you say something?' I struggled to understand, waiting for the words that would shed light on his thinking.

'To begin with I feared I might be wrong, that you weren't really like me at all. Then when Granny Tess assured me I wasn't, I couldn't shake the worry I've always lived with. What if you still didn't believe me? I didn't need yet another person to think I was off this planet.'

'Like Mum?'

He slid his glasses off and rubbed the bridge of his nose. 'Yeah.' He positioned the black frames back onto his face. 'I've held onto hope for so many years, but I don't think she'll ever fully understand what this is, what it's like.' And for the first time I saw a sadness in his eyes and his need to cover up his affliction better than I ever had.

'What's it like for you? What things do you dream?'

He hesitated, but I held my eyes firm, sharing my understanding with him. 'It depends on the week. It's often local, because of what I do. Ski accidents, work type injuries, break-ins, car accidents, that sort of thing. Basically whenever someone is hurt. I can't always fix it, but without fail, I always try.'

'Does it get confusing? When things've changed?' I'd had Tyler to remind me what I'd missed, but without someone beside him to help, Dad had been on his own.

'I work at the newspaper, remember. Why do you think I pore over those pages every morning?' Funny how I'd always likened Dad to Clark Kent: reporter for the local paper, raven hair like mine, black-framed glasses. How did I completely miss that he had a whole other Superman persona going on? Batman and Superman under the same roof – life could get interesting. He continued, 'As much as I love helping the world in this small way, part of me always hoped you weren't like me, hoped you wouldn't have this burden. So I kept quiet and watched.'

I pressed my fingers into my palms. 'That's like watching me break my leg and letting me walk on my own without help.'

'No, it's not. I never knew for sure, at least not until Granny Tess said something. And part of me also wanted you to figure it out for yourself without me giving you any pre-meditated ideas. If I told your brother how good he'd be at basketball, or even medicine, would it help him become as good as he could? He'd become complacent or he'd be frightened off by my premature admiration. I needed to let you discover for yourself.'

'That my leg was broken? You know a normal dad would carry his kid to the car and take her to the hospital for help.'

'Well, I'm not a normal dad, and truth be told I never thought you were sick, that your leg was broken. That's what Mum's always thought, and it's why she's always wanted to get you fixed.' He smiled at me. 'But you know what, you're not broken. You're anything but. You're just learning to live with the limp of this responsibility, which, when you do, could very well become a gift.'

'What if I don't want the gift?'

'We don't always have a choice. Talent is given to us whether we like it or not. All you can choose is if you're going to make the most of it, to go along for the ride, or if you're going to neglect it.'

'I'm not going to neglect it. I love saving lives. I might have lost my own in the process, but I'm used to things being unfair.' I let my head fall against the wall, my shoulders slumping.

'No one said it'd be fair. Life usually isn't, but it can be good.'

'Not if you've lost the person you love.' I hadn't meant to talk about Tyler.

'No, that can make it hard.' He dropped his eyes momentarily, and I had a feeling he wasn't talking about me.

'I'm sixteen years old. I'm meant to be worrying about exams, and boys, and what clothes to wear.'

'You never worry about what clothes to wear,' he said, surprising me again with his insight.

'I know, but my point is, that's the sort of thing I *should* be thinking about, not how I can save an entire plane from flying into the ocean.'

'What plane, when did that happen?' And the journalist had arrived.

'Exactly. It didn't.' I sighed. 'I changed it. They all died and little ol' me brought them back to life.'

His eyes widened. 'You brought people back from the dead? Granny Tess never told me that.' His surprise surprised me.

'Now can you see my dilemma?'

'I can. I can also see the power.'

'I don't want power. I just want to help people.'

'Of course you do. You always have.' He shook his head, as if only just comprehending what I could do. Admiration overflowed, until softening as he looked at me with eyes that pleaded and said 'I won't let you down again'. He opened his arms. 'Come here.'

I shuffled across the bed, into his outstretched arms and he squeezed me tight. 'I'm so sorry. I'm sorry for not being brave enough to protect my little girl. Will you forgive me?' My eyes welled and I nodded into him. 'You know, you'll come to get used to it in time, like I did. Promise.'

I knew he was right. I'd been able to do it once before, to come to a place of acceptance. What I wanted to know and wished he could give me, was a promise I'd be able to live without Tyler.

—11—

'TELL ME WHAT YOU know,' Amber said, making herself comfortable on my bed. I sat on my chair in the middle of the room and put my feet on the mattress.

She'd given me two days to settle back into school and, now we were at Friday afternoon, she was more determined than a dog with a bone. She wouldn't be giving up until we found Tyler. Her enthusiasm scared me; like, would this mean we'd actually find him? I still wasn't convinced it was a good idea, because what then? What would that mean? The chance of seeing him might grow, but so would the prodding agony that he remained out of reach.

Amber kicked my foot. 'You look like you're heading to your execution.'

'Maybe I am.'

'Come on, Luce, the boy of your dreams is out there.' She waved at the window, and her face, with more than enough enthusiasm for both of us, finally rubbed off on me and my smile betrayed me.

Boy of my dreams – understatement of the century. 'You're right.'

'Of course I am.' She laughed. 'I can't believe you didn't find out what school he went to.' Neither could I.

'We had other things on our mind.'

She shook her head. 'Never mind. We can figure it out.' She grabbed her pen and notebook. 'So?'

'He surfed. I know he usually walked to the beach, but it was far enough away that his mum sometimes drove him.'

'Would three k's be too much?'

'With a surfboard I reckon, yeah. Maybe just one?'

'Let's go two to make sure.' She wrote it down, then putting the pen to the side of her mouth, said, 'But that was his house. His school could've been anywhere.'

I frowned, drawing on all our conversations. 'I think a lot of his mates went to the same school, and they all surfed. I feel like it'd be a school close to the coast if there were that many into it, don't you?'

'Five k's then?' Her stare probed me with the question. 'Ten?' *Was that enough?* She raised her brows. 'Fifteen?' I nodded.

'And he said something about Manly, so we should focus our search on the north.' She wrote it down. I closed my eyes. 'The uniform is maroon and white.'

'How do you know *that* and not the name?'

'Saw it in a photo. He had on like a woollen type jumper with a white shirt underneath.'

'Private then?'

'Dunno. Hard to tell. It didn't look that fancy.'

'But they do meditation. I can't imagine that at a public school. Can you imagine them trying that at our school?'

I laughed. I couldn't. 'Yeah, it's probably private, but let's not rule out public.'

Amber scribbled on the paper. I let my gaze drift out the window to the trees over the back fence and the snow-capped mountains in the distance.

'Anything else?' Amber spoke gently, luring my attention back into the room.

I paused before offering a slow shake of my head.

It took ten pieces of A4 paper to print out a detailed enough map of northern Sydney. We drew a big fat red line at roughly fifteen kilometres from the beach. Amber handed me half the sheets of paper and collected up her own. 'You work on that lot, I'll do these.'

She settled back on the bed, and silence descended over the room as we searched up schools and ticked off our requirements. Maroon uniform? Check. Offers meditation? Check. Within our estimated close enough distance to the beach? Check.

After two hours we'd only managed two pages each; it appeared I had some homework to do.

By the end of the following week I retrieved my crumpled but completed map sheets from my bag. 'Here you go, Miss Jones.' I handed them to Amber.

Her eyes roamed the list, her mouth moving slightly as she counted. 'Eleven. That's a total of nineteen potential schools.'

'Now what?' Max plucked up the sheets, casting her eyes over our work.

Amber snatched back the papers and slid them into a folder. 'Now I call them all.' She placed her palms flat on top of the folder, a large, satisfied grin plastered across her face.

'All? Why aren't you doing any?' Max quizzed me. 'I mean I know I wouldn't want to cold call the schools, you're much braver than me, Amber, but it's your guy, Luce, I thought you'd be keener.'

I rubbed my nails on the wooden table, picking at a rough piece. 'I'm still not sure I want to just...' I paused thinking of the word. 'Confront him.'

'Don't say confront, that sounds brutal,' Amber said. 'Think waft.'

'Like a bad smell?'

'Okay, no. Breezily walk over to him, flick your hair, flutter your eyelashes.' She demonstrated the action and I laughed at how absurd she looked.

'Who walks breezily? What is that anyway?'

'Oh I don't know.' She waved her hand, dismissing my objections. 'I haven't thought that far ahead. You know him, you know what he likes. That's the bit you need to think about. Homework, Miss Piper.' She pointed her finger at me.

I groaned. That was worse than the last lot of homework she set for me.

*****

THE FOLLOWING WEDNESDAY, AFTER finishing up a massive assignment for English, I headed up the hill for a run before dinner. With the wind in my hair, and the comforting sound of Twenty One Pilots' 'Holding onto You' playing in my ears, I gained momentum as I steadily jogged along the track. I wound through the trees, the crisp air piercing the back of my throat whilst the spring sunshine warmed my shoulders.

At the end of the track I bent over, placed my hands on my bare knees and sucked in a lungful of air before climbing through the fence and onto the hilltop. This was the only place I could reach the peace needed for the meditation I'd continued since returning from Granny Tess and Pop's.

Granny Tess had called a couple of times to continue her mentoring, wanting to find out how I'd progressed, if it was getting easier, and if it had helped with the dreams?

'I'm still doing it, at least a few times a week,' I'd told her when we spoke the day before. And yes, it had become much easier. 'I'm still dreaming, finding people to save.' Just the week before I'd saved a little boy who died in a farming motorbike accident. He likely continued to ride his motorbike dangerously around his property, but I couldn't control that any more than the snowfall on the mountain. He was alive, that had to be enough.

Granny Tess suggested I use the meditation to fall asleep. 'When you've got control of your mind and you take that straight into a sleep, it's amazing, trust me.' And I did trust her. More than anyone.

I tugged the music from my ears and eased myself onto the ground, allowing the tranquil silence to wrap itself gently around me. Once upon a time I came here to escape my life, my dreams, and the thoughts ever rampant in my overactive mind. Now, in a sense, I came for the same thing, but I also came to be with them. My thoughts of Tyler became part of me up here, on our hill, and part of me knew I would always find him here.

I closed my eyes. Inhaled. Exhaled.

Lowering myself back into the browning grass, my breathing slowed and I fell asleep.

I STOOD UNDER A canopy of branches. Under the gorgeous maple, that in reality had re-birthed a vast magnitude of green leaves, but in this dream displayed the full colours of autumn. The tree under which I'd shared many moments with my friends and even better ones in my magical dreams with Tyler.

Not this time. This time, I was all alone. Peacefully – but monumentally so.

Standing there, under the luminous light of the dream, I imagined I wasn't so alone. I imagined what it would be like to see him here again. Would it be the same? It'd been so long.

I faced away from the tree, but sensing a change, I turned toward the fat trunk – and him. Tyler. Standing casually with his hands folded behind his back, leaning against the tree, one foot crossed over the other. I startled, gasping.

His eyes lit up as he stared over my left shoulder into the distance.

I glanced behind me, and back to him.

'Tyler.' I said his name softly, hoping to gain his attention but not scare him away.

He pushed off the tree and strode toward me, but his gaze remained on something else. He'd almost reached me, was almost beside me, but it was as if he wasn't truly there, like I only saw a memory. My hand flinched, wanting to reach for him. I held it shakily by my side.

I said his name again, however fruitless it might be. He marched straight past and disappeared into thin air.

I startled awake. A piece of grass poked me in the nose, and I brushed my hand to shift it. I sat up and a smile formed without trying, because even though I felt an overwhelming sense of loss at having seen Tyler, I'd still seen him. He didn't see me, but it felt more real than any of the hundreds of drawings I'd pencilled in the weeks since he'd gone. And even better than that, I'd made it happen. I'd intentionally thought of him and he'd appeared – I was a magician. Chuckles of excitement bubbled out of me and echoed across the hills.

I had to find him. If seeing him in reality gave me a fraction of that feeling again then I wanted a great big chunk of it. Consequences and embarrassment be damned.

*****

'How many schools have you called?' I asked Amber the following day as we settled behind our easels in art.

Guilt flooded her eyes. 'I'm really sorry.' She dropped her gaze. 'What with work and exams coming up...I've only managed to call a couple. And schools aren't open on the weekend.'

'Why are you sorry?'

'Because I wanted to find his school for you sooner.' She stuck a loose thread of hair into her lilac headband.

'Do you think I'm upset with you? Because I'm not. It's not your responsibility.' I grabbed my work from my portfolio case and positioned it on the easel.

'But I told you I was going to do it, and I haven't gotten very far.'

'That's why I'm going to help you.'

'You are?'

I shrugged. 'Yeah. I want to see him again.' My eyes fluttered closed, bringing his face to mind. 'I just really want to see him.'

Amber squeezed my knee. 'You will.'

I called a school that afternoon during lunch. Away from ogling eyes and ears at the table, I paced the lawn on the other side of the tree, awkwardly pretending to be Tyler's mum, Sally, asking if I could get a message to Tyler Sims.

'Tyler Sims?' The lady queried over the phone.

'Yes. Year eleven.' I bit into my thumb nail as I listened to the *tap tap* of the keyboard on the end of the line.

'I'm afraid we don't have a Tyler Sims enrolled here.'

'How strange.' I strangled out the words. 'Thanks anyway,' I said quickly and hit the end button.

I rounded the tree and slumped onto the bench. 'That was horrible.' Amber's face showed pity and a big wad of understanding. 'How do you manage, Miss 'I never lie about anything'?'

'I *don't* manage. I spend ten minutes talking myself into it before I press call. That's another reason I haven't gotten far.'

'Why didn't you tell me?'

'I didn't want to frighten you any more than you already were.'

I sighed. 'It's fine. We'll pace ourselves.' Amber screwed up her nose, and I bit the inside of my lip. 'One call a day.'

One call a day and soon I'd be closer to seeing Tyler again. The thought wrapped around my heart like a warm hug. The hug fell away and my chest constricted. *One call.* He wouldn't be the only thing I'd be seeing. I couldn't forget the real reason for my trip and the more urgent need to go to Sydney. *One call.* Why hadn't I thought of that already?

I jumped off the bench, typing the business name into the web browser as I strode away.

'You've done your call for the day,' Amber yelled after me.

I held my phone in the air, my back to the group. 'Different one,' I shouted, marching around to the other side of the tree. My pulse thundered in my head as I hit the green telephone icon.

My heartbeat grew heavier with each shrill of the ringtone, and right when I thought I might pass out, it cut off.

'Salander Computer Repairs, you're speaking with Benjamin Webb.' A wave of nausea rose through me as the voice from the plane flowed down the line. He'd only spoken to me once, but I recognised that same curt huskiness.

The phone shook against my ear. I hadn't taken enough time to consider what I needed to say. I had his name now, but what else did I need to find out?

'Hi...hello. I was...um...I brought my laptop in the other day. I think I spoke to the owner, the guy with...uh, black hair, a bit curly on the top, tall.'

'I'm the only one who works here love, you musta been talkin' to me. What do you need?'

'So, you own Salander Computer Repairs?'

'It would seem so, but what's that got to do with your laptop?'

I startled. 'Oh, nothing. Just making sure I'm talking to the right person. Thanks.' And I yanked the phone from my ear and pressed end.

My shoulders still heaved with exertion and fear when I slumped back at the table, the ringing in my ears doing little to block out the concerned expressions on the faces of my friends.

'Here, drink.' Max shoved a bottle into my face, and I took a big swig of water, the trembling in my hands slowly easing.

'His name is Benjamin Webb,' I finally said. Not Salander; that part was only a sick joke. Because didn't another book come out in the Dragon Tattoo series? Something about a spider web? I shivered as a bristling dread climbed up my neck.

*****

FOR THE REST OF the week, in between calling schools to find Tyler, I searched up everything on every Benjamin Webb I could find. Which wasn't a lot. I pored over every online article with his name. No reference of any past police-related offenses, but I did find mention of him in his local newspaper in an article about the opening of his business. How he had years of experience in the industry and how his aunt, who'd raised him, had encouraged him to finally open the business.

'I think she just wanted me to move out of home,' he said. The article was dated five years earlier.

I hadn't gained anything to add to my evidence for the police. But at least I now had his name. I wouldn't need to approach him when I went to Sydney, just go to his business and hope to see his van so I could get the rest of the number plate.

*****

THE LUNCH BELL HAD yet to go and I sat alone at our table at the end of yet another week, making it nearly six without Tyler. I had my book out, drawing something I didn't normally draw: a scene from my dream, inside the room in the middle of the bush. The bed, the apparatus on the walls, the table and stool. I couldn't remove the image from my mind and hoped by drawing it, like with the faces, it might remove its hold on me. If only I knew the location of the shed so I could send the police straight there instead.

The bell sounded, startling me from my daze, the pencil slipping from my fingers. Blue and white uniform-clad students poured from the buildings, a familiar blond one strode directly toward me, a slight skip in her step. Amber's grin widened as she drew closer before dropping onto the opposite bench.

She slapped her palms face-down on the table. 'I got the car. Mum and Dad said yes.'

'They did? That's awesome. For when and what did you say we were doing?'

'Girls weekend. Next weekend.'

'Without Max?' I asked. Amber raised her eyebrows and nodded over my shoulder. Max smiled sheepishly sliding in beside me. 'You're coming?'

'What, you thought I'd just sit around here while you're off on exciting escapades, saving damsels in distress?'

'And seeing Tyler,' Amber piped up.

'But I'm not.'

'Are too.' She shoved a piece of paper across the table. I gaped at the blank piece of paper, its edges fluttering in the breeze. Quickly plucking up the valuable piece of paper before it blew away, I turned it over and read the two words on the page – *Macquarie High.*

I looked up. 'You narrowed it down to one?'

Amber nodded repeatedly, eyes alight. 'Yes.'

'You're sure?'

'I've called the school. They have a Tyler Sims enrolled in year eleven.'

I gulped and stared at the words slowly distorting on the page, solid evidence that he truly was out there.

'You should probably say thank you,' Max whispered in my ear.

'Right, yeah. Thank you.' My voice quivered. I couldn't believe this tiny piece of paper held the key to seeing him. I still had no idea what I'd say when I did, but right now, that concern stood in the shadow of the absolute and sheer joy that I'd soon be seeing Tyler again.

*****

The waves crashed behind me, the heartbeat of the steady rush of water against the shore calmed me, wooed me, but I was cast under a different spell today. The spell of her beauty. I couldn't take my eyes off her. Dark hair fell over her shoulders and she flicked it back as she glanced over at me with eyes that killed me every time I stared into them. Then she smiled, and I knew in that moment, she was so much more than just a gorgeous girl: she was mine.

—12—

I CLENCHED MY JAW, anticipating the days ahead as Amber slowed the car to a stop in front of the backpacker's hostel we'd be staying at for the next two nights. A street light flickered up ahead, illuminating the gardens it towered over, and plunged it into darkness again. Swallowing hard, I tried not to think of all that could go wrong.

Amber opened the back door for me like a valet. 'Come on, lovely. Anyone would think we'd lured you to your death.'

'It could be, we don't know yet.' I climbed from the car.

Max retrieved our bags from the boot and dumped them on the curb. 'Stop being so melodramatic. Can we just get inside and go to bed, I'm knackered.'

Picking up my bag, I followed her into the fluorescent green building, the smell of stale cigarette smoke and mouldy linen hitting me the moment I stepped in the foyer. A young, gum-smacking woman, with blue highlights in her otherwise black-as-night hair, sat behind the front desk scrolling on her phone. She threw us a quick glance, turned back to her phone, scrolled some more, and put it down before giving us her proper attention.

'Got a booking?' She reached for a pen and dragged an opened book across the desk, eyeing us expectantly.

Amber stood on tiptoe to peer over Max's shoulder. 'Amber Jones. We booked the family room.' It'd been one of the parental stipulations of this trip. Still cheap, but safer they said.

'Nope, no Amber, sorry. The family room is being used by the Cooper family this week.' She said 'family' as if the fact we weren't one was reason enough not to give us the room.

Amber dropped back onto her heels. 'But I called last –'

'Ah, here it is. You've got the booking for next week.' She tapped her finger on the page.

Max stepped forward, tired and in need of a resolution. 'We don't want the booking for next week. We booked it for *tonight*. Have you got another room we can stay in?'

'Not a *family* room.' She did it again, this time staring down her nose at us. 'I can give you three singles in one of our regular rooms?'

'In a room with strangers?' I choked out.

'Yes, the rest of our rooms are five bunk rooms. I'll put you in room three which only has a couple, and two single men.' *Only?*

Amber and Max turned to me, resignation in their eyes. *Not like we have a choice.* I shrugged in unavoidable agreement.

We approached the room with caution and glumly dragged our bags behind us, awkwardly assessing our home for the next two nights. The room was larger than I expected. Five bunks were evenly spaced against the walls, and propped below a large window on the opposite side of the room sat an armchair and a green faux leather beanbag. A young man, maybe in his early twenties, relaxed in the armchair tapping at a laptop resting on his knees. Another man of similar age laid on the bottom bunk beside the window, arm behind his head, chatting to him.

'Hey wasup,' Laptop Guy said as we stumbled into the room.

'Hi,' we chorused, sounding braver than I expected.

'These beds taken?' I asked, pointing left of the door to the only two beds not rumpled or obviously occupied.

'Nah man, they're good, all yours.'

The guy on the bed sat up as we set our luggage in the corner between the two bunks. 'So, where you girls from?'

'Oh, we've come from Antil Springs,' Amber said and I shot her a glare, wanting to smack her. What happened to stranger danger? We might be sixteen but we were probably in more danger than we were as six-year-olds. I remembered Tyler's motto of trust until proven otherwise. How stupid, how dangerous. We didn't know this guy.

'Really? I was there last month. What brings you to Sydney?'

After learning the newly introduced Paul and Dan were travelling around the country from Perth, Paul returned to tapping at his laptop and Dan left the room to join in the common room activities.

We shuffled about near our beds, a little lost until Amber plucked out a Tupperware container Laurie had sent along for us. She raised the container, her eyebrows arching. 'Dinner?'

'Yes,' Max and I said simultaneously.

*****

I HELD THE CRUMPLED piece of paper tightly in my fist, but I didn't need it, the address of 'Salander Computer Repairs' was permanently etched in my mind. Staring out the bus window, I clutched my backpack to my chest. Why was I so nervous? It wasn't like I'd be seeing him or anything. I just hoped to God his van would actually be there, and I wouldn't have to bunker down somewhere and wait.

I was in luck.

The bus stopped at the end of his street, and I set my eyes on a small but fat tree protruding from the curb directly opposite his house. Twice my height, and a spray of soft green foliage to hide behind. I paused once I stood behind the trunk, catching sight of the van. Anger swelled in my guts knowing what went on behind those tinted black windows. But I didn't have time to dwell. I poked my head out and focused on the number plate – BNP 49A. My skin crawled, I wanted to get the hell away from there, but I didn't trust myself to remember the letters, not when they were so important. I knelt down and slid my book from my backpack. I flipped to Megan's page and scribbled the missing piece of the number plate.

My heart pounded as I stood on shaky legs. I slung my bag over my shoulder and chanced a last glimpse of the place. Webb opened the side gate and stepped into the driveway.

Crap.

I ducked my head behind the tree. My breath hitched as I willed my body to shrink. Did he see me? My feet prepared for flight, but I couldn't draw attention to myself.

A twig snapped under my Converse. *Shit.* Now I had no choice but to move. I gripped the strap of the bag at my shoulder and stepped back onto the footpath away from his house. I held my head high, nothing to see here.

I resisted the urge to peer over my shoulder, instead eyes fixed on the yellow and blue bus stop sign fifty...forty...and finally ten metres away. I reached the end of the street, crossed the road and reached bus stop twelve. I turned and stared back down the street, my stomach lurching into my throat.

He stood staring at me.

Standing beside the front door of the van fifty metres away, yet it felt like he might have the power to reach me in five steps. I yanked my eyes away. I couldn't let him think he was anything more to me than any other passer-by on this ordinary Sunday morning. I peered up the road, never more grateful to see the bus in the far distance.

I waved as it neared, determined not to glance in Webb's direction. I climbed onto the bus, catching a blur of white from his direction, the van reversed out the driveway. *Shit.* Blood pulsed heavily behind my temple. I sat halfway down the bus and fixed my eyes on the road ahead, willing the driver to speed up and whisk me away. I swivelled in my seat. The van drove three cars behind us. Was he following me? I didn't know if I should ditch the bus and throw him off my scent or stay on and hope it was a coincidence he trailed me.

Ten stops later and he remained two cars back. Three more stops to go. One arm held the grey backpack on my lap, the other gripped the pole attached to my seat, poised to press the stop button. I let stop twenty-five sail past. I'd get off at the next one. I pushed the button. When I stood by the door, I carefully peered out the back window. No white van. I turned to see if he was next to the bus. In front? Nothing. The bus lurched to a stop, and I flew down the steps.

I needed to backtrack, but first I wanted to make sure I was out of sight in case the van suddenly reappeared. I dashed across the road and hid in the shadow of a tall building. A bank. Whipping my eyes down the road, I darted through the opening doors, relief surging out of me. That was close, too close. Cal would have my head when he heard how much.

After five minutes I plucked up enough courage to leave the safety of the bank. No van in sight. Feeling an overwhelming sense of being followed, I scratched at my neck and picked up my pace. I couldn't see anything out the corner of my eyes, his van was long gone, but the unease remained until I stepped, trembling, through the doors of the backpacker's.

Amber and Max were watching T.V. when I entered the common room. Their calm expressions filled instantly with nervous concern the moment I came into view. They jumped from the couch, rushing to my side.

Max grabbed onto my arm. 'You okay? You're shaking, what happened?' Failing to form any words, I covered her hand with my own.

'Lucy, talk to us, you're freaking me out.' Amber's worried voice broke through my daze.

'S-s-sorry,' I stammered. 'I think it's the adrenalin wearing off. Nothing happened. I'm fine.' No need to freak them out any more than they already were. I held my lips firm as they led me back to our room. I lowered myself onto my bed. 'I think I'm gonna lay here for a minute if that's okay.' I closed my eyes.

'Did you get the number plate?' Max whispered.

I cracked open an eye. 'Yeah.' I patted the backpack still clutched to my side.

'Good.'

My heart slowly subsided until it no longer felt like I'd run a marathon. But going there, seeing him, him seeing me, made me need a rest as if I had. I slept for a couple of hours.

When I woke, the girls were already dressed for the evening. I showered and changed into denim shorts, a small, plain blue top, and white Cons.

We marched out of the hostel doors, Max on one side, striking in her tight cherry top and long bare legs below a black skirt, Amber on my other, blond hair glistening under the remaining sunlight. She looped her arm through mine, and pressed into my side, her white dress swishing onto my bare legs. A large smile spread across her thin mouth. 'All right, so part one of our mission is complete. Now for the exciting part.'

'Today was plenty exciting, thanks very much.' And scary, and a touch too close for comfort. I shuddered.

'Tomorrow will be better exciting. Do you have a plan?'

I swung my attention her way. 'No, do you?'

She squeezed my arm. 'That was your homework, remember.'

'Yeah, but I kinda got caught up in some serial-killer hunting thing.'

'Not anymore. Get your head in the game.'

'Do we even know he's going to be there? What if he's home sick, or he's got extra lessons after school?'

'Stop talking yourself out of this,' Max said.

'I'm not, it's just that...' Okay, maybe I was.

We found a nice-looking Italian joint around the corner, and while we waited for our pasta to arrive, we came up with a plan.

Later in bed I spent ten minutes wrestling with the thin covers on the strange mattress before the delicate sound of Amber's steady breathing filled the room. Still awake, I lay quietly as each of our roommates shuffled into the room, climbed under their own covers, and muttered quietly to one another. Dan's snore started up in his bed by the window; Paul had a small reading light on and held a book open above him. The couple, who we still hadn't met, slept on the bunk on the other side of the window from Dan and Paul. Once everyone in our room had settled for the night I thought I'd be able to relax, but images of my close encounter continued to surface. I practised my meditation techniques, concentrating on the slow rise and fall of my chest, and finally sunk into the mattress and into sleep.

*****

I CRACKED OPEN MY eyes, taking in the strange, echoed sounds of the large room, the odd smell, and the rough blanket under my fingertips. I dragged it up under my chin, feeling on edge and exposed in a room of people I barely knew. Thoughts from the previous day returned to mind. I wanted to roll over and go back to sleep, but paired with the knowledge of what we were attempting in a few hours, I was suddenly wide awake.

A couple of metres away, Max stirred in her bed. I could barely make her out with only the sliver of light filtering through the edges of the large window at the other end of the room. I wiped the sleep from my eyes and stretched as I propped myself up.

'She awake yet?' I asked Max, gesturing to the bed above me.

Max yawned and shook her head. 'Think the excitement got to her.'

I grinned and reached under the bed for my backpack. My hand found empty air and my smile fell away. I lowered myself to my stomach and hung my head over the side. Nothing. *What? No.* I threw myself out of bed and onto the ground. On hands and knees, I scanned the floor in the near dark, trying to locate my gear.

'I can't find my bag.' I panted, heart in my throat.

Max shuffled into a sitting position. 'It's right there.' She pointed to the end of my bed.

'No, my backpack. It was under the bed, it's gone, someone's taken it.' I marched to the other side of the room and ripped back the curtains. Dim early morning rays spilled into the room.

'Hey,' Dan said.

I ignored him and bolted back to the door and flicked the switch, sending artificial light bouncing off the walls, the intensity burning my eyes.

Someone swore, another person groaned loudly.

'Where is it?' I said, rummaging amongst some of the piles of baggage and clothes strewn on the floor, at ends of beds, even *on* some of the beds. 'Someone's taken my bag.'

My invasion wasn't taken lightly. Curse words were thrown my way, and Paul slapped my arm as he tried to shove me out of his gear. Max grabbed onto me and dragged me back to her bed. Amber climbed down her ladder and sat beside me. I glared around the room, but the matching daggers propelled back were just as fierce. I lowered my eyes and held my balled hands tightly in my lap. *This is why I don't travel.* Crap like this didn't happen at home.

'It's gone.' My shoulders sagged heavily at the dawning reality.

'Was there much in there? Your wallet?'

'Yeah, but I'm not worried about that. My phone, all my music, and my book...my book was in there. It has everything in it.' My guts twisted at the thought of anyone going through my sketch-book. The only other people who'd seen my dream book were people I'd chosen to share it with. This time the choice had been violently snatched away without my permission. A bitter taste swirled in my mouth and I bit back the need to cry.

Amber gasped. 'Oh no.' She lowered her voice. 'The number plate.'

Max hitched herself up on the bed. 'Crap. Please tell me you remember.'

Yes, thank God. No way I wanted to go back there. 'Big, nasty predator four nine arsehole.'

'What?'

'The number plate, BNP four nine A.'

'BNP...bad...naughty...person,' Amber suggested, and we huffed our agreeance.

'Bastard, nose picker,' Max said, and after a slight pause, our laughter invaded the room.

'Think you can turn the light off now?' Dan called from the other end of the room.

WE FILED A COMPLAINT at the hostel after we'd made a thorough search of the entire place, but the chick at the counter, in the supposed reception, cared more about her fingernails than the fact I'd been robbed on their premises. I had a feeling even if it showed up I wouldn't be seeing it ever again. Dread barrelled into me, without my book and phone I may as well have lost a limb.

I called home to let Mum and Dad know.

'Why were you in a shared room anyway?' Mum asked. 'I thought you were getting a family room.'

I knew she wouldn't be happy about that. 'They double booked it.'

'I hope you got a refund.'

I sighed. 'Only for the difference. Anyway, are you able to call the bank for me and cancel my card?' I didn't have a credit card, but with Pay Wave, my thief would have access to my whole life savings of one thousand, six hundred and twenty dollars. That was more than a return flight to Canada, and I didn't want to lose that too.

'Sure, honey. So where are you staying tonight? You won't be sleeping there again, will you?'

'No, we're leaving Sydney, heading to Granny Tess's a bit later today.'

'All right, text me when you arrive.'

'I don't have a phone.'

'Right, get Max to then, will you?'

'Sure. And thanks for sorting the bank out.'

'Of course.'

Within minutes of leaving the backpacker's we'd found a phone booth for me to make my call to the police. My hand shook as I pressed the numbers and held the phone to my ear, relaying my anonymous detailed recount of what I'd seen outside the gym, including the number plate of the van. I clicked the handset back in place, stepped from the booth and hoped, with heart-pounding desperation, it'd be enough to stop him.

—13—

T HE DRIVE ACROSS THE city took forever. It gave me far too much time to comprehend what came next – Tyler. I was going to see Tyler. How could this be real? Butterflies lurched themselves against the walls of my stomach, and by the time we jerked to a stop outside the school, I thought I might pass out.

'Just go in there and do your thing,' Max said. 'You got this.'

Amber reached over and squeezed my hand with calm reassurance and the flick of her head. 'Go,' she said.

My pulse drummed in my throat, and I made my way across the front of the school until I stood outside the main office. I squared my shoulders; I could do this. The automatic doors slid open.

A lady with short, blond hair and a polite, round face glanced up from the screen in front of her.

'Can I help you?' She grinned with obvious delight. That helped.

'Hi. I wondered if you could get a message to Tyler Sims for me. Sally, his mum, sent me in; she's lost her phone and couldn't call. I bumped into her earlier, and she asked me if I'd come past for her.' My words were fast, but hopefully convincing.

'Yeah sure, what's the message?' Wow, that easy?

'She'll be here later to pick him up. She said to tell him to come out the front of the school, that she'll be waiting for him there.'

The lady's brow creased. 'Doesn't he have a car?'

What? No, he doesn't have a license. *Does he?* Heat flared in my cheeks, panic rising in a tidal wave, ready to sweep me away. I wanted to let it. *What do I say?*

'Ah...yeah...but she needs to see him. Can you let him know she'll be there?'

'Sure, can I tell him who left the message?'

'A friend.' I flashed her an enthusiastic un-Lucy-like beam, and offered a quick 'thanks' before turning to leave.

I slumped back in the car, the adrenalin flowing freely. I felt like I could fly, or puke – or both.

'So?' Amber bounced in her seat, barely containing her composure.

'Now we wait.'

Thirty minutes later the girls shoved me out of the car when the bell rang out, and I wandered back along the footpath toward the school entrance. It wasn't a massive school, but it had a wide front yard, leaving plenty of options for where he'd appear. I hoped I'd see him when he did.

I stood across the road and leaned against a brick retaining wall, beside a car park. If he had a car, like the woman suggested, this would likely be the way he'd leave the school whether he received a message or not. I struggled to come to terms with Tyler having a license. He didn't even have his Ls when I knew him. Did his dad's death stop that progression? It wouldn't surprise me, what with having to take care of his mum and Jada instead of himself.

The sounds of activity spread as students filed from the buildings, seeping onto the front lawns and over the road to their cars.

My nerves amplified, and I tapped my clammy hands restlessly on my denim shorts. I don't think I truly believed in the prospect of seeing him again; how could I until I laid eyes on him? I didn't want to hold my breath for fear I'd pass out if he never showed.

And then he did, only twenty meters away over the black

bitumen road, striding out of the school with his mates. So close that if I called, he would've heard me. My slow inhalation at the sight of him came to me like a gentle breeze on a warm summer's day: subtle and needed.

Oh, Tyler, how I've missed you.

I felt like all I'd done in the last seven weeks was wait. Wait for each of those painfully long minutes to tick by on the clock as I waded through a life determined to drown me. I didn't realise I'd been waiting for this moment, but those endless days ceased to exist as I stood admiring him, alert to the fact he was also staring at me.

His eyes bored into mine, and for a fraction of a moment I convinced myself he recognised me, but I think it was simply my own desire projected back at me.

I held his gaze and seized tightly to my hope, an essential requirement that'd help me take the brave steps needed to reach him and say hi. That's all I'd thought of; the rest I'd figure out if I got that far.

I pushed myself off the wall, testing to see if my shaky legs still worked, when another group of friends arrived beside Tyler. A petite girl with shoulder-length, brown hair bounced up to him, slung an arm around him and snuggled into his side. He didn't hesitate before he removed his eyes from me and turned to her. He beamed, then leaned forward and kissed her squarely on the lips as he snaked his own arms around her.

The arrow pierced my heart, in one side, swiftly out the other, ripping a gaping hole in my chest. Blood flowed freely, leaving me empty, hollow. I fell back against the wall, thankful for its strength and ability to hold me up.

I always knew he'd go back to a happy life. I hadn't doubted I was returning him to something good, but I never imagined this.

Not in my wildest dreams.

I wanted to run, but my feet were planted firmly on the concrete footpath, my eyes fixed on the harrowing scene in front of me.

His neck craned, and he glanced back at me. Almost a question in his eyes, as if I were a puzzle he hadn't quite figured out yet. I certainly had one in mine. Why?

I know he hadn't betrayed me or cheated on me, but heaven help if it didn't feel like he had. But it wasn't fair to be angry at him; my anger grew from more than what I saw in front of me. Anger at my life, for my dreams putting me in this situation in the first place.

His attention shifted again when a friend said something beside him and then their laughter filled the air, flew over the road, and wound itself around my heart in agonising torture.

I turned away from it, from the pain of their laughter, reminding me of his happiness, but mostly my sadness. I staggered back to the car.

The girls expected much more from me when I slumped into my seat, but only one word came out, 'Go.'

WE DROVE FOR FIVE minutes when Max's phone broke through the depressive quiet in the car. She placed it to her ear, said hi, and fell silent as she listened to the caller.

'That's great. We'll be there in about twenty minutes. Thanks. Bye.' She pressed end and twisted around to face me. 'That was the backpacker's. They've got your bag.'

'You guys stay here, I'll run in.' I slammed the door and ran straight to the reception where the girl smiled with one side of her mouth, chewing gum in the other. She dumped the backpack on the counter.

I let out a sigh, relief for so much more than I even knew, but the ease disappeared as soon as I rummaged through my bag. I found my phone in the front pocket where I'd left it, but my wallet and sketchbook were gone. My heart rammed against my ribs, as if my book had been ripped out of my hands all over again, even though I'd never had it returned. I didn't know what was worse. Losing my entire bag, or having it returned and knowing what someone chose to keep.

'All there?' the girl at the counter asked.

'No. There's a few bits gone,' I replied but she'd turned her back, interest already shifted. 'Can I ask you something?'

Her hair flicked over her shoulder as she studied me. 'Sure.'

'The guy who brought this in, what did he look like?'

She waved her hand at me. 'Oh, he wasn't the one who stole it.'

I fiddled with the zipper. 'How do you know?'

'Said he found it out the back early this morning before his shift.'

'He works here? Wouldn't that make it more likely he's involved?'

She put a hand on her hip. 'Careful throwing that kind of accusation around.'

'It was stolen during the night on your premises. If a staff member didn't take it, then someone broke into our room. Which accusation would you prefer?'

'Look, I'm really sorry your bag got stolen. We have lockers in the main room for valuables. Perhaps next time you can use one of those.'

Next time? As if. I gritted my teeth. 'Perhaps.' I marched out the doors and over to the waiting car.

The bag sat clutched on my lap as Amber drove away. 'I need to tell you something,' I said, twisting the bag strap around my fingers.

'What?'

'I don't think it has anything to do with this, but I feel like I should tell you.' I hesitated. 'He saw me.'

'Tyler?'

'No, I mean, yes he did too, but no...the kidnapper. He spotted me outside his house and watched me walk to the bus. And he followed the bus in his van for a bit.'

Max spun around. 'Jesus Christ, Luce, why didn't you say anything?'

'I thought it would freak you out.'

'Gee, I wonder why.'

Amber's knuckles turned white against the steering wheel. 'Do you think *he* stole your bag?'

I flinched as a sense of foreboding anxiety crept over me. 'I don't know. I lost him before I even got off the bus. I don't think he followed me to the backpacker's...like, I'm certain he didn't. There's no way I would have led him back there to you two.'

'And wouldn't he have kept your bag?' Max asked leaning her head against the head rest. 'I mean, he seems like the sort of person to want to know as much about someone if they had an interest in them. Stalker-like, you know?'

Which would be why he kept my book and wallet. I opened my mouth to speak, but they were jostling and giggling over Max's stalker comment. I couldn't bear to push the idea. It wasn't like it changed anything. I scrolled through my Spotify list and plugged my earphones into the phone.

'And you have the bag back now, so it can't be him.'

'Hmmm.' I inserted the music into my ears, 'Too Proud' by Broods. With my head flopping back onto the seat, I tried to appreciate the view outside the window as I settled in for the sombre ride out of Sydney.

Fifteen minutes later, and no longer able to bear my extended silence, the girls coaxed me into telling them what happened at the school. I didn't embellish the story, told it like I saw it – the most painful sight I could imagine. The wound continued to bleed onto the floor of the car.

Amber caught my eye in the rear-view mirror. 'I'm so sorry, Luce. If I'd known, I never would've insisted on making you see him.'

'It's not your fault, you couldn't have known. Maybe it's a good thing.'

Max twisted to face me. 'How can seeing him kiss another girl be a good thing?' Yeah, it wasn't. Tears flooded my eyes as the image of his lips on hers sprang to mind again. 'Oh, hon.' She reached over the centre console and clasped hold of my fingers.

'I mean…maybe it'll help me get over him, move on. I feel like my whole life since he left has been a stalemate. Just waiting for something to happen. Well, it has, and now it's game over.'

Max and Amber stared at each other.

'What?' I frowned.

'Nothing.' Amber swung a glance over her shoulder. 'I really don't know what to do. We've used up my game plan. I don't have any more ideas. You?' She turned to Max.

'No, nothing, I'm so sorry, Luce.'

'It's perfectly fine. It's not your job to fix my problems.'

'I know, but I still feel crap about it all,' Max said, sounding almost as torn up as I felt. 'I'm glad we tried though. I mean, you're probably right, now we…you…can move on. We gave it a shot, it didn't work. I just wish it wasn't so painful for you.' She squeezed my hand.

A tear rolled down my cheek, the saltiness landing at the edge of my half-raised lips. 'I know, me too.'

*****

I'd never seen anything so perfect. The water, the sky...her. She floated like an angel, her dark hair swirling lazily behind her like brush strokes on the water. A masterpiece, as rare as any I'd seen, and I wondered what made me so special I was rewarded a glimpse.

−14−

T HERE'S NOTHING MUCH MORE frightening than a future without hope. It felt like by letting go of Tyler and the hope I'd kept
snug in the pit of my stomach for all those weeks, there'd be nothing
else to keep me going forward. I yearned to go back; back to before,
when he'd been beside me giving me the air I needed to bear the
burdens life threw at me.

But he'd gone and taken all my breath with him, and when I
saw him across the road and felt maybe, finally, I could fill my
lungs, he'd snatched it away again.

When we arrived at Granny Tess's I fell into her arms and held
tight. She knew what we'd gone to Sydney for; I'd told her when I
arranged our stopover.

'C'mon, let's go paint. Painting always helps.' She tugged me
into her art room, the sun pelting through the windows and glass
panels in the roof. I inhaled the paint fumes and the roses in the
glass jar sitting amongst the paint pots and brushes. Granny Tess
found me a blank canvas, and I hitched myself onto the stool behind
it. She positioned herself at her own partly completed work.

I wasn't as familiar with this medium, more used to my pencil
than the brush, but swirling the paint across the canvas had a way
of calming my aching heart with each stroke. The kaleidoscope of
colours coming to life wasn't unlike what we witnessed at the lake
as the sun went down. I couldn't paint Tyler, for the first time in

two months; seeing his face would only hurt more. A tear fell.

Granny Tess turned to me as I wiped at my cheek. 'Oh, my darling girl. I may have overestimated the power of the arts.' She waved the wooden brush in the air.

A sad smile crept to my lips and with a sniff I said, 'If only it were that easy.'

She sighed. 'Yes, if only. It's harder for you than it was for me, I think.'

'How?'

Brush still in her fingers, she lowered her hands to her knees. 'When I lost Thomas, I wanted nothing more than to have him back, but I couldn't do anything except move forward. It wasn't easy, it was the most painful thing I've ever had to do, to take a path forward when all I wanted was to go back. But it's a good thing I didn't, because when I looked up, I saw your pop.' Warmth radiated with her words. 'But *you* have to choose this. Tyler's not gone, he's alive, and so for you it's harder to walk away from something that hasn't been separated by something as final as death. You did something wonderful, you lost something wonderful, but it might be time to accept it and try to move your feet forward.'

I nodded, she was right. But moving forward, away from him, was like visiting Paris and not stepping into the Louvre, or cutting off a limb while my blood seeped into the carpet. My acceptance was little more than a lack of choice in the matter, but either way nothing lessened the burning ache in my chest or slowed the falling tears when my head landed on my pillow later that night.

*****

CAL LANDED WITH A thump onto the bench, his backpack dropping to his feet. 'Have you seen the news?' My least favourite words in the world.

We'd been home for two days, back into the routine of school and the normality of a life without Tyler. I folded my arms across myself. After the reeling effects of a distressing weekend, I didn't think I could keep thwarting the punches coming my way.

'No.' I shifted to rest my chin in my hand. 'We're taking a break. Our relationship hasn't been on good terms lately.'

'I can understand needing to put some distance between you both, but the news has...well, news.' Cal's eyes lowered, dejected, and the worry on his face frightened me.

I sat up straight; he had my attention. 'What is it?'

His gaze flitted around the table, hesitating to say the words. 'Your serial killer is not the serial killer.'

'What do you mean?' I shot back in my seat, teetering on the edge, before collecting myself. 'Of course he is.'

'The cops don't think so, they've released him. Not enough evidence apparently.'

'What! No, no.' I shook my head, denial in every movement. 'This can't be right. Are you serious?'

'It's not something I'd joke about, Luce, even for me.'

I put my head in my hands, my elbows on the table. I needed to stop the spinning.

'What do we do now?' Amber said gently.

I clenched my jaw. We couldn't do a thing. That trip was a big frickin' disaster, a waste of time. Instead of everything we hoped for, we failed miserably. 'There's nothing we can do. Girls will die and I can't do anything about it.'

'None of us can, Lucy.' Amber placed her hand on my arm. 'Why do you insist that you have to?'

'Because I can,' I snapped.

'Not this time. This is too big. I think you might need to let this one go.' Like I did with Tyler. I was losing control of my entire life.

My grip slipping on everything that mattered to me.

'Girls are going to die.' My lip quivered.

Worry crept over Cal's face, and I clung to his concern, hoping he could offer some comfort or fix the impending disaster. He couldn't.

'Yep, it sucks,' he said.

*****

I OPENED THE TOP drawer of my bedside table and found the unopened packet of pills. I slid the foil pouch from the cardboard box, tempting myself with the idea. Could I do it? Ignore the call to help the lives taken too early. I could live with the dreams if it meant I could save lives, but what if Webb hurt more girls? Seeing it would be torture if I couldn't stop it. Guilt seared behind my eyelids, but if my attempts to help would only be in vain, I wanted no part in it.

And even though I hadn't had any more dreams of Tyler, I couldn't bear the thought of seeing him again if that's all I got. A pressing of my nose to the glass, a view from a distance, but nothing more. And I couldn't have more; he was with someone else. He'd moved on.

No, he hadn't moved on. He'd moved back. To a past where I didn't exist; to a past of easy happiness. He didn't need me anymore, and I had to accept that and find a place where I no longer needed him either. I wouldn't welcome the dizzy spells, but the tablets would be the numbing gel required to help me through the pain until I came out the other side.

I reached into my school bag for my water bottle. It was empty.

I struggled down the stairs into the kitchen and filled a glass. Dad sat at the kitchen table, tapping on the keys of his laptop. I scraped out a chair and eased myself into it. He eyed the water and foil pack, his eyes coming to meet mine in acknowledgement.

'What happened?' he asked gently, pushing his glasses higher onto the bridge of his nose.

I shook my head. I couldn't tell him what happened in Sydney, about my failed attempt to stop a serial killer by going to his house. He'd have heart failure. 'I just...I'm not coping, Dad. I don't want to see so much death.'

He patted my hand. 'Okay, honey. It'll get easier, but you do what you need to get through. If this is what you need for now, I fully support you.'

'Thanks, Dad.' I punched out two tablets, dropped them onto the back of my tongue, and swallowed a mouthful of water.

*****

I CLOSED MY EYES and pressed my finger to my forehead as a deafening pulse thrummed below my temple. Sitting at our outdoor table during lunch, our food spread in front of us, sprinkles of mist hitting us through the thickening branches of the maple tree above, my world began to spin.

Brilliant. It'd taken less than forty-eight hours for the side effects to begin.

'You okay, hon?' Max whispered, rubbing my back.

'Mmm, just a bit of a headache. I'll be fine.' I offered a half smile.

'We're going boarding on the weekend, don't even think about bailing on us.' Cal pointed a finger at me.

'I'm not bailing. I've got a headache.'

'Poor excuse,' Cal said, dismissing me. 'You can give up on Tyler and your dreams, but the snow hasn't left yet.'

I rolled my eyes. 'I'm not giving up, ya jerk.' I shrugged. 'Well, not on the snow.' I huffed out a laugh. It was the last day of term. We were about to have two solid weeks up on the mountain, and although sailing down the mountain without Tyler left me with a big ball of sadness in my throat, no way would I ditch the last thing that gave me any pleasure.

I wiped at my damp hair clinging to my forehead and ripped off a chunk of bread roll. The sky displayed a depressing pallet of grey and white and, together with the drizzle, matched my mood perfectly.

I stuffed the bread into my mouth, the voices of my friend's chatter and merriment swirled around my throbbing head, the pain careening through my veins. I shut my eyes to create a thin barricade, anything to block them out for a moment. Easing my eyes open, a shape caught my attention. I shifted my focus beyond the school yard, over the fence and across the road. A tall and broad dark-haired man stood in the rain, hands in the pocket of his coat, watching me.

It was him, the man from the plane – Megan's murderer.

My eyes widened and I inhaled, lodging the bread in my throat and sending me bent over in a cough. I righted myself, swiping at the tears trailing down my cheeks, and darted my gaze back across the road.

'You all right?'

I ignored Max and stared into the distance. Heads whipped in the direction of my focus, but he'd gone.

'What is it?'

I sprung to my feet and ran to the fence, scanning the length of the road. He'd completely vanished in the few seconds it'd taken to compose myself.

Sean appeared at my side. 'Whatcha lookin' for?' His brows furrowed as he searched the street.

'There was a man across the road, you didn't see him?' I turned in a full circle, taking in the rest of the guys at the table, and scoured the school grounds in case he'd gone that way

'There's no one here. You said you had a headache – you sure you're okay?'

I glared at him. 'I'm not seeing things if that's what you're suggesting.' I marched across the grass.

'Sorry for caring.' Sean landed at the table. 'You lot see the dude over the road?'

A collective mumble and shake of heads indicated I'd been the only one. But it wasn't just a dude, it was a man who kidnapped young women and killed them. That was a vastly dangerous difference. But the way Amber snuggled into Cal's side as he kissed her forehead and Max picked at something under a fingernail suggested they had no clue of the danger. How could they; they didn't see him.

Or maybe I really was seeing things. Turning my fear into a reality. Could it be from the drugs? I hoped they weren't messing with me that much. Although, I much preferred that option than the man following me.

'Sorry, Sean, I didn't mean to snap. You're right, I think I might be seeing things.' I huffed nervously, hoping they'd buy my fake delusion, but immediately stopped laughing as their faces blurred in front of me. I closed my eyes and focused on the rise and fall of my chest to ease the dizzying effects coming back. Yeah, definitely the drugs.

*****

MY LEGS HUNG LIMPLY over my bed, warm sun filtering in through the window. Books were piled around me, my laptop resting on my legs. Like most year eleven students across the country, I had no life except one that existed for exams and final assignments. Without my dreams I'd been able to immerse myself completely, and I went in hard, using it as the perfect way to keep my mind off other less desirable thoughts. I couldn't think of Tyler anymore: it hurt too much. And I avoided thinking about Webb for the fear that lurched in my guts when I did. He hadn't shown up again, and I began to think it really had been my imagination playing a wicked trick on me. But as long as he stayed away and I never had to see him again, I didn't care if it was a trick or not.

I jotted a note in the book to my side. These numbers were screwing with my brain. Tapping my pen on my lip, I stared at the edge of the mountains appearing in the frame of my window. It was a mild spring day, enough warmth for short sleeves, but not so much that we – the town that lived for winter – couldn't handle.

Antil Springs had reduced in size once again since the snow had melted. Hordes of tourists and winter workers had deserted us for either the winter snowfields overseas, summer holiday destinations, or more commonly, and far less exciting, their own version of regularity.

I got used to the busyness each year, but by the time I began to wonder if all these strangers would ever leave, the sun came out and they ever-so-slowly vanished, leaving the town with a subdued silence, and a slight ringing in our ears.

I ought to be feeling some of that spring peace I knew so well, but I was like a deflated balloon – no air, no joy, no life

If it weren't for my friends, my schoolwork, and the time I spent at the homeless shelter, I'd be completely numb.

The feeling reminded me of a time during one of my first shifts working for Laurie when I locked myself in the fridge. I'd been sent to the storeroom trailer outside the marquee kitchen to put away some cakes, and forgetting to prop open the door, accidentally locked myself in the icy room. Amber hadn't been rostered to work the shift with me, and no one noticed my absence for a whole twenty minutes.

I wore a skirt, short sleeved shirt, and no gloves – and it was two friggin' degrees. My fingers began to burn, my teeth chattered, and everything from the tip of my nose to the ends of my toes went numb. I paced the trailer, my steps slowing as the minutes ticked by, until my body didn't feel quite like mine anymore, and my breathing became less like breathing and more like surviving. I contemplated how it might be the end of me.

It'd been a little under three months since losing Tyler, and now I contemplated the same thing. People say give it time, but that's a load of crock. No amount of time would help me acclimatise to a life without him, but I did adjust to the slow, cold beat of my heart and the numbness that enveloped my whole being.

—15—

3 <small>MONTHS LATER…</small>

I TIED UP MY laces and bound down the stairs for a run, stopping halfway when the wall tilted away from me. Damn those drugs. I steadied myself before coming into view of Mum in the kitchen. She stood over the chopping board, slicing pumpkin and carrots. My mouth salivated from the rich scent of the roast in the oven.

'I'm heading out, what time's dinner?' I grabbed a chunk of carrot.

Mum tried to smack my fingers, but the carrot had already reached my mouth. She rolled her eyes, but it didn't hide her amusement. 'Should be ready just after six. You going for a run?'

'Yeah. See you in a bit.'

'All right, honey, have fun.'

I left the house, winding my way up the long street towards the top of town, and turned right onto the steep road that led to my track. I stopped across from the house that had been Tyler's in my other memory. I bent over to fill my lungs and take it in. I don't know why I had to stop each time I ran past. As if I expected to see something different if I stood there long enough – I never did. The grass grew long and brown, and even taller around the base of the 'For Sale' sign that sat pegged into the middle of the yard, as lifeless as the day after he'd disappeared from my life six months ago, all trace of him, and his mum and Jada removed.

I moved my feet away, breaking back into a run. The music worked its way through the muscles driving me up the hill. 'Turn' by one of Tyler's favourite bands, The Wombats, once again drawing attention to all that remained even though he was gone.

School had ended, Christmas and New Year's had come and gone uneventfully. Thanks to the drugs, my nights were now filled with vast and empty sleeps. But the side effects had set in like a hurricane, wild and strong. I'd become the weird friend who occasionally resembled a drunk stumbling around the school, who wobbled when she stood, and tripped on things that weren't there.

Once exams had finished, I distracted myself with extra hours at work and time at the shelter trying to help others find some joy over the Christmas period. Eventually, my distractions failed to keep my mind busy and I'd returned my focus to Tyler. I bought a new sketch-book and each day I opened it and drew something to remind me of him: his dimpled chin, him sitting against the trunk of the maple tree, his hands. It was painful to remember him, but I found it just as painful not to.

And when I wasn't drawing my summer away, I'd slide my sneakers on and run. Around the corner, up the road, and to my hill. Yes, it had become mine again – there was no us.

I'd come to accept it, and as hard as it was to step into the future without him, I felt ready to embrace my senior year on my own. I had one last day before I'd be expected to be a responsible final year student, to get steady good grades, and start figuring out what the hell I wanted to do with my life.

Escaping the heated rays of the sun, I left the road for the track in the trees, welcoming the cool relief. I didn't much like running in the dripping heat, but I didn't have much choice during this time of year. The dry, hard track was brutal even beneath my expensive sneaker-clad feet.

Jake had moved to Canberra and now lived with Granny Tess and Pop. He'd finally got the score he needed for medicine and had packed his bags and driven away in his van four days ago. And the other thing I did over the break: got my learners permit. Without Jake and his van, I'd lost my ride.

I'd hesitated to get behind the wheel, having seen how dangerous cars were in my dreams. But if my skill and ability helped me fly happily down the mountain as fast as I did, I needed to do the same with the car so fear didn't dictate my limits.

I reached the fence and the cows and my hill. The mountains glistened with the reflection of the sun, barely a sprinkling of clouds in the stark blue backdrop of sky. I lifted the wire and climbed through the flimsy fence. I wandered amongst the tall brown grass and picked a few dandelions as I headed for my new summer spot. A quiet place not far from the track but out of view from anyone who might venture as far up as I did. I no longer rested out in the open, but settled myself closer to the fence, where the shade of the trees protected my skin from burning.

I lowered myself into the grass and folded my legs, soaking up the view before I closed my eyes.

Meditating, especially after a run, had become almost as easy as falling asleep. I focused on the constant thump of my heart and allowed the monotonous beat to take me away to a place of nothing.

After a solid thirty-minute session, I stood and wandered back along the fence.

A man appeared halfway down the hill, striding toward me, sandy hair blowing in the breeze. I squinted. Had he bought the land? I didn't want to think about it belonging to anyone but me. I bet he was some big hot shot pacing out the perimeter, ready to build a subdivision. He raised his arm in a hearty wave. I hesitated before waving back, but he was probably trying to gain my attention to tell me to bugger off and leave his cows alone. Dropping my arm, I backed away, my hands clenched at my sides. I'd be back. He couldn't scare me off that easily. I climbed through the fence and started down the track without hesitation.

*****

I DOWNED AN EXTRA strong coffee in the morning, as if the extra strength would not only help me through the day but the entire year. *I wish.*

For the first time in a long time Mum drove me and Ollie to school, a reminder that life wouldn't be the same without Jake. A lump of sadness swirled in my stomach, because although I hadn't said it aloud, I really did miss him.

Cal and Amber were climbing out of Cal's car as I approached.

'Hey guys, ready for the big year?' I hugged Amber.

'Of course, but the bigger question, Luce...are they ready for us?' Cal said with a chuckle.

His laughter rubbed off as it so often did, and I joined in. 'Probably not.'

We linked arms, Amber between me and Cal. We strolled into school, a force to be reckoned with as we began our final year. This was it – *our* year. But as soon as Amber's arm slipped from my grip and I headed to my own class, I felt like nothing to be reckoned with, just a fallen leaf blowing in the wind.

I inhaled and closed my eyes – geography.

My heart surrendered to my aching loss as I sagged into a seat at the back of the room and peered out the window. The glass had been cleaned over the break, and I could see clearly through, yet couldn't focus on anything, too absorbed in thoughts of Tyler and the fact he wouldn't be taking this class with me again. I slipped into a little fantasy where I pretended Tyler had simply chosen not to take geography this year, enjoying my delusion far more than the burning reality he was gone. I smiled at the idea.

I always took a long time to wake in the morning. I blamed it on my dreams, but lately, without them, I could only point the finger at myself. Still hazy with the remnants of sleep and my usual persistent dizziness from the meds, I turned as more classmates filed into the room. Eagerly chatting, full of new-year enthusiasm that'd only last the next two days before reality set in.

It boggled me how anyone could be that perky, so early in the day. I liked the slow rise of my alertness as it eased itself on me like the sun rise; too much too soon and it was blinding.

Well, today I *was* being blinded. Slapped, shaken and stirred, my body on full alert within the space of point-zero-five of a second – Tyler had just stepped through the door.

My heart stopped.

I didn't move a single muscle, my eyes fixed on him as he walked in slow motion toward a seat.

His eyes darted around, appearing unfamiliarly nervous. Something I hadn't noticed the first time he moved to our school, too distracted with my own thoughts, I guess. But today, a strong awareness of everything about him gathered in my chest. His hair sat slightly longer, but otherwise it flopped onto his forehead exactly as I remembered. Strong cheekbones and a dimple on his chin you wouldn't find unless you peered closely, but I knew it was there. Headphones sat on his head, positioned snugly over his ears, and I desperately wanted to know what he was listening to. He slid his backpack off his shoulder, his lean and muscly arms awakening a gentle familiarity.

I nearly passed out, but he lowered into his seat and broke the spell. My pent-up air discharged in a whoosh. He sat only a couple rows in front of me, but knowing I could stand and take four steps to reach him – to touch him – made my skin prickle. Could it really be him? Maybe my mind and meds were playing tricks on me. Oh, God, nothing could be crueller.

'Welcome back, everyone,' Mr Beck boomed from the front of the class. 'I trust you all had fabulous holidays. What parts of the world did you venture to?' He tapped the world map attached to the wall behind his desk.

People called out, as was common for this lesson.

'Gold Coast.'

'Bali.'

'Thailand.'

'Nice, nice. All very nice. And for those of you who stayed local, I hope you went and explored somewhere new.'

'Does Alexander's pool count?' Zach called out, and laughter erupted.

'If that's the only new place you explored then you're only doing yourself a disservice, Zach. The world has so much more to offer than a good swimming pool, but you have to be willing to go and find it.' Mr Beck's grin broadened, it was one of the things I loved about this lesson, his unadulterated enthusiasm. 'Does anyone want to know where I ended up for the holidays?' The class let out a simultaneous moan, which he ignored. 'At the top of Mount Kilimanjaro. A mere five-thousand-eight-hundred and ninety-five metres above sea level. Now there's something to aspire to, Zach.

'Now before we start, I'd like to introduce you to a new member of our class and our school, Mr Tyler Sims.' He waved his arm in Tyler's direction, and I could no longer deny reality. He was definitely in my class. 'Please make him welcome and come and introduce yourself after class. All right, let's get started.'

Did running up and jumping into his arms count as introducing yourself? Too much? The image played itself out in my mind, until a big, fat goofy grin spread across my face that I couldn't remove if I tried. He was here. He'd come back.

Throughout the remainder of the lesson my excitement level went from giddy Christmas Eve expectation all the way to heart-pounding exhilaration before a first run down the Canadian mountains. I'd never experienced that before, but I imagined it might feel something like this.

Okay, so he had no idea who I was *and* had a girlfriend, but they were details I'd sooner forget for the sheer tingling pleasure at having him near me again, and I clung to the feeling as if that was all that mattered. And it was. Because he was here, and that alone was more than I ever expected to have again. Happiness draped around me like one of Pop's hugs, offering a calmness I hadn't felt for an eternity.

But then my head began to spin, from Tyler or the drugs in my system I couldn't be sure, maybe a cocktail of both. I closed my eyes to quiet the invasive dizziness taking over, a sensation I'd grown to live with over the summer, like a pimple on your chin, or a yappy dog that won't shut up.

By the end of the lesson, after completing zero amounts of work, except a marathon for my heart and eyes, I was on full alert. Should I leave first? Stay seated and wait until he left? Do I go over to him? What would I even say?

Crap, too late. He dashed from the room. I jumped up, flung my bag over my shoulder and bolted after him. My pulse drummed in my temple. I peered over the heads of all the bodies swarming the corridor, he'd gone. Damn it, Lucy, you and your daydreaming.

—16—

B Y MORNING BREAK I bounced off the walls like I'd had ten double shots of coffee. I almost skipped to our lunch table under the full green of the maple. No one had arrived yet, and too on edge to sit, I paced the grass. Tree to table, table to tree.

'You right, Luce?'

I jumped and spun around. Sean dropped his bag on the ground and leaned a hand on the table.

'What? Huh, yeah, I'm good.' My face beamed brighter than the sun, and I couldn't turn it down.

'What's wrong with her?' Cal said, striding towards us. 'What's that thing on her face?'

Sean shook his head. 'Dunno. Is that a...it is, isn't it? It's a smile.'

Cal stepped in front of me and poked the edge of my mouth. 'Dude, you're right. It is, and a genuine one at that.' I shoved his hand away.

'Haha. Funny,' I said, trying, and failing, to form a frown.

'Feels good, doesn't it? Happiness.' Sean slid into the bench.

'Yeah, it does.'

'So you gonna tell us what brought this on?' Cal asked.

'Brought what on?' Max crammed onto the bench with Amber. Her gaze darted from Cal and back to me. 'Oh, this. Someone's happy. You do know it's the first day of school and not the last, don't you?'

'I do. And you know what happens on the first day of school?' I paced at the end of the table.

'We get new books?' Amber pressed her hands on the table.

Sean's eyes lit up. 'Hot new girls at the school?'

'Exactly.' I shot my arm out, my finger directed at him.

'What?' He screwed his face up. 'You're excited there's new girls in the school?'

'Not entirely...' I let my voice fade away.

'No way!' Amber sat up straight. I nodded, and squeals accompanied her clapping and fist pumping the air. 'Where?' She scanned the school yard.

'I don't know, I lost him. He was in geography this morning.'

'He's here?' Max's eyes widened.

I nodded, pressing my lips together but not losing the grin.

'Tyler's here?' Cal glanced over his shoulder.

Sean frowned. '*Your* Tyler?' I couldn't pick the emotion in his voice, disbelief, dejection?

'Yeah, sorry.'

'Sorry? Why are you sorry?'

I lowered myself onto the seat. 'I don't know, you seem sad or something?'

'Not sad, a bit disbelieving I guess.'

I threw my hands up. 'I knew you never believed me.'

'What, no. This just makes it very real. Before it was only you telling us, and this is kind of evidence.'

I tilted my head, slanting my eyes. 'You needed evidence for this too?'

Sean let out an exasperated sigh. 'No, but I guess there's no denying it now, is there.'

'No one was denying it, Sean,' Amber cut in.

'She's right, ignore him. We've always believed you, Luce.' Cal flung an arm over my shoulders.

'Seriously, guys,' Sean said. 'You think I never believed her?'

I waved my hand in his direction, brushing away my concern. 'It's fine, Sean, just leave it. As long as you're okay with it.'

'With you being in love with the new kid who only started at the school what, like two hours ago? Totally.' He might be mocking but his face was full of light. 'No really, I am. It's weird, but it's okay.'

I nodded, acknowledging all that his words meant for him, but also for me. 'You know you're going to love him too.'

'Pretty sure he's not my type, but thanks,' Sean said with a straight face, running a hand through his dark hair.

'No.' I laughed. 'You all are. He's a good guy.'

'So, what now?' Max asked.

'Yeah, how did he come into our circle in the first place? No one scales these walls very easily,' Cal said.

'It was soccer. He joined the soccer team. It's all down to you, Cal.'

The grin on Cal's face fell away. 'But there's no soccer at the moment, we're not in season.'

'Oh. Right, okay.'

Amber leaned forward. 'What classes did he take? Maybe we can catch him that way?'

Sean huffed. 'You make him sound like a prized animal on the loose.'

'He kind of is.' I chuckled, my euphoria bubbling out. I folded my hands together. 'Okay, so he did geography with me. French, which none of us take. I think he did history, and also maths, but not with us, Sean. And I think he did P.E. too, but not our class, pretty sure that was with you boys. That might be where you met him.'

'We've got that before lunch, haven't we, Sean?' Cal grabbed his timetable from his bag and read it over. 'Fourth lesson. Let's hope he's doing it this year too, hey.'

'Then what, we sidle over to him and say, "Hey we know the perfect girl for you, she's in love with you, wanna meet her?"' Sean shook his head with a laugh.

'Sidle?' Cal said. 'That's a bit creepy, dude. We should probably just walk or we might scare him off.' Everyone erupted in laughter. Easy, relaxed, whole. How long since we'd done that together?

Break ended and we parted ways, ready for the hunt.

'Hey,' I called to Cal and Sean as they strode away. I plucked one of my small art books from my bag and flicked to where I'd already been sketching pictures of Tyler.

'You do all of those today?' Sean asked peering at the pages. I couldn't concentrate on a single thing after I'd seen him earlier, I may have drawn a few.

'Shut up.' I found a decent-looking picture and ripped out the page, handing it to Cal. 'Just in case.'

He grabbed the thin piece of paper from my fingers. 'Not bad.' He smirked.

'I know, right.'

'But we won't be needing this.' He handed it back. 'I think we'll notice the new boy. Besides, if anyone finds that on me, my creep status will rise considerably.'

I folded the paper. 'You don't have a creep status.'

'I will if that's found in my possession.'

'And my creep status doesn't matter?'

'Luce, you've got half a book full. But it's normal for you to go around drawing everyone, you're safe.'

FIVE MINUTES INTO FOURTH lesson, whilst I sat behind my art easel, my phone buzzed in my bag. It went against all school rules, but no one on earth could make me follow the rules today. I opened my phone.

Cal: *Eyes on the prize. Eyes on the prize.*

My lips lifted of their own accord, and I held the phone for Amber to read the words. She let out a tiny squeal and jiggled her knees.

Mrs Mac paused her instructions from the front of the room and sent us a reprimanding glare, but as her top student, she also had a friendly glint in her eye. I popped the phone away and returned to listening to the workload ahead of us for the new year.

I didn't receive any more messages from Cal. Partway through class, I snatched up my phone, my thumb hovering over the reply button. My heart hammered, my impatience growing, but what would I say anyway? It'd only prove my anxiety and distract him from the important task of luring Tyler with his charms. Resigned to sit on my hands if need be, I dropped the phone back in my bag.

WITH MY EARPHONES ALREADY in, I lay on the bench, knees bent and hands placed behind my head. Late afternoon sun filtered through the branches overhead, and I stared out at the flawless sky beyond, grateful for the next hour in which we could bathe in it, because days like this were such a waste to be holed up inside. I closed my eyes.

A shadow fell over me and I opened an eye. *Did I fall asleep?* Max and Amber stood above me, serious expressions on their faces. I tugged a bud from one ear.

'You might want to sit up, lovely.' Amber shuffled on the spot, a slight twitch at the corner of her lips.

'Why? I'm sleeping,' I moaned.

'No really, get up now.' Max's pleading eyes made me bolt upright and nearly fall off the seat. I squinted, the harsh sun adding to my 'what's going on' face. She flicked a glance over my shoulder. 'Don't look now, but the boys are heading over here with your man, so act natural, okay?'

A roaring pulse thundered in my ears. 'Natural?' I wiped at my eyes, at the edge of my mouth, and pressed down on the loose strands of my dark hair. 'Okay?' I peered up at the girls.

'Fine,' Max said. 'Now breathe.'

'Ha, that's a joke, right?' I choked out.

Slowly, with jellied limbs, I twisted on the bench as Cal, Sean, *and* Tyler strode across the grass.

Oh my God, what do I say, what do I say?

With each step toward us I remembered every detail of his stunning face, and when his head lifted and our eyes met, my heart stopped. This was the moment all his memories came rushing back, and he ran over to me and said, 'I told you I'd come back'. My little fantasy laughed in my face as Tyler gave me a small, 'hello stranger in the yard' smile.

'Hey girls, look what we found?' Cal even made it sound like he'd returned from a hunt with the prize. 'Tyler's new here, thought I'd make him welcome, introduce him to some of the ladies. Amber, Max, Lucy.' Cal stared straight at me. I wanted to whack him across the head, but instead shot him a friendly glare that said 'behave yourself'. His eyebrows arched, his mouth rising in a taunt – who me?

'Lucy,' Tyler said in an almost whisper. My breath hitched in the back of my throat as my eyes darted to meet his. 'Uh, Cal said he had a gorgeous friend he wanted to introduce me to. I'm guessing you're Lucy?'

Cal shrugged and sat on the bench.

I couldn't speak; a huge lump had wedged itself in my throat. I choked on a little cough and extended my hand. 'It's nice to meet you, Tyler.' I gazed into deep blue eyes, eyes that'd once upon a time gazed as longingly into mine.

He studied my face before putting his hand in mine and sending a shock wave up my arm and my pulse into high gear. His mouth turned up in a small delicate grin, and then his brows creased. 'Hey, I remember you.'

'You do?' The words tumbled out in a strangle. Could he really remember? Were all our memories hurtling down from the void, a swirl of love, affection, and kisses? Of promises, laughter, and dreams?

'You came to my school last year. I saw you.'

The memories swirled into a ball and slammed into my guts – he recalled nothing.

'Uh, yeah.' My hand still rested in his, exactly as I remembered it, smooth, gentle, firm. He observed our joined hands, hesitated and removed his from my grip. I wanted to yank it back, reclaim what'd once been mine.

'So, what were you doing there?' he asked.

Coming to see you.

I rubbed a palm on my thigh. I needed a lie, quick. Amber put a hand on my arm. 'Lucy has a cousin in Sydney; she was meeting up with her. Wow, same school as yours. Who'd have thought?' Amber and I traded nervous laughs.

'Oh yeah, what's her name, I might know her?'

C'mon, Lucy, think of something. 'Probably not, she's a bit younger than you.' I scrunched my lips, pausing to figure out the next part of the lie. 'Alice's in year ten this year, I think.'

'Hmm, I'll have to ask my sister if she knows her. She's year ten this year.'

Crap. I should've thought of that.

'So, Tyler, what brings you to Antil?' Amber asked, breaking the tension as we all slid into the bench seats around the table.

'Mum and Dad wanted a change.' Tyler sat directly across from me, and I lowered my gaze. Staring was rude at the best of times, and my level would have him running for Cape York if I wasn't careful.

Amber pushed her golden hair off her shoulder. 'You didn't?'

'Would you wanna be uprooted right before final year?' I couldn't help but notice the bite in his words. 'Nah, I didn't wanna move here. My life is the sea, and unless I'm mistaken, you guys don't have one of those?'

'No, but we do have a lake,' Cal said with a grin, completely unaware of Tyler's bitter tone. 'We'll take you sometime. It's not the ocean, but with a set of skis and a speed boat you won't even miss it.'

'Sounds great, thanks.'

'And no sand and salt to worry about either! Ugh, hate the sea water,' Cal said like a true inland born. 'What's so great about the sea anyway?'

'He surfs,' I jumped in too quickly and Cal's eyes widened, reminding me I didn't know this boy any more than they did. 'Right?'

'How did you know?' he asked with a slight frown.

I shrugged. 'Good guess.'

'Do you snowboard?' Amber asked, drawing his attention away. 'Nope.'

'Well, you're gonna love it if you're a surfer,' Cal said. 'You'll pick it up in no time.'

'They're a bit different though, aren't they?'

'One lesson from a good teacher,' I started with a sly grin, 'and you'll be gliding down the mountain beautifully.'

'Wow, your confidence in me is impressive.' He shared in my delight, his high cheekbones rising and causing a flurry of ecstasy to stir in my stomach.

'I just have good insight.'

'Really? What else does your insight tell you about me?'

More than I could probably confess, and the warning glares on Cal and Sean's faces on either side of Tyler reminded me to proceed with caution. Oh, but this could be fun.

'Mmm, let's see. I know that even though you're unhappy about being here, you've never once complained to your parents, because you know how much it means to them.' The smile on his face faltered. 'And the truth is you're actually happy to be here, even if it has taken you away from the sea, because you're excited to see a new part of the world.'

His eyes narrowed slightly before he turned away and asked, 'Is she always this smug?'

Sean stifled a laugh, but Cal did nothing to hide his. 'You'll get used to it, dude.' He slapped Tyler on the back.

Talk moved to other things, and every now and then, so did my eyes. I didn't want to come across as a complete psycho. But he was so beautiful. I'd dreamt of this day for so long, and now, I was mesmerised.

'Pinch me,' I whispered to Max.

'What?'

'You heard me.' She grabbed my thigh under the table and squeezed hard. I yanked my leg away with a yelp and rubbed at the spot.

Max leaned into me. 'He's real.'

I glanced up as his gaze fell on me, and my mind blew into smithereens.

* * * * *

I PRACTICALLY SKIPPED THE rest of the way through the day. I had no idea what lay ahead, if Tyler would one day be interested in me the way he'd once been, but the anticipation tingled through my body as if I were climbing a roller coaster.

Mum noticed my mood when I got home after school but asked nothing of it, best not to mess with a good thing.

'You're looking happy,' Dad said later as I stood at the kitchen sink helping Mum peel the potatoes for dinner. He planted a kiss on the top of my head. 'Have a good first day back?'

I focused on the potato in my hands, my grin growing. 'Could say that.' I didn't have to see them to know Mum and Dad's eyebrows just had a conversation over the top of my head.

'And so you know...' I faced them, peeler still in hand. 'I've stopped taking the tablets.'

Mum pursed her lips tightly, concern pooling behind her eyes.

'That's great,' Dad said, ignoring Mum. Satisfaction flowed around his genuinely pleased smile. 'When did you do that?'

'Today.' I spun back around, picking up another potato.

—17—

'HEY, WE'VE GOT GEOGRAPHY next. Wanna walk with me?' Tyler asked the following day. Surprisingly, and much to my relief, he hadn't been deterred by all our excitement and weirdness. 'You can show me the way from this part of the school, I'm still getting lost.'

'Love to.' I beamed. 'I mean, sure, why not.' Max's shoulder brushed mine with her chuckle.

Tyler and I strolled side by side, and it took all my effort to maintain a normal distance between us and not close the gap like my accelerated heart was inclined to do.

'So Mr Beck's great, you'll like him. He likes to talk, but he's pretty fair, and as long as we get our work done he doesn't mind what we do.' I couldn't stop from jabbering. My fingers tapped my legs as we ambled into the room.

Tyler and I sat beside each other, second row from the back of class. I grabbed my book and laptop from my bag and pretended, with a concentrated stare straight ahead, that being beside him wasn't the single best thing to be happening in my life.

We went our separate ways for the next lesson and met up as we neared the maths rooms, because Tyler now shared maths with me and Sean, which meant I now had another class with him. I wanted to do a cartwheel, but instead offered a quick wave when I spotted him outside the building. Was I being too obvious?

He lifted his chin in a friendly hello. 'So, maths, you like it?'

'Does anyone?' I tilted my head and guilt filled his eyes. 'Really? No, you don't.' How did I not know this?

'Only this much.' He used his thumb and finger to indicate about an inch worth of like. He laughed at the astonishment on my face. 'What's our teacher like?'

I groaned. 'Awful. He'll be on your case if for one second you don't pay him the attention he thinks he deserves. And it's so hard too, 'cause he's stupid boring. And he wears the most hideous woollen vests every single day...I swear they're each a different shade of vomit.'

'Nice.'

I shook my head. 'No, not nice.' My heart soared with happiness, and when he smiled as we marched into the building I nearly melted. We climbed the stairs and stepped onto the linoleum corridor, reminding me of our first dream together, soap-skating past the classrooms and landing in a heap.

Tyler mumbled something inaudible.

'Huh?'

Blinking, with a shake of his head, he said, 'Oh, I said I trust you.'

I creased my forehead.

'About the vests, that they're all a different shade,' he said, quickly answering my unasked question.

'Right.'

'Gee, this place is familiar.' He scanned down each direction of the wide corridor.

'Really? Your old school have the same dismal choice of tiles and paint as this one?'

He huffed out a small laugh. 'No, the opposite actually. It was an invasion of colour, like the place'd somehow be happier if they used every colour of the rainbow.'

'Was it?'

'Not really. You stop seeing it after a while, but still, it's nothing like this. That's what's weird, I feel like I've been here before.'

My pulse quickened. 'Maybe in another life,' I joked and a pathetic little laugh burst from my throat.

His brow furrowed. 'Yeah, maybe.'

We reached our room and I motioned being sick with my mouth and finger, pointing into the room. His gaze followed my direction.

'Ugh, schnitzel and tinned peas,' he said.

'What?'

'The shade of vomit.' He nodded to Mr Blythe.

'Ew, gross.'

'You're the one who said it.'

'I never classified them.' I laughed. 'Tinned peas? Is that a thing?'

'Yeah, and they look like that.' He jerked his head again. 'My grandma used to make us eat them. I remember how floury they felt. Definitely vomit-inducing.'

'You two care to join us?' Mr Blythe barked from his desk, and we slid into seats beside Sean up the back.

Break came immediately after maths, and I floated on air as the three of us strolled to our spot. Sean rolled his eyes at my delight, only obvious to him, but I couldn't care less. Tyler walked beside me, and all was good in the world.

Light-hearted conversation kept up around the table as everyone got to know each other, and I reacquainted myself with something long gone, but never forgotten. At times I acted disinterested, balancing the scales against the times when I was overly so, but always pricking my ears up at something new and interesting.

'What do your parents do?' Cal asked even though he knew

what one of them did. 'There must be something that brought them here, yeah?'

'Kinda, but mostly it was to get away. Dad's a pilot, and I think he's hoping to set up tourist charter flights or something like that.'

'Cool.'

'And Mum's a travel agent. She's already got a job lined up. I think she starts in a week or two.'

I thought of Tyler's mum, Sally, and her monumental sadness that kept her from sustaining a job. A feeling of pride swelled inside me at the mention of his mum and dad and the huge change I'd made. I must've had a strange expression on my face because Sean pointed it out moments later.

'Stop,' Sean said, poking a finger in my direction. 'It's freaking me out.'

My grin fell away.

'What, she's not allowed to smile?' Tyler asked with one of his own. 'What are you Kim-Jong-il?'

'Oh, no, she's allowed to smile, but this is over the top, it's not normal, it's not Lucy.'

'The normal Lucy doesn't smile? Who've I met then?' Tyler glanced my way, warmth in his eyes. Was he defending me?

'Dunno,' Sean muttered. 'Some new happy-reincarnated version.' So much for behaving themselves.

'You know, I *can* hear you, Sean.'

He ignored me and continued. 'We normally get quiet gloom and glares. I miss the glares.'

I speared him one right in the centre of his temple. 'Better?'

'Much.'

*****

TYLER SLUMPED INTO THE bench across from me, startling me out of my solitude. I gasped and slammed the book shut, yanking the earphones from my ears.

'Sorry.'

'It's fine, you just scared me.' I pressed my hands over the cover of my art book. My pulse drummed in my ears. Under my fingers were pages and pages of images of him.

He combed his fingers through his hair and nodded at the book. 'You like to draw?'

'Ah, yeah. Love it, one of my favourite things to do.'

'Can I see anything?'

Hell no. Plucking up the book, I clutched it to my chest, my eyes brimming with horror. What was I thinking?

'I'll take that as a no.' He chuckled. 'Maybe another time. If you change your mind.' *Yeah, not happening.*

'Sorry...I love to draw, but sharing this...' I jiggled the book still snug in my arms. 'Not so much.'

'Tell me then, what else do you love to do? Besides drawing, snowboarding, and colour-coding your maths teacher's clothing?'

'I don't do that, you're the one who started naming them.'

'I'm not the one who came up with rotten banana smoothie yesterday.' We'd come up with a new name for each lesson except for today when, shock horror, Mr Blythe wore a blue cardigan.

'No, but how spot on was it?'

'Very, I could almost taste it.'

I screwed up my face. 'That's just gross.'

'So,' he said. 'You love...?'

You. I love you. My gaze wandered to his lips, then flew back to his eyes, still fixed on mine and waiting for me to speak.

'Oh, I love...to run,' I sputtered.

'As in athletics? Sprints or long distance?'

I shook my head. 'No, not competitive. I just like to run. Stick music in my ears.' I held up the earphones strung around my neck. 'Open my door and run.'

He rubbed the side of his jaw, as if the idea baffled him. 'Where to?'

'Anywhere. But mostly to the edge of town. There's a hill a couple of k's away from home, I go up there. It has an awesome view of the mountains. I've claimed it as mine, even though it belongs to the cows more than anyone. They don't mind sharing while I sit.'

'I thought you were running?' He tilted his head, confused.

'Yeah, then I reach my hill and I...' I paused, should I say it? It felt so private, and no one knew what I did up there. But it was Tyler, and I told him everything. 'I meditate.'

'You meditate?' A huge grin stretched across his face, his eyes lighting up. 'Me too.'

'I know,' I blurted. My hand shot up to cover my mouth, and I coughed to mask my slip-up. Composing myself, I continued, 'I mean, I wondered. It seems like something you might do.' *Argh, what does that even mean?*

I hadn't heard the bell, but all at once, Cal, Sean, and Max were there. Tyler's eyes were locked on mine, but the voices and activity around us cried for our attention. Reluctantly, and painfully, we shifted our attention away from one another.

I shoved my art book into my bag.

'Whatcha got there, Luce?' Sean asked, edging around to my side of the table. 'You got some new drawings to share?' The singsong tone of his voice prickled the hairs on my arms.

Jerk. He knew full well what was in that book. Ignoring his taunts, I dropped my bag at my feet, but Sean hopped behind me and plucked it off the grass. Without a flinch, I lunged for the bag, clutching hold of the strap as Sean yanked it away. His laughter echoed in my ears, but anger boiled inside me, firing my resolve.

I gripped my fingers around the strap like my life depended on it. Right now, it did. Sean's eyes danced with delight, and I wrenched hard, ripping it out of his grasp and sending me flying off the back of the bench. I landed on my back, the contents of my bag spilling onto the grass around my head. My art book flung open; the pages thankfully facing down.

Slamming my arm over the book, I slumped my head back onto the ground. That was close. The clouds spun above me, nausea swirled. I shut my eyes and the swaying floated away.

Max knelt quietly beside me, and I rolled over to help her collect my books into my bag. I zipped it closed, lifting the bag as I stood but it remained upturned on the grass, the torn end of my strap hanging from my fingers.

Pressing on my matted hair in an attempt to tame it, I aimed my scowl smack bang at Sean's guilty eyes. 'You're a dick.'

He dropped onto the bench. 'Sorry, I was being stupid.'

'You got that right.'

'Seriously, Sean. You owe her a backpack.' Max slapped him over the head in true sibling style as she marched back to a spot at the table.

'I didn't tear it. Luce was the one...yeah okay.' He dropped his gaze from Max's glare.

I rested my hands on the table with an exasperated sigh. 'No, it's fine. I mean it's so not fine, but I've got another bag at home I can use instead. Forget it...and don't do that again.'

'You weren't kidding, were you?' Tyler said with a gentle slant of his lip.

I hadn't forgotten he'd witnessed the entire humiliating scene, but my cheeks flamed hot now that I had to look him in the eye. 'About what?'

'Sharing your work.'

'Oh...yeah.' I attempted to laugh, as if it was all a big joke. 'Nope, not kidding.'

• 144 •

—18—

T HE FOLLOWING MORNING, I sipped coffee, music pouring from the speakers in my room, allowing a moment's reprieve and motivation to get through the enormous stack of homework in front of me. If I had this much work after one week, I dreaded the year ahead. The image of Tyler's face filled my mind, and anticipation buzzed through my veins. No, it was going to be a great year.

But I was exhausted. I'd been riding one hell of an emotional roller coaster all week with no letup; the bar holding me in place hurt more with each twist of the track and downhill run, and although exhilarating, the turbulence had been dizzying.

Yet with all the excitement, there remained the growing amount of homework the teachers threw at us. Later that afternoon after doing more maths than I'd ever wished to do on a Saturday, I shoved my feet into a pair of sneakers and ran downstairs. The full brunt of the February heat slammed into me the second the door opened. The cool inside air beckoned me. I hesitated on the door mat, enduring a silent standoff with the sun. I always preferred the cold to the heat. But I needed a run, and I wouldn't admit defeat without trying.

My feet drove me forward, down to the corner and up the steep road. The heat clung to me, entered my pores and refused to let go. Sweat ran down the sides of my face. Reaching the top of the hill, I bent over and gripped my legs, panting heavily. I heaved myself to standing again and climbed through the fence. Where was a waterfall when I needed one?

And where were the cows? Squinting into the sun, I held my hand against my forehead. No cows in any direction, but my eyes focused on something else striding up the hill from the opposite direction. Crap, it was that man again. I'd finally been caught trespassing. What were the penalties for that?

I stepped back toward the fence, my heart racing as I prepared my explanation.

'Hey.' He raised his arm, in greeting or to shoo me away I couldn't quite tell. Was he smiling?

I waved back. 'Sorry,' I yelled, my chest still heaving. 'I'm just leaving.'

'No need. You must be our new neighbour.'

Huh?

I peered up at the approaching man, now blocking the glaring sun behind him and coming into view. I gasped. My vision became hazy. Tyler's raised-from-the-dead dad stood before me. I reached for the fence, but my fingers found thin air. I staggered and fell into the grass.

'Woah, you all right?'

'Just lost my footing.' I tried to reassure him with a smile, but the shock held firm. I should be used to it by now, but seeing people after they were previously dead still did incredible things to my mind. My mouth hung open as I appraised the man standing over me. Calmer, more relaxed than the one I remembered, but then that wouldn't be too hard. Lack of stress had smoothed out the lines etched into his face since I'd seen him on the plane, but he was unmistakably Tyler's dad.

He extended a hand and helped me stand. 'The name's Charles. We must be neighbours.' He beamed in candid delight, and a dimple appeared on his chin, exactly like Tyler's.

'Uh, no I don't think –'

'Sure we are, we just moved in. House down the hill.' He pointed his thumb over his shoulder.

'You bought the land?' That's why the other house was still for sale; they'd chosen something else. Relief stirred in my stomach. 'That's great.'

'It is pretty great.' He turned to appreciate the view I'd seen hundreds, maybe even thousands of times, but to him was like his first sunset. 'So what are you doing up here?'

'I come up here when I go for a run. We're actually not neighbours. This here...' I nodded to the scrub over the fence. 'That's public land. I come up from town. I'll stay over that side from now on. Sorry 'bout that.'

'Oh, no, you can come on over, that's no problem. There's plenty of land to go around. Hey, you might know my boy. Do you go to school locally? His name's Tyler.'

My cheeks burst with the fullness of my joy. 'Yeah, I know Tyler. He's been hanging out with me and my friends.'

'Well, what d'ya know. Let me guess, Amber? Lucy? What's the other one?' So he hadn't told him about me specifically, but he'd mentioned me. That would do, I suppose.

'Max,' I said.

'That's right. Nice to meet you, Max.' He held out his hand.

A small chuckle escaped and I placed my hand into his firm grip. 'No, I'm Lucy. It's nice to meet you too.' He had no idea how much.

'Hey, why don't you come down to the house? Tyler's bored senseless with all this unpacking. He could do with some company. And you look like you could do with a drink.' He turned and started down the sloping grass.

I stepped forward, paused, hesitated. Beads of sweat dripped down the sides of my brow, attaching the wisps of hair to my skin like glue. Did I really want Tyler to see me like this? What did I smell like?

Tyler's dad glanced over his shoulder. 'It's not far, you'll be able to see it in a minute.'

Oh, what was I thinking, who cared about any of that? I'd be seeing Tyler. I leaped forward and joined Charles's long strides down the hill.

The house came into view, nestled at the bottom of the hill on a flat expanse of land, lush with an overgrowth of natives and greenery. Built from deep terracotta-coloured mud bricks, with a gabled roof and loads of windows. It might only be a few blocks away, but this home was worlds away from the other one. Where the first house said 'who cares', this one shouted love. A vine crept up one side of the house, and pots of plants stood amongst the garden beds around the home. An abundance of flowers sprouted alongside the paths. Pink roses, purple lavender and – my heart soared – Tyler's mum got her white daisies.

Charles led me to a gravelled path, and we wound our way through the garden toward the house. He opened the large front door and waltzed inside. I stopped on the doormat, feeling exposed and silly all of a sudden. I fiddled with my fingernails.

'Hey, guys, I bumped into our neighbour. Tyler? Sally, where's Tyler?' he called into the kitchen where I could make out the back of Sally as she unpacked a box of glassware.

'I think he's in his room, hon,' she said over her shoulder.

Charles moved to the other side of the open area in front of me. He yelled up the stairs, 'Tyler, get your butt down here.' I giggled.

This house had more life in it after one week than the other place did after four months. The house itself had a more homely feel, more boxes had been unpacked, but it was definitely the people – namely the one who'd been dead last time – that made the place more alive. I liked it a lot. I hoped Tyler did too.

Tyler's bare feet appeared at the top of the stairs before he bounded down them two at a time, coming to an abrupt halt the moment he laid eyes on me in the doorway.

'Lucy?'

'I bumped into your friend. She's our new neighbour, thought you could do with some company.' Charles pointed a finger at me. 'And I was going to get you a drink. Come in, I'll grab you a nice cold glass of water.' He trudged away and left me standing awkwardly in the doorway. Cool air-con to the front, sweltering heat on my backside. If I took one step back I might melt right into the ground. But then again if I took one step toward Tyler I might suffer the same fate. I was doomed.

'Sorry.' I wiped at the hair plastered to my temple, brushing it behind my ears. 'Is this weird me showing up here? It's weird, isn't it? I should've said no.'

'To Dad? I don't think he'd understand, it's not in his vocabulary,' Tyler said, the gentleness in his eyes quieting the pounding rhythm of my heart. He trundled down the last of the stairs.

'I'll just grab the water and head off.'

'You don't get out of it that easily,' he said with a kind smirk.

I scrunched my brow. 'Huh?'

'Unpacking. That's what he dragged you here for, right?'

'Not exactly, said you could do with some company.'

'Yeah, and another set of hands. It's never ending.'

'Great, well at least I know what I'm good for.'

He didn't reply, just kept a goofy grin on me that said he knew something. If only I couldn't read him so well. Not knowing what that face meant would be so much easier.

Charles returned with a tall glass of ice water. I ran it across my forehead before drinking half in one go. 'Thank you so much.'

Tyler's mum swept into the room wearing a vibrant red halter neck dress. 'Hi, I'm Sally.' She placed a hand on Charles' shoulder, leaning into his side. She exuded genuine joy and contentment – no fake smile this time.

'This is Lucy, Tyler's friend from school. She's our neighbour.' He was really keen to have a new neighbour.

'Well –'

'It's so lovely to meet you. Sounds like you and your friends have made Tyler very welcome at school.' She rested a hand over her heart, warmth emanating from her. 'That means a lot to me, thank you.'

'No thanks needed. It's great to have him around.' *Really, it's my pleasure.*

What a strange transformation. Seeing the reverse of a tragedy in someone's life. It was normal to witness the happiness die; to see the overwhelming sorrow in someone's eyes as they dealt with heartache and loss of a loved one. Less normal was seeing the light restored in their eyes and a bounce returning to their step almost overnight. That's what I witnessed now – Sally as a new person. It only proved how much more I'd given to Tyler when I brought his dad back. Pride swelled in my chest.

'All right, you two,' Charles said. 'Why don't you scoot? Do the books on the landing if you get bored. But have a rest first, Lucy, you still have to run home later.'

—19—

'C'MON.' TYLER LED THE way up the stairs. This time I didn't hesitate to follow. 'Have you really been running in this weather?' he asked as we reached the top of the stairs. The landing was a small room of its own, already fitted with armchairs, a sofa, and bookcases – empty bookcases.

'Rain, hail, or shine, the weather doesn't dictate if I run.'

'Hail? That's gotta be painful.' Tyler manoeuvred around the piles of boxes, aiming for a clearing on the other side of the room.

I ignored the thumping pulse in my neck and screwed up my face in answer. 'It is. I had bruises to prove how much.'

Tyler's eyes widened. 'No way. How big?'

'The hail was about the size of a bouncy ball.' I demonstrated with my fingers. 'But I ended up with bruises much bigger.'

'Ouch.'

'Yep.'

'Apparently you have to rest.' Tyler waved to indicate the armchair under the window and settled himself onto the edge of the sofa.

I lowered myself into the seat. 'I don't really need to rest. I do this all the time.'

He raised an eyebrow in warning. 'Dad will know if you don't.'

'You know, I'm not really your neighbour. I tried to tell your dad.'

'Let me guess, he didn't listen?'

'Not really, no.'

'Whatever, wouldn't care if you were.' He shook his head. 'Sorry, that came out wrong. I mean, makes no difference to me if you're our neighbour or not. How'd you get here then?'

'The track I mentioned yesterday leads to the edge of your property. I've been sneaking over to this side of the fence since... forever. I like to sit and take in the view with the cows.'

'The cows?' Astonishment clouded his features.

I let out a tiny laugh. 'They make great company.'

Tyler scrunched his mouth and hesitated. 'We got rid of the cows.'

I sat up straight, tears pricking behind my eyes; I loved those cows.

'No, not as in killed them. Dad wanted empty land, didn't want the cows. Maybe I could come up there and give you some company instead.'

My heart steadied at his reassurance and the calming lull of his voice. 'You think you'd make a good cow replacement? That's a tough gig.'

'What's so great about the cows?'

'They don't pay me any attention.'

His cheeks turned a soft shade of pink. 'That *is* a tough gig.' He tucked his bare foot casually under his knee, as if he were oblivious to the reaction his words had on me.

The heat in my face intensified, and I lifted the cool glass of water to my parched lips. 'And they're really good listeners.'

'Well, what do you know, so am I.' He grinned, and I couldn't help but smile at his enthusiasm. 'So you just sit and talk to the cows up there? You know, I think there's places for people like you.'

'It sounds so much worse than it really is.'

'You're right, it does.' Tyler bounced to his feet. 'Okay, enough rest.'

We cut open the top of the nearest box, folding back the cardboard flaps to reveal the biggest stash of books I'd seen outside the school library.

'You guys read all these?' I grabbed up a handful and slid them onto a shelf.

'They're Dad's mostly, but I've read some. You like to read?'

'I prefer movies.' I didn't tell him the details were difficult to conjure up because images from my nightmares crammed for space in my head. That I preferred the music and the pictures the movie director created for me.

'Movies are pretty awesome.' He heaved out two giant books from the box, his arm muscles tightening from the weight. I wanted to run my fingers along their length, get to know them again. *Him* again.

I shook my head, clearing the thoughts away; I couldn't go there. 'Are we supposed to be doing this a certain way? By colour? Alphabetical order? Height?'

'If it was meant to be done a certain way, we wouldn't have been given the job.'

'Right.' I pulled out another couple of books as Tyler reached in for more, and the back of my hand brushed against his. I stilled as a surge of lightning ran up my arm, jump-starting my heart to abnormal speed again.

Tyler's eyes locked on mine, the intensity of their heat warming my cheeks and likely turning a similar shade of pink to the book in my hands. Tyler swivelled toward the shelf to arrange his books, and I reluctantly followed his lead.

'So, what do you all normally do around here on the weekends? Other than help strange families unpack their furniture.' His eyes returned to me, lit up with the light from his smile, the heat of a few moments ago now gone.

My mood lightened and I relaxed once again into his casual presence. 'Not much. In the winter we're up the mountain from lifts open 'til lifts closed.' I pointed in the general direction of the snow fields. 'Life feels a little less busy in the summer, we just cruise along with it really. Movies in Mayfield every now and then, we often hang out at Slice of Heaven, the pizza joint in town, I go running. Cal has a huge room with almost every gaming console you can think of, that keeps him and Sean happy most of the time. I'm sure you'll end up there eventually.'

He nodded. 'Already got an invite for tomorrow.'

We reached the bottom of the box and dragged another one close, slicing open the top.

'Oh and you've heard of the lake house? One of my favourite places in the world, after the mountain of course.'

'Of course,' Tyler said, the edges of his eyes crinkling with his smile.

'Every time I'm sure we've overstayed our welcome, but Cal's mum, Marie, laps it up. She'll love having another son.'

'Another son?'

'You. That's how she treats us all when we're there. Like her children. Cal's an only child. They lost his older brother, Richie, six years ago.' It felt strange telling Tyler this again, more than any other fact, this was something you only wanted to say once.

Tyler's eyes softened, sadness creeping in. 'Shit, that's awful.'

'Yeah. He was twelve, would've turned eighteen last year.' I thought of his birthday the year before and how my memories of that day were so perfect, the day Tyler and I learnt we shared something extraordinary, the ability to share dreams.

Tyler exhaled, turning his face to the ceiling. 'Do you ever imagine how different things could be if one small thing changed. Like how different your life might be?' I stared into his eyes, grasping at the seriousness of his question. Blood rushed through my veins.

I held his gaze, the pounding of my heart drilling in my ears. 'All the time.' My breathing deepened; something was happening here. I didn't know what, but he had to mean something by that, surely. 'But nothing could change what happened to Richie. He didn't step out in front of a bus...he got cancer. That's not something that a simple should've done things different would have prevented. Molecules and cells aren't so easily manipulated.' I spoke from too much experience, and Tyler regarded me like I'd elaborated on a lie I hadn't needed to. I should've just said yes.

'What, and those other things are?'

Crap.

'No, I guess not.' Actually, yes. 'But you know sometimes we can look back and say, I wish I'd done such and such differently, then things could be different. But not with cancer. He was eight when he got it, nothing he did could've changed his course.'

'Sucks, huh.'

'Balls.' And we laughed at my elaborate choice of words.

After another three boxes and goodbyes to Tyler's parents, with their profuse thanks for my help, Tyler and I stepped out into the heat.

We strolled up the hill, slipping back into the awkwardness of unfamiliarity. It was a strange feeling for me, because although I knew him so well, or had done the last time he'd been in my life, it did feel as if I were getting to know a different person. And he *was* a different person. A regular teenager unburdened with the weight of losing a parent and becoming the man of the house. He no longer had the responsibility of his mum and sister on his hands, just the regular demands of being a teenager.

There were so many obvious differences to me, noticeable to a person who'd seen the other him – he had a license and a car for one – but I also knew, that inside, the same gentle and caring Tyler I'd come to love still existed.

But to feel so at ease and yet miss what we'd had left me dizzy with emotions. I swallowed and kicked the grass under my sneakers.

Tyler broke the silence. 'Do many others use that path? Will we be flocked by dozens of locals every weekend?'

'Doubt it. In all the years I've been using it, I've bumped into maybe a handful of people. Scares the life out of me when I do, because it's so unexpected. The mountains steal everyone in the winter, and then it puts its charms on in the summer too. Doesn't bother me. I like having this place all to myself.' We reached the fence and stopped.

'Then we came along, *désole*. Sorry.' Tyler shifted on his feet.

'No, I like your company.' *More than you know.* I held back the enormous grin wanting to flood my face.

'Yeah, I like yours too. It was nice to spend the afternoon with you.'

My head bobbed in agreement. 'Yeah, it was. Thanks.' I bent and lifted a leg through the fence wire, coming to stand on the other side. Tyler frowned, studying me. Sweat glistened on his scrunched brow. 'What?'

'Nothing. Just feels like I've known you for a lot longer than a week,' he said, pressing his hand to the back of his neck.

Fierce panic roared through my veins and I stepped back, raising an eyebrow. 'Maybe you have,' I teased with a quiver in my voice, and his eyes speared me with a million questions. I spun on my heel to escape into the thick of trees. I fixed my sight straight ahead and ran hard away from him. Fear ignited my legs. Afraid of what his questions could be, wanting so much for them to be what I hoped... that he remembered me.

—20—

I worked later that night, and despite my fatigue, the smiles were easier to dish out than they'd been in a long time. Amber placed her empty tray on the stainless-steel bench in the kitchen. 'So when are you two getting together?'

'Ha, I don't think it's that easy.' I slid a tray to the edge of the bench and positioned it onto my palm.

''Course it is. You're gorgeous, he's gorgeous. You're like magnets, drawn to each other.'

'No. I'm drawn to him, but last time he was into me because of the dream he saw me in. It kinda made me stand out somewhat.'

'All right, you two.' Laurie stepped through the back door into the kitchen. 'Less talk, more food. Save it for clean-up. Those people are ravenous.' She picked up a tray of mini bruschetta and placed it in Amber's hands and shooed us away with a clap-clap and wave.

'And you don't think you stand out now?' Amber asked over her shoulder. 'With your lush dark hair and big brown eyes, not to mention your athletic body. I've seen the way he stares at you.'

'You have?'

'Yes, he looks at you like you're a God.'

'Well...' I tipped my head to the side, thought of all the lives I'd saved, and raised my tray of Gruyere cheese and asparagus tarts into the air. Amber burst out laughing, and we thrust into the throng of party goers.

The guests filtered out of the marquee, music had ceased blasting from the speakers, and we collected the last of the food from the party area.

'You girls were on fire tonight,' Laurie said, packaging up the uneaten cupcakes and mini cheesecakes for the shelter. 'You handled the situation beautifully.'

I brushed at the remains of the beer down the front of my shirt. The guests had been loud and rude and probably the most intoxicated party goers I'd ever had to manoeuvre around. But no amount of spilt beer could dispel the unmistakable love-struck grin on my face.

'It's 'cause she's in love.' Amber brushed past me, and I elbowed her in the side as we piled our dishes into the sink.

'Now that would explain it.' Laurie grinned.

'I'm always like this.' My voice pitched a little in defence.

'Not quite like this, my dear Lucy.' Laurie pointed at my face.

I shoved my hands into the soapy water, scrubbing the trays with overzealous enthusiasm. 'What, so this is too much now? I thought you wanted big smiles.'

'Oh, I do. Whoever he is, he's a keeper.'

Amber laughed and reached for the tea-towel and silverware on the sink. 'And if this is what you're like now,' she said quietly, 'imagine what you'll be like when you eventually get together.'

I flicked her with the dishwater. It wasn't worth defending myself or my position at this point.

*****

THE WEEK BEGAN WITH another intense pummelling of summer heat, even the shady maple struggled to keep it away. I grabbed my water bottle from my bag and took a swig.

'Bet you're missing the surf on days like today,' Sean said to Tyler.

'You've no idea.' Tyler shook his head, his eyes holding regret at the reminder of his beloved surf.

'You two going to your dad's this weekend?' I asked Max and Sean. They went to their dad's place in Sydney for one weekend a month. I didn't think this was their weekend, but Tyler didn't need reminders of what he missed about home, not when I desperately needed him to want to be here.

'Nah, next weekend,' Sean said

Amber and Cal dropped onto the end of the bench.

'Okay, lovelies, guess what I've got.' Amber pushed a box into the centre of the table, followed by a knife. 'I've only got three though, you're going to have to share.' She was like Mary Poppins, the things she managed to bring to school in that bag astounded me.

Tyler peered into the cake box. 'Wow.'

'Banana Caramel, Toffee apple, or Lemon Meringue?' Amber paused, waiting for Tyler's choice.

'Man, that's like asking me to choose between surfing in Hawaii or Fiji. They're equally appealing.'

'Don't worry, dude, you'll get to taste them all eventually,' Cal said.

'Okay then, lemon, please.'

Amber passed him the more intact of the two cut halves, and he bit into it with a sigh as his eyes virtually rolled into the back of his head.

Cal took the other half.

'Luce?'

'Ooh, the apple please, Miss A.'

Cal bit into his cake. A large chunk landed on the bench between us, and he shoved himself aside to locate it.

Amber squealed, and the knife clattered to the tabletop. 'Ow, ow.' She held her thumb in her fingers. Blood pooling where she'd made the cut.

'Shit. I'm sorry, babe. You got any tissues in your bag?'

'I think so, I dunno.' She hissed again, staring at the mass of red growing larger and brighter on her pale skin.

'I'll have some napkins from the canteen.' I grabbed my bag at my feet, the grey one I'd taken to Sydney because Sean killed my other one. I trailed my hands around my books and found nothing, no mass of spare napkins like I stuffed in my usual bag. Everyone was rummaging, trying to find something to stop the flow of blood. I opened the front zipper, nothing. I opened the main part of the bag again. I might have something in the mesh pocket at the back of the pack.

My fingers made contact with something smooth and flat, not soft and crumpled like I'd hoped. I found the corner of the white card and tugged it free. My eyebrows drew together. Who put a photograph in my bag? I turned it over and the walls of my world narrowed.

Everything around me vanished and I sat alone, the photograph held in my trembling fingers. An image of us strolling out of the backpacker's in Sydney, Amber clutching onto my arm and leaning into me, Max on my other side, smiles on all our faces as we headed out for dinner. I lowered the picture below the barricade of my backpack still on my lap. A deathly drum pounded in my temple. We were completely oblivious when this picture had been taken, of the person standing up the street watching us. And worse than that, of the danger it posed for us. Amber's head was thrown back in laughter, her blond hair cascading over her shoulder, and drawn in thick red marker, was a circle around her face.

I whirled my gaze up to her. He'd been watching us. I led him straight to her.

'Luce?' Cal's hand brushed my arm.

I started, my eyes flashing down to the picture and back up at him, widening with fear. Cal would kill me if he knew. My fingers were on fire. I needed to get rid of this picture. I slid it inside my art book and shoved it far into my bag.

'Are you okay?' he asked. 'You're pale as.'

'Huh, what? Oh great, you found something for the bleeding.' Amber held something white around her thumb, the bloodied knife left untouched while Max broke the cakes in half without it. 'Sorry, none in here like I thought.' I hugged my bag to my lap trying to rid my hands of the shaking and dispel the terror in the depths of my core.

*****

THE TREES BRUSHED PAST my face as I ran along my path, winding my way through the bush to the edge of Tyler's property. I placed my hands on my hips, panting as I caught my breath, the sweat running down my neck. I shuffled over to the fence. Do I do it?

Climb the fence and run the risk of Tyler seeing me meditate. Even if he did do it himself I'd still look like an idiot. Could I even do it with him so close by? Besides, I didn't want to close my eyes when I got up there; I wanted to keep them peeled open in case he showed up.

But I needed something to calm me down. Since seeing the photo earlier I'd been on the precarious edge of a teetering tower. I couldn't shake the constant fear encasing me. I needed to steady my erratic heart.

I climbed through the wire, found a shady spot further along the fence-line and lowered myself into the grass. The view of the mountains loomed in the distance, comforting me in their familiarity. I closed my eyes.

Easing out of my induced state of relaxation, my eyes fluttered open, but the feeling remained like a soft blanket covering my shoulders, and with a sigh, I wrapped it tightly round my body. It always felt like I'd had a sleep after I came to, but without the tired, need-to-go-back-to-sleep sensation.

With the feeling of peace surrounding me I let my mind return to the photo. He'd followed me. I mean I knew he'd followed me, I'd seen him, but I thought I lost him. A chill ran down my sweaty neck at the thought of being watched. Instinctively I flicked my gaze over my shoulder. Nothing.

I climbed through the fence and strolled along the scrub-lined track. I picked up a dead branch from the ground and plucked at the leaves.

I didn't know what to do. Should I call the cops? What would they do with a photo? It proved nothing. Except his guilt in the stealing of my backpack. Not that the cops would care about that. And I had no new evidence to get him arrested again, not that I'd try, not if it put Amber in danger. Because when he slipped the photo securely in the pocket of the backpack, he'd sent me a pretty chilling message that it would.

But he'd put it there over four months ago. Surely that meant the warning had expired, and if the threat had gone away what point would there be in telling my friends. It'd only worry them. No, I might be sharing a lot more with them lately, but this, I needed to keep to myself.

—21—

'How're you feeling about everything?' Max asked during P.E. the following morning. We ran beside each other on the track, the rest of the class dotting out in front and behind us.

'Okay. It's a bit surreal, but I really couldn't be happier.' Tyler had become a favourite topic of conversation since he'd appeared on the scene the week before, not that I was complaining.

'Even if he has a girlfriend?'

'What?' I jerked my head toward her, my feet stumbling on the track.

Max slowed as I regained my footing. 'Didn't you say he was with someone when you saw him in Sydney?'

I'd forgotten that piece of information. 'Why did you have to remind me?' I picked up my pace, irritation flowing readily.

'I didn't think you'd forget. Sorry.'

'It's fine, but damn, that makes things even worse.'

'Worse than what? You just said how happy you were.'

'Worse than the fact I have to get him to fall for me all over again. Having another girl in the equation was never part of the plan.'

Max's expression softened. 'Maybe they broke up when they moved? That happens, right?'

'I dunno. Guess it depends how much they were into each other.' The thought of him being more into someone than he'd been with me filled me with dread. What if he loved her?

'I'll ask him.' Max said. 'Want me to ask him?'

My ponytail slapped me in the face as I whipped my head around. 'If he's into his girlfriend?'

She laughed. 'If he still has one.'

'He'll wonder how you know he even has one.'

'Don't worry. I won't give anything away. I'll figure something out.'

I raised my eyebrows.

'Ye of little faith.' Her mouth rose in a sinister grin.

When break rolled around my legs wobbled with anxiety under the table. I wiped my palms on my shorts. I loved that I had my friends on side to help fight my peculiar battle, but the nerve-racking unknown of what they might say or do next rattled me.

Typically, Max handled it as smoothly as she did her bar routine. It came up perfectly in conversation right after Cal mentioned how long he and Amber had been together.

'You have a girlfriend back home, Tyler?' she asked casually.

'Oh, uh –'

Amber skipped up to the table. 'All right, lovelies, you guys are gonna love me.'

'Already do.' Cal slid an arm around her waist and kissed her neck.

'More,' she said, and Cal nuzzled into her neck again. She swatted him. 'No, you're going to love me more.' *And I'm going to pass out in a minute.* 'Mum accidentally cooked twice the amount than her order.' She deposited a cake box on the table.

'Six peanut butter chocolate cupcakes if you will.' Her eyes were alight as she lifted the lid off the box.

'Oh my God.' Hands dived into the box and we all sighed in ecstasy.

'I knew these'd be good,' Tyler muffled around a mouth half full of cake. 'But these are bloody amazing.'

'How'd you know?' Amber tipped her head to the side.

'Look at them.' We peered into the empty box, showing no sign of the beautifully made cakes of moments ago. The table melted into a sea of laughter.

Max wiped at the corner of her mouth. 'So?'

Tyler's gaze flitted from Max to me before answering the non-forgotten question. 'No, no I don't.' That didn't sound convincing. I couldn't help myself.

'But you did have?' I said, a heated blush rising up my neck. 'I saw you with someone when I came to the school. Sorry, you don't have to answer that, not my business.' No, I demanded an explanation. How long ago did he break it off, or did she break up with him? I twisted my fingers together in my lap.

'No, you're right, I was still with Chloe then. We broke up not long after, I think. Turns out she wasn't the girl of my dreams after all.' He didn't catch my eye when he spoke, but I startled as the air whooshed right out of me, because every ounce of my being screamed for him to remember that I was the girl of his dreams. What I wouldn't give to know how to remind him of that?

*****

THE REST OF THE week turned out to be uneventful and yet amazing; a done-to-death ski slope, covered in fresh powder. Tyler being around turned everything from melancholy and flat into something enjoyable, his mere presence masking how dull everything had been.

And him being around helped keep my mind off the insistent reminder of the photograph. I knew I couldn't do anything about it, so I refused to think about it too long. Besides I had other more enjoyable things to think on. Things I desperately wanted to speed along, but how do you encourage something with someone who has no memory of their love for you? I had to start from the ground up, like a garden. Before we could flower, we needed nurturing, watering, but most of all, that intolerable thing called patience.

I wished my dreams would come back, because with them returned the possibility of sharing a dream with Tyler. He'd been back in my life and I'd been off my tablets for almost two weeks, but so far, nothing.

I worked on Friday night and again on Saturday afternoon, grateful for the chance to stay busy. By the time I came home from my shift on Saturday, my feet were too sore for any running. I plopped on the couch with some leftovers Laurie, the best boss in the world, sent home with me.

I switched on the T.V. turning it up to block the hum of the bass from the music in Ollie's room upstairs.

'...he'll face court again later this week.'

Crap. I'd turned on to the news. No, this was great. I sat up straight and focused on the flickering screen.

Footage of a man exiting a courthouse appeared on the screen, then cut back to the news presenter sitting straight-backed behind the news desk. My eyes were glued to her, even though I knew it'd be bad, even though I doubted I could help anyway.

'Two children and an elderly woman have drowned at a beach in North-East Queensland earlier today. Emergency crews responded to a call at midday, but due to the remote access of the location were unable to reach them in time. Family members are said to be reeling from the tragic loss of ten-year-old Skye Larson and her six-year-old brother, Archie, along with their sixty-eight-year old grandmother, Fay.'

My stomach dropped. An aerial of the small beach where it

happened and their faces filled the screen, sending an overwhelming sense of regret through me that I wouldn't be able to fix this. I couldn't undo anything because I'd selfishly taken those tablets and they were still in my system.

I watched the rest of the news, attempting to catch more stories I'd missed, but I couldn't remove those innocent little faces from my mind. They were so etched into me that when I drifted to sleep that night, even though I could've sworn I wouldn't dream them because of the tablets, I found myself on that beach.

WARM GRAINS OF SAND *scratched around my bare feet, and a gentle breeze from the ocean blew my hair around my face. Grabbing the wayward strands, I scanned the area. I stood in a small secluded alcove, the semi-circle of sand and water enclosed by short but rugged cliffs, with only the doomed family in sight. Skye and Archie played in the shallow water, jumping as the white waves crashed to shore and chased them back to sea. An elderly couple relaxed on low-lying lounges further up the beach, both reading, periodically flicking gazes over the top of the pages.*

Sweat gathered on the back of my neck as I squinted out at the water, the reflection of the sun stinging my eyes. I padded toward the water's edge and dipped my feet in.

'Skye, cream time, your turn,' the Gran called.

Skye turned and marched up the sand and wrapped a towel around her shoulders. Her gran rubbed the towel over her skin before squeezing a blob of cream into the palm of her hand and rubbing it into Skye's near-dry skin.

Archie chased another wave out and trudged further into the water. Ankles, knees, waist. He waded toward a line of rocks just past the waves. The rocks were dotted along the beach, some big, some small, but all shadowing the depths of the water around them.

My heart hammered; he was too little to go any deeper. I stepped forward. 'Don't do it, buddy,' I mumbled.

He reached a large boulder about thirty metres out and climbed onto the rough and wet surface, lifting himself out of the water to knee depth.

'Check this out!' he called with a wave from atop his rock. The grandfather peered over his book and waved back, the gran too busy rubbing the cream over Skye's neck to notice, and Skye's face pointing to the sand at her feet. All oblivious to the danger in the water.

Archie stepped off the back of the rock and slipped silently into dark water twice his height. I lunged forward, hands pushing through the water at my sides. 'Hey!' I called to shore. 'Hey!' They couldn't see or hear me. They hadn't seen or heard Archie either.

He burst through the surface, coughing and spluttering, moments before he disappeared again.

The sound along with his silence finally reached the shore.

'Archie!' Skye screamed. The sunscreen bottle landed in the sand, and the book flung aside. All three of them bolted into the water.

Skye latched onto her gran's arm. 'You can't swim.'

'I have to get to him, it's not that deep. You stay here. George, call for help.' She plunged into the water, her short, plump body bursting through the waves, knees lifting high to propel her forward. She caught up to me in no time, overtaking me in her terror to reach her grandson. With her hands on the rock and the water sloshing around her thighs she stepped around to the side but slid under the water before she could take a breath. I let out a scream, shocked she could lose her footing so easily, and moved myself closer. I stumbled up to the rock, a sudden wave nearly knocking me over. The ground under my left foot disappeared and I squinted at the almost distinct line that ran beneath the water where the seabed dropped off massively. A roaring pulse resonated in my head.

Archie spluttered, while his gran's hands groped at him, trying to push him to the surface even through her own struggle. Another wave surged on them and threw the gran against the rock. Her head slammed hard and she vanished below the surface.

Skye appeared beside me and jumped right into the black depths with her gran and brother.

'Skye!' the grandfather yelled from the shore, a phone held to his ear, panic etched in his eyes.

Archie's arms flailed and latched onto his sister, dragging them both under. I pitched myself into the water, sinking, drowning right along with them. I surfaced and gasped for air, giving me a quick view of the grandfather running into the water. No, no. Not him too. His agonising scream sliced through me before I got dragged under again.

My lungs filled with water, searing at the walls, tearing me inside. The burning so intense I opened my mouth and screamed, but no sound came out. Skye and Archie's eyes bulged open like mine; fear, so much fear. Then they softened, our bodies resigning to the fate delivered upon us, descending further into the clutches of the agitated water. Peacefulness settled over me and the world faded away.

I woke and gasped for air. Sucking in a couple of sharp, deep breaths, I sat up in the hopes it might help fill my lungs. Slowly – in...out...in. My heart pounded beneath my ribs, panic filling the emptiness in my chest – out...in.

I'm not dead. I didn't drown. I'm okay.

The silent words echoed in my head, reassuring and calming as I surveyed my surroundings. I blew through my lips, easing the tightness from my shoulders, and steadied my pulse.

For the first time in months, I reached onto my bedside table, found my jet bracelet, and slid it onto my shaking wrist. It'd been four months since I'd experienced a death; I forgot how overwhelming it felt. My panic had been so real I failed to remember I could wake myself up.

When the fear subsided and eased itself off my shoulders,

I lowered myself back onto my pillow, but my clock read 6:52. I wouldn't be going back to sleep now.

Thoughts hurled around in my head like loose cannons, images from my dream battling with questions of how it'd all escalated so quickly. *How would I be able to save them all?* I shuffled to the bathroom for a scolding shower, scrubbing at my skin to remove the salt still clinging to me from my dream.

The house stirred, and I made myself a super strong coffee and a ham and cheese croissant. I moved about in a daze, once again becoming that solemn, reflective girl most people knew me to be; most people except the new Tyler. He wouldn't recognise this. I hardly recognised this.

—22—

A FEW HOURS LATER I wandered into town to meet the crew for lunch at Slice of Heaven. My mind in a fog, still unable to erase the images of my dream, I ambled along the footpath, my head bent, focusing on the cracks in the pavement.

I'd explored all the possibilities of what could've been different for those children to change the outcome. Why did the grandmother only call Skye from the water and why weren't they worried about Archie being in the water on his own? The words 'it's not that deep' echoed in my head. She couldn't swim but she didn't think it was a problem. No one had seen the dangers beyond the rock. But Skye had tried to hold her grandmother back, instinctively knowing it wasn't a good idea. Not bad for a ten-year-old. Maybe I could use her maturity to change things.

'Lucy,' a voice called, jolting me awake. I'd marched straight past the pizza place. I turned around to my lot waving and laughing at me from their table, a huge yellow umbrella canopying them from above.

'You sleep walking?' Sean asked as I slumped my tired body beside him.

'Something like that,' I mumbled.

Their concerned stares followed me to my seat, picking up on my sombre mood, turning their worry into questions. Had my dreams come back? Tyler glanced around the table, but he had no idea what I could do, what we were all thinking. We couldn't discuss it here.

Sean tossed an arm over my shoulder. 'Well, wake up, we've got business to do.' I scrunched my forehead and he waved a menu in my face. 'Pick the pizzas.'

'I'm easy, you guys choose.' I pushed the menu away, my bracelet glinting from the reflection of the sun.

Tyler's gaze wandered to my arm, and his eyes widened when they settled on the jet on its wrist. Why? Because I wore a piece of jewellery? He peered up at me, and I wanted to lose myself in him and never let go, but before I had the chance to get lost, he looked away.

The pizza arrived and we all dug in, our chatter moving seamlessly from soccer, to our next weekend at the lake house, to schoolwork mounting up. Like a radio station drifting in and out of reception, I only heard sections, my mind still on that beach, my lungs filling with water as I drowned below the depths.

'What about you, Lucy?' Tyler's voice dived into the water and plucked me out.

'Mmm?' I glanced up to all sets of eyes on me.

'I asked if you'd done that piece for geography yet. Cal reckons I'm nuts for getting it finished already.'

'Cal thinks anyone who gets work done on time is weird,' I said.

'They are. Who does that?' Cal said through a mouthful of pizza.

Amber swivelled on her seat. 'I do.'

'See, weird.'

'Hey.' Amber nudged him with her shoulder.

'I don't think it's weird to hand it in on time,' I said. 'I'm going home to finish it this afternoon, but to have it done early, yeah, that's weird.' My lips angled with amusement.

His face softened, like he was pleased I'd finally relaxed. If only he knew it was all a pretence, that inside I still screamed from miles away in my dream.

'You okay?' Sean spoke softly in my ear, dragging my attention from Tyler. 'You had a dream, didn't you?'

I faced him and closed my eyes with a small nod.

'Was it awful?'

'Yes.' They always were.

His whole body sagged. 'I'm sorry.'

'For what?'

'For never being there when you needed me. For not seeing the pain it caused. I can see it now.'

'I managed.' I didn't need him feeling bad about something that was now history.

'I know you did. And I think it was easy to believe you could because you covered it so well. You don't have to anymore though, you know that, right?'

'Yes, I do. He doesn't know what I can do.' I tipped my head sideways, my heart thrumming with the hope he couldn't hear our muffled conversation.

'Why don't you tell him? You'll have to eventually, right?'

'I know, but I can't just come out and say it. I'd known you my whole life and look what happened.'

Sean lowered his eyelids as if in shame for how it played out when I tried to explain it to him the first time.

'Sorry, I'm just scared.'

'I know, but whatever happens, you need to know you're not alone. Don't forget that.' He slid his arm around my shoulder and tugged me close, pressing a kiss to the side of my head.

'Thanks.'

Tyler's eyes met mine and almost as quickly moved away.

'Right.' Cal slapped his knees and stood. 'Time to get this

gorgeous girl home. We have homework to do, apparently.' He gave us a wink.

'Homework, is it?' Sean said to a table of laughter.

'Yes.' Ignoring us, Amber slid her hand into Cal's. 'Homework.'

'Catch ya's.'

They crossed the street to Cal's car, and the rest of us stood to make our way home. Max and I hugged, the strength of her squeeze telling me she was also aware of my returning dreams. 'See you in the morning.'

Sean waved, and he and Max strolled down the street in the opposite direction to my route home.

'You walking?' Tyler slid his hands into his pockets with his phone. 'Want some company?'

I scanned both directions of the street, trying to locate his car. 'You didn't drive?'

'Nah, Cal was at my place before we headed out.'

'What, and he just left you here?' I said with a small laugh. 'What a friend.'

He shrugged. 'I don't mind walking.'

'At least it's not raining.'

'Or hailing,' he added with a grin, and we started up the street towards home.

'Now, wouldn't hail at this time of year be quite the phenomena.' I tilted my head up at the cloudless blue sky.

'It'd melt the instant it hit the ground.'

I shook my head. 'I reckon it'd melt on the way down.'

'Wouldn't that be called rain?'

'I prefer bruise-less hail,' I said with a puff of a laugh.

We passed the last of the shops and the most recently built backpacker's on the corner of the street, with its hip raw-food café underneath the accommodation. We turned right and onto the winding road to my place.

✳✳✳✳✳

I CONTEMPLATED TWO THINGS as I lay in bed trying and failing to fall asleep: how to save the family who drowned and my walk home with Tyler.

It'd been pleasant, nothing more beyond the surface-level chat you have with any regular friend. I didn't make any confessions about my dreams, but I couldn't decide why I hadn't grabbed the chance to share more. Sean said I should tell him, but how did I do that without coming across like the freak I was. The first time around it had been a gradual process. He admitted he'd seen me at the airport, then we shared a dream before finding out it was mutual, then came the final blow at discovering the effect my dreams had on people's lives – or deaths, depending on which way you viewed it. It had been a slow descent into the depths of my world; a dipping in of the toes, then the ankles, until finally he'd been fully immersed in my reality. This would be like pouring a bucket of icy cold water over his head. I couldn't do that to him, not if it had the potential to ruin any possibility of an 'us'.

No, I'd made the right decision. I would wait, and when the time was right to take the plunge I'd know.

When peace over my decision finally drifted over me, so did sleep, and my eyelids closed.

'SKYE, CREAM TIME, YOUR *turn.*'

I stood back on the beach, the warm sand collecting between my toes as I inched closer to the water's edge.

'Okay,' she called from the water, ignoring the annoyance edging onto her gran's face. She surveyed the expanse of water beyond the protruding row of rocks and swam toward the boulder further out near the waves.

'Archie, watch this. Stay there but check this out.'

Archie stood with eagerness in his small eyes, the water bobbing and splashing above his knees.

'Skye, what are you doing! I said to come here.' The gran shielded her eyes with a hand to her forehead, her other one resting on her hip.

'Just a minute, Gran.' Skye climbed onto the rock. 'Archie, the water's really deep out here, it doesn't look like it, but watch this.' She stepped off the rock behind her and disappeared below the dark surface.

'Skye?' Archie's lip trembled and he pushed through the water to find her.

Skye swam around the rock and resurfaced. She stood when she reached waist-high water again and flicked the sodden hair from her face.

'It drops off big time, so don't go out there, okay.'

He nodded, eyes wide. 'But how did you know?'

'It's darker, can you see?' She pointed to the water beyond the rock where the seabed suddenly dropped away. Archie nodded again. 'Right, so I'm getting out for a minute, but you have to stay in the shallow, 'kay?'

She waded through the water onto the shore and stepped into the towel her gran held out to her.

She rubbed at Skye's shoulders. 'What took you? What was so important that you couldn't wait until after I'd done this job?'

'I wanted to show him how deep it is out there. He can't swim and it gets really deep on the other side of the rocks.'

Her gran squinted into the distance. 'So it does. You're a good kid, Skye. Too good sometimes.'

Archie sat splashing in the shallow waters, giggling at the arrival of each new wave over his legs. I stepped to the water's edge and lowered myself into the sand beside him. The water licked my toes, caressing my legs, and sea salt sprayed in the air. A smile crept across my face.

I FORGOT HOW GOOD it felt to save lives, and this time no stalker, crazy dude would come along and kill my victim again. I tried not to think about my failure last year and what part I'd played in Megan's death. I couldn't let that thought taint my happiness. I visualised the faces of those dear children and their grandmother, alive and safe from harm because of a smart little girl foreseeing a danger to her brother.

Their shadows wouldn't haunt me anymore; only one thing followed me after my new dream – peace.

I opened the big double doors at the start of the school day on Monday with a generous smile on my face. Not because I was at school, but because I'd finally started my tally for the year – three lives.

—23—

A WARM BREEZE BLEW my hair around my face, and I tipped my head to sweep it over my shoulder. I held the page of my book flat as my pencil scraped across the paper, drawing the lines of the children from my dream. I'd already saved them, already drawn them in my dream sketchbook that morning, but I had the urge to do them again after months of not pencilling many faces.

The leaves of the maple tree rustled above me, their shade offering relief from the blasting sun. The bell sounded and I scribbled the last of the hair of the little boy before shutting my art book. Laughter closed in around me with the arrival of my friends, and I pressed my palms over the cover.

Tyler's gaze landed on me and my throat went dry.

Sean nudged my side. 'Drawing again?'

I tossed him a glare. He wouldn't dare. I plucked up the book and bent to cram it into my bag. When I straightened, Sean had hold of something. His eyes were downcast, staring at the thing in his fingers – the photo from Sydney. It must've slipped from my book.

'Sean, give me that,' I whispered through my teeth.

He turned to me. 'What is this?'

'Please, give it to me.' My words wobbled, and I reached to grab the photo from his grip.

He tugged it away.

'What the hell is that?' Cal asked, and Sean placed the photo face-up in the centre of the table, the glint of the reflecting sun doing little to hide exactly what the hell it was.

'That's us in Sydney.' Max pressed her fingers to the picture, her eyes projecting me with a thousand questions I didn't want to answer.

I glanced across the table, at Cal's seething expression, and the deathly pale complexion of Amber's face. I didn't dare look at Tyler.

'I found it in my bag last week. It's been there for four months. I thought telling you would just freak you out.'

'Got that right.' Max squirmed. 'He was watching us.' Her voice faded away, a bit like I wanted to.

'I thought some rando stole your backpack?' Sean said. 'Why would this guy steal it and then return it? Why not just slip this in there if that's what he wanted?'

'He didn't return all of it,' I croaked out. 'He kept my wallet and sketchbook.'

'You didn't tell us that,' Max said.

'I'm sorry, I didn't mean to keep it from you…I just –'

'You led him to Amber.' Cal's voice was thick and dark. Amber still hadn't said anything. She sat quietly by his side clutching hold of his hand.

My eyes stung with the threat of tears. 'I thought I'd lost him.'

'You knew he followed you?'

I only nodded.

'We should call the police,' Max suggested.

'And tell them what?' Cal projected some of his venom toward her. 'That you've got a threatening photo someone took of you. Anyone could've taken this. You gonna tell them how you know who took it? That he followed Lucy after she went to his house because she saw him in a dream?'

I dragged in a breath. *Don't look at Tyler.* My eyes betrayed me, and they swept across the table. His face said everything I expected it to: unease, concern, interest. I shifted my attention away. 'That's exactly why I didn't tell them myself.'

'But you could've told us,' Cal said. 'I could've been watching Amber at least.'

'I'm fine, Cal.' She finally spoke up. 'Like Lucy said, it's been four months. If he really wanted to do something, he would've done it by now.'

'And you know this how?'

I lowered my eyes from the heat of his question. Should I tell them more?

'What?' The seriousness of the question deepened Cal's voice.

I curled my hands into tight fists, the nails biting into my flesh, urging me to speak. 'He came here, last year, less than a week after we got back from Sydney. I saw him across the road. I mean...I think it was him. I wasn't sure at the time, and then when I found this, I knew it must've been. But that was over four months ago and nothing's happened since.'

'Like that means anything.' Cal's anger slapped me across the face again. His shoulders sagged. 'I'm sorry. I'm just freaked out. I'm not letting you out of my sight.' He buried himself into Amber's side.

'Great, thanks a lot, Luce.'

I found a small huff of a laugh from the depths of my aching heart for what I'd done to my friends, what I was putting them through.

'What are we going to do then? Besides keeping Amber under lock and key?'

'You don't think that'll be a bit suss to the parent folk?' Sean asked. 'And if they find out, they will definitely want to call the cops.'

'So, we don't let them find out. I can be stealth. I've done it plenty of times before.' Cal winked.

'I'm so sorry. For everything. I wish I knew why he sent me this. I think it was a warning. Telling me to stay out of it.' I held Amber's gaze. 'I won't put you in danger again. If I'd known, I never...' I placed my fingers to my lips to quiet the trembling.

'But now you do, promise you won't get involved in any more superhero, vigilante business?' Sheer terror and love dominated Cal's face.

'I promise.'

Tyler's eyes rose, transparently clear with something like fear.

'Shit, Tyler, forgot you were here.' Sean chuckled. 'Bet you're wondering what sort of freak show you've stumbled on.'

'A little.' He let out a half chuckle. 'I have no idea what's going on, but I'll admit I'm freaked out.'

'Will the short version do?' Sean asked.

'I have a feeling that's all I'm going to get, so yes?'

I jumped in before Sean shared too much. 'Last year, when we went to Sydney to visit my, uh, cousin, we also went to find more details on a man who I think is involved in the murder of that girl, Megan, last year.'

Tyler lifted his chin and narrowed his eyes. 'And you suspect him because you saw him in a dream?'

'Right.'

'Hmm.' The whole table quieted, the stillness amplifying the raging thrum of my pulse. 'Yeah, okay, so I can understand not wanting to go to the police.' And his smile turned into a nervous laugh that made the whole table erupt in laughter, myself included. Except it didn't feel like the happy sort of laugh that comes after a joke, but the crazy sort that escapes when you have no idea how you're supposed to react.

*****

WE DIDN'T TALK ABOUT the photo for the rest of the week. I had another dream which helped distract me for a couple of days, a workplace accident that involved a lot of blood. But once I'd saved the man, the nervous thoughts surrounding the photo returned, remaining a constant undercurrent below the surface I couldn't kick free from.

Cal, true to his word, found every excuse to spend as much time beside Amber as he could. When we worked on Thursday night, he drove us, and when we knocked off, his car sat across the road like a surveillance van, until he followed Laurie's car home, assuring himself of Amber's safe arrival.

'I assume you're spending the weekend together then?' I asked the following morning as we climbed out of the car. Sean now had his Ps, and he parked beside us moments after Cal turned the ignition off. We all crossed the car park toward Tyler, and my heart lurched into my throat at the familiar yet unusual sight of him. He leaned against the bonnet of his car, and spotting us, pushed himself to stand and strode over.

'He won't let me out of his sight.' Amber rolled her eyes.

Cal snaked an arm around her waist and tugged her in tight. 'You weren't complaining last night.'

'And who's watching Luce? We're off to Dad's later, otherwise I'd offer my services.' Sean puffed out his chest and we broke into laughter.

'I don't need anyone to keep me guard, I'll be going for a run or two, but otherwise I'll be spending the weekend holed up in my room doing homework.'

'You think running's safe?' Max asked.

'He's not here. It's been four months. I'll be perfectly fine.'

Her flawlessly shaped brows curled into a high arc. 'Like you were when you went to his house?'

I held her stare.

'I'm not busy,' Tyler said, his voice uncertain, nervous perhaps. 'We could do something together.'

My mouth formed a smile, no effort involved. 'Why, have you got more boxes to unpack?'

His nerves vanished and were replaced with a full grin. 'Probably, but I was thinking of something more exciting than that.'

I rubbed my hands together. 'Tell me more.'

'Well exciting for me, might not be for you. But all week, no, all three weeks we've been here, I've been desperate to go up to the mountains.' He pointed in the general direction of the range, obscured by the orange brick of the school building. 'Mum and Dad want to go, but they're still too excited playing house. Unpacking boxes is their idea of fun these days.' He shook his head as if not understanding their madness.

'You want to climb it? Hope you've got good hiking boots.'

'Climb it? Are you crazy, in this weather? No way. I wanted to go for a drive up there. Want to be navigator? You know the way, right?'

I lifted my eyebrows, conveying a look that said, you're kidding right? 'Tyler, I grew up on that mountain.'

The light in his eyes grew, as did the dimple on his chin. 'That only proves you're the perfect person to ask.' *Was that the only reason?* 'Want to take me?'

Did I ever.

—24—

'Have you always lived here?' Tyler asked as we drove up the winding road to the mountain.

'In Antil?'

'Yeah.'

I raised my arms, taking in our surroundings. 'Born and bred. What about you?'

'Only moved here three weeks ago,' he said with a straight face, and I pretended to hit him with a swipe of my arm, breaking his composure into a laugh.

'No, what about you? Have you always lived in Sydney?'

'Yeah. Moved house a couple of times, but pretty much stayed in the same area. Then Mum and Dad decided it'd be a great idea to uproot us from the only life we knew and move us to the middle of nowhere.' He half-smiled at the sarcasm, but the dig at his parents tainted the grin. 'Hey, how did you know I didn't kick up a fuss about it? That first time I saw you, you said I was secretly okay about moving here, even though I'd just told you all how annoyed I felt.' He studied me before turning back to the road as he waited for my answer.

'Was I right?' I didn't need him to tell me I was. 'Left here.' I pointed.

'Spot on. But the thing is, I didn't even realise until you said it. It kind of freaked me out.'

'Sorry,' I said.

'No, it's all right, I'm growing used to you freaking me out.'

I spun to face him. 'What?' Was that supposed to mean something?

'No, that came out wrong. You don't freak me out, you fascinate me. I...I just haven't figured you out yet, and *that* freaks me out.'

'You're trying to figure me out?' I stumbled over the words, gulping down the lump in my dry throat.

Tyler pressed a hand to the side of his forehead, as if he were trying to rub away the lines of confusion. 'Do you ever feel like the universe is hiding things from you? That your life is a big riddle and someone's playing games with you?'

A surge of laughter broke free. 'Oh my God, all the time!'

Disbelief and humour clouded his eyes, crinkling as he grinned at my reaction. 'Really?'

I nodded. 'Yes.'

His eyes focused on me as he grew serious again. 'Sometimes I think you're part of the riddle.'

I held my breath, afraid to say what I wanted, that I wasn't the riddle, but the player. I'd messed with his life, and the universe *was* hiding things from him; a life where he was in love with me. I also wanted to ask him why he felt this way, what'd happened to make him question his life as anything other than ordinary. I bit the inside of my cheek. I couldn't say any of those things.

Tyler drove into the entrance of the ski resort where a few other cars had parked. The resort, normally alive and kicking in the middle of winter, stood eerily still and barren like a deserted theme park.

I kept my eyes peeled straight ahead and attempted to lighten the mood I feared might become too thick to wade through. 'Well, I hope you figure the riddle out soon.' I opened the car door.

'Me too,' he said across the roof of the car.

'Any clues I can help with?' *Crap.* What the hell possessed me to ask that? I rubbed my palms against my shorts, panic surging through me, and I spun away from Tyler to wander around the building.

He caught up to me. 'Let's start with why you knew that about me when we first met.'

My footing slowed and I closed my eyes in thought. 'I don't know. I think I saw a tenderness when you mentioned your parents and how unhappy you were about moving. You don't seem like the sort to lash out at your parents.'

'I'm not, but how did you know that?'

'Good guess?'

His hand combed through his hair, his eyes narrowing. 'Good guess...mmm, I'm not buying it.'

Finding my innocent face, I shrugged. 'Well, that's all I have, so either take it or leave it.' We were slipping into shaky territory, and I needed to back away swiftly.

'I'll take it, but only because I can't think of any reason not to believe you.'

'Trust until proven otherwise,' I said.

'Exactly.' He pointed at me, his footsteps faltering. 'That's what I would've said.' Damn, I forgot they were his words first. I didn't slow, kept my steps even, as if all of this confrontation meant nothing to me.

I brushed him off. 'It's part of the riddle. Keeping you on your toes.' I skip-hopped a step.

'Like a ballerina.'

I laughed, hoping he didn't notice how shaky it sounded. 'I'd like to see that.'

'No, you wouldn't.'

We continued the short trek around the resort building, and I pointed out some favourite ski slopes, now a patchwork of brown and green from a summer of heat.

When the car park came into view again, Tyler broke the silence. 'Can I ask you something?'

'Another part of the riddle?'

'Different one, I think.'

'Okay?'

Tyler lowered his head when he spoke. 'You and Sean...you're not together, are you?'

Tingles of anticipation shot right to my toes. I hadn't been expecting that. An easy smile spread across my heated face, because I knew what a question like that meant. 'No.' We leaned against a stone wall near the car park as we surveyed the mountains.

'Oh, okay. I wondered, because...well you seem real close, that's all.' He shifted against the stone and positioned his elbow behind him.

'We are. We've known each other our whole lives. It shifted briefly into something more a while ago, but it didn't feel right.' I stared into the intensity in his eyes. 'He wasn't the one for me.'

'No?'

'I fell for someone else. I was madly in love with him.' My thunderous pulse careened around my body, a slight sway making me grip the edge of the stone.

'Was?' He ran his hands through his hair.

'Still am actually.' My heated gaze did nothing to sound convincing, and questions soared in his eyes, followed briefly by hurt. His hand fell to his side and I wanted to shout 'It's you', but in truth it was the other Tyler. I loved this one too, they were one and the same, but without his knowledge of me – of what I could do – or had done, he couldn't be the same person.

I wanted nothing more than to tell him how much I loved him and how I'd missed him, but I couldn't profess something like that after only knowing him for three weeks. He'd run a mile. Besides, I wanted what we had before, a mutual belief and trust in each other. He needed to know the complete me – including how I'd interfered with his life – before the possibility of anything more.

'Have you ever loved someone so much it hurts?' I asked, not sure I wanted the answer.

'No. But sometimes I think I know what it might feel like.'

'It feels bad. I mean good, but also bad. Especially when you can't be with that person.'

'You can't be with him? He doesn't love you back?'

'No, I don't think he does.'

'That sucks.'

'In more ways than I can explain right now.' More riddles. *Damn it, Lucy, stop making it harder.*

'You don't have to explain anything,' he said. 'I like you, Lucy. Like I said, you fascinate me and...I dunno, I thought there might be something between us –'

'There is.' I took an involuntary step toward him. What was I doing? I was pushing and pulling him all at once.

He half-frowned, his eyes narrowing. 'But there's someone else. Or at least to you there is.'

'No, there's no one, just some feelings I'm working on.'

'Right, well, let me know if you need any help shifting those feelings aside,' he said with mischief in his eye. Heat crept into my cheeks. I couldn't help but admire his attempt to get closer to me but also his chivalry at not stepping over the threshold until invited. He cleared his throat. 'So, how do we get up there?' Tyler shifted his focus from me and waved an arm at the towering peaks of the taller mountains.

'We walk, or we wait until winter and ride a ski lift. You want a view, don't you?' Right over the other side of the mountain was where we spent most of our time on the slopes, where we had our favourite lunch spot, and we'd be able to find a more impressive view. But without hiking we had no way of getting there at this time of year.

'Yeah, that's kinda what I hoped.'

'There's a good lookout spot a little bit further up the road from where we pulled off. Wanna go up there?'

'Sure.'

'And then, come winter, I promise to personally take you up to that peak.' I squinted, pointing to the tallest peak in the distance.

'Already looking forward to it.' Tyler's grin trailed from the view down to me. The corners of my mouth rose, my heart soaring to similar heights. I couldn't agree more.

*****

'BLOODY COMPUTER.' CAL TAPPED repeatedly on his laptop keypad. 'I swear that virus I had last month never went away, it keeps coming up with the same stupid message every time I try to upload my assignments.'

'Have you had it checked out properly?' Tyler peered over Cal's shoulder.

'Yeah, but I don't think the chick was that good.'

'What about Mr Mason?' Amber asked. 'Isn't he supposed to be good with that stuff?'

'He is, but Dad wanted to use his friend who's started up some kinda computer repair business. Help her out, you know. Except I need to get this assignment submitted ASAP.'

A hazy image of Salander Computer Repairs surfaced, the black and white sign positioned above the dull grey door to his home. I swallowed and closed my eyes. I couldn't think of him, couldn't go where I'd only be reminded of what I'd done.

My eyelids fluttered open to Tyler's scrutinising gaze causing a flurry of nerves to buzz inside me. I hadn't expected so much wariness from him, not after our honest conversation on the weekend, but maybe I'd done more damage than I thought by telling him I was in love with someone else.

Had I made the single biggest mistake of my life? Because hadn't this been exactly what I wanted? For him to feel something for me so we could go back to being together. And yet I'd stopped it dead in its tracks, right when it appeared to be heading that way.

His eyes interrogated me, but I had no idea what questions they asked. Was he still trying to figure me out, solve the riddle? I wished he would stop. Now he'd started freaking *me* out. I averted my eyes, lowered myself to the bag at my feet and grabbed my lunch.

The sun belted down, darting around the clouds and hitting us with the force of a summer nearing its end, as if it intended to use up all its stock before time ran out.

I took a bite, chewing, while Cal continued to curse and hit his laptop. Chicken, lettuce, mayo, and brown bread churned around in my mouth, sweat pooling on my neck. Damn this heat, multiplied by a hundred from Tyler's stare.

Eventually the bell rang out and my torture ended. I held my half-eaten chocolate bar between my teeth as I closed my bag and hefted it onto my shoulder.

'Lucy?' Tyler's footsteps quickened to catch up to me. 'Can I talk to you for a sec?'

I slowed, hesitant, concentrating on keeping my voice steady. 'Sure.' I said, sticking the last of the chocolate into my mouth.

'I was chatting to Jada last night,' he said in a tone that had every nerve ending in my body standing to attention in fear. I stopped chewing, a chunk of chocolate in my cheek. 'I was telling her about this girl I've met who seems to know me better than I know myself, and yet we'd only just met.' Silence descended, thick and heavy. His eyes were fixed on mine, and our feet slowed. 'Then I remembered that you'd come to my school last year. Nothing odd about that, but then I began to wonder.

'So, I know we've got this whole trust until proven otherwise thing going on, and I promise I wasn't out to prove anything, but...I asked Jada about this Alice cousin of yours, the one in Jada's year.' He paused. I blinked. 'There is no Alice in year ten.'

I swallowed, willing the remains of the chocolate to melt, trying to act calm despite the jackhammer in my chest. I'd lied plenty of times, this was an easy one. I smiled, the perfect accompaniment to any lie.

'That's because she's Ally to anyone who knows her.' My heart acknowledged the lie, racing at full speed. The clouds drifted in front of the sun's glare, providing a fraction of relief. I'd never felt so stifled in my life.

'Ah, of course, that makes sense.' He lifted the side of his mouth – he'd bought it. 'Oh, is it Ally Foster?'

I exhaled. 'Yes, that's her. You know her?'

'Know her? Not at all. She doesn't exist.' His lips turned up, but his eyes didn't. A look that didn't come from pleasure at catching me out, but sadness I'd lied. I stepped back against the cool bricks.

Silence existed as a physical force, enclosing around us like a heavy fortress, trapping me against the side of the building. Tyler's silence was even worse than my own, coated with accusations and a lie so big I couldn't keep it locked up anymore.

'Fine.' I sighed. 'But not now. Tomorrow. I'll tell you what you want to hear, although I'm pretty sure once I'm done, you'll wish you never asked.'

'Riddles are meant to be solved, Lucy.'

—25—

I COULDN'T SLEEP. His words rolled round and round in my head. I twisted under my covers, turning over, squeezing my eyes closed and seeing the hurt in his face. I needed to make it stop, but how would I be able to say the words?

The following day I showed up to school puffy-eyed and walking like the dead. I wanted desperately to run back home, curl up in bed and not come out for a week. And if everything sorted itself out while I was there, even better.

Unfortunately, hibernation wouldn't help in the long run – Tyler deserved answers. I needed to face this head-on, with as much transparency as I could muster, and hope he wouldn't run away like I imagined he'd want to.

I shuffled to the library for my free. Bile rose in the back of my throat at the mere thought of talking to Tyler and offering him a few pieces to the riddle. I figured if I drip-fed it to him it might be more tolerable. That was the plan anyway. But the thing with plans, they're meant to be broken.

Tyler had beaten me to it, already settled at a table, in my seat. The rectangular window lit him up from behind. Heat-filled terror travelled up my neck. I'd have to have my back to the room. He focused on a row of books halfway up a shelf to his right. He tilted his head and scrunched his brows.

'Hey,' I said, pressing my fingers into the back of the chair, afraid to sit down.

His gaze flicked up. 'Oh, hey, I'm in your seat. You sit here, I'll grab that one.' He stood, but instead of coming to sit, stepped over to the shelf and dragged out a book. A large gold book – Queen Victoria. My eyes widened, fear and shock descending with a force that rooted me to the spot.

'What's wrong?' he said, catching sight of my face. 'Which seat do you want?'

'Huh, oh, that one, thanks.' I moved my stunned feet to the other side of the table and eased my wobbly body onto the seat.

Tyler slid into the chair, the book perched on his lap. 'You look like you've seen a ghost.'

'Perhaps I have.' I feigned a smile.

He raised his eyebrows. 'Freaking me out again.'

'I'm just getting started.' I couldn't do it. *How do I say it?* My hands shook, and I lowered them into my lap before he noticed the trembling. Curling my fingers around the hem of my skirt, I kept my voice painstakingly even. 'So, what's the book?' Diversion, brilliant.

'It's part of the riddle, I think.' He heaved it onto the white table, and Queen Victoria stared up at him. He ignored her and found my eyes instead.

'You think you'll find answers in a book about Queen Victoria?' I tried to laugh, but a garbled lot of nothing came out.

'I'm hoping.' He didn't hesitate when he opened the book. Flipping open a chunk, he turned a few pages and stopped. I didn't need to see the page number to know which one he'd turned to and what words he read.

Blood roared in my veins. Certain I would pass out at any minute, I stuck a finger between my shirt and neck, my school uniform suddenly ten sizes too small and choking me.

How did he know? How could he remember?

Obviously he didn't remember, that's why he was asking so many questions. I was a riddle, but where were the pieces coming from?

The dreams.

I gasped and he glanced up momentarily before returning to the book. Had he remembered the dreams? I fiddled with my fingers in my lap, willing my heart to slow.

Tyler peered into my eyes. 'What does this mean?' Tears blurred my vision. I didn't know what to say. 'You're killing me, Lucy. I know you know something, I can see it in your eyes. I've been seeing things and I can't make sense of them, but I think you might be able to help me.'

'Seeing things?'

Tyler tapped his fingers on the pages. 'This's probably gonna sound nuts –'

My laughter erupted. 'That's hilarious coming from someone else. Believe me, it won't sound nuts.'

Mrs Oliver shot me a glare, and I bit my tongue, stifling my chuckles.

Tyler's chest rose as he inhaled deeply. 'All right...so I've been having these dreams.'

I swallowed. 'Dreams?'

'Yeah, they don't make a lot of sense, riddles remember, but the feelings I get when I have them are so intense, good intense. It's like nothing else.'

Desperate for more details, I forced the words out my dry throat. 'Who's in them?'

'Me,' he said softly and not taking his eyes away added, 'and you.' I fell back in my seat, his words jarring into me.

He remembered our dreams.

'I knew from my dream that I needed to open this book to page fifty-five. I didn't know why, and I still don't understand what it means, but I'm hoping you might...because I told you in my dream to read it. Please tell me you know something, because I'm slowly going insane.' He huffed out a small nervous laugh and I joined in. My laughter grew, and I could no longer keep it contained. I hadn't expected this. Never did I anticipate that Tyler might remember the dreams. I wanted to jump up and fly over the moon, but instead threw my head back in ecstasy.

'Way to make me feel better,' Tyler said. 'Laugh in my face.'

'No no, I'm not laughing at you – this is happiness.' I pointed emphatically at my face, laughing again.

Mrs Oliver marched over to the table. 'Lucy, I think you need to take this outside. You've already had a warning.' She stood with her hands firmly on her hips while we packed our bags. Tyler put Victoria back on the shelf, and Mrs Oliver ushered us from the library.

We pushed on the double doors leading outside. 'Oh my God, you remember.' I beamed.

'I don't remember anything, what're you talking about?' Tyler's brows creased, his confusion mounting.

'But you do.' I bounced on my feet as we stepped into the fresh air and headed to our spot under the tree.

'Can you please stop laughing, I'm freaking out over here.'

I put my hand over my mouth. 'I'm sorry,' I said, stifling the giggles.

By the time we arrived at the foot of the tree, my laughter had subsided, but my grin remained on full display. We plonked our bags at our feet and sat on the grass behind the tree facing the road, the massive trunk enough to hide us from any passers-by in the school.

I crossed my legs opposite Tyler, his face a mix of worry, amusement, and impatience. I couldn't relax against the tree. I held my trembling hands in my lap and sat straight-backed like a toddler on the first day of kindy.

'Right,' I said still grinning ear to ear. 'Tell me everything.'

'I have, I gave you everything, now it's your turn.'

I collected my hair back and twisted a band around it. 'Can I ask some questions first?'

'Sure.'

'How many and how often?'

'The dreams?'

I tilted my head. 'What else?'

'I don't know how many different ones, it's like I get fragments every now and then. Like a puzzle. I can tell what bits go together, like the ones by this tree. Then there's the water ones, they fit together, but they're never in any particular order. The only thing that's the same is you. You're in them all.' My chest tightened at his words. He'd continued to dream of me, of us. Oh wow, he'd dreamt of us kissing before he met me. Heat crept up my neck onto my cheeks.

'How clear were the dreams?'

His eyes sparkled with humour. 'They were hazy. Like you know when you're really tired and you rub your eyes and make everything blurry? Bit like that. But clear enough to know exactly what was going on.' He added a flush of his own. Did he know I knew what happened in those dreams too? 'I feel like I've had a whole life with you in my dreams, and I know that sounds stalkerish, if that's even a word, but what's weird is it started before I met you, before you even showed up at my school. Oh man, that sounds even worse when I say it out loud.'

We both laughed. 'It does, but it won't sound as bad as what I'm about to say.'

'As long as you can help me make sense of it all.' His eyes pleaded with me.

'I can try. It's a long story, so bear with me, okay.'

'I have supplies.' He patted his backpack.

'Chocolate, I hope. I'm gonna need chocolate for this.'

He unzipped his bag and found a pack of M&M'S. He held it up with a cheeky grin, then grabbed my hand from my lap and placed the bag silently into my fingers. The heat from his touch flowed through me, but then he let go and my entire body repelled the distance he created.

'Go,' he said with a nod.

'I'll start with the dreams.'

'Good choice.'

I inhaled as much air and bravery as I could to start. 'Your dreams: the tree, swimming at the lake house, surfing in Bondi, soap-skating in the school corridors...'

His eyes widened.

'They weren't just *your* dreams...they were ours.' I paused, giving him time to process. 'You're recalling each of those dreams because we once shared them.'

'What? When? How?' He stuttered, shaking his head.

'I don't really know how, well I kinda do. But it all happened last year, before the dreams probably even started for you.'

'What does that even mean?'

'All right, I'm going to go back to the beginning.' I fiddled with the packet of M&M'S.

'There's more?'

'Way.' I held up the M&M'S. 'Chocolate?'

He chuckled. I poured some into his outstretched hand, needing to rewind five years to when my dreams started and explain how

I'd been plagued for years with experiences so real and clear as if I were living them.

'You know how I was a bit off last weekend when we were out at lunch?'

'Yeah?'

'I'd watched two children and their grandmother drown that night, but I also drowned myself. It's not like a dream to me. I wake up and it's as if it actually happened. Except instead of being dead, I'm alive.'

All sorts of emotions flashed across Tyler's face: awe, horror, and a whole lot of shock. 'Holy crap.'

'Yep.'

He shook his head, dismissing the shock, and rubbed his palm on the side of his face. 'That sucks, but what does that have to do with this? With me?' His hand flew out, touching my arm, before placing his fingers in his lap. 'Sorry, that was harsh. I just mean I don't get the connection, apart from the whole dream thing.'

I nodded. I got it. 'Yeah, okay, so a bit over a year ago I had a dream. Two things happened in the dream; I saw you saying goodbye to your dad at the airport, and I was in a plane crash...in a dream that is. Then you showed up.'

'What, in a dream?'

'No. Here.' I pointed to the ground. 'At school.'

'I am so not following.'

'You know how I said my story would sound worse?' He nodded, and I rubbed my hands on my pleated skirt. Time to find out if he believed me. 'Here goes...you moved to Antil last year, in April, with your mum and Jada, about a year after your dad's plane crashed and he died. You've lived here before.'

Tyler's face froze, his mouth slightly open. Disbelief? I had to push forward.

'You remember the soap-skating dream?' Another small nod. 'That was the first time you and I shared a dream. We were at Cal's place, and sleeping in the same room –'

'Hang on, what?' His back straightened.

I smiled. 'I'll explain later. Anyway...because we were near each other –' he raised an eyebrow '– it meant we were able to share a dream. That first dream you spoke to me in French, you called me –'

'*Ma petite rêveuse.*' His mouth remained serious but his eyes were laced in wonder.

I held his stare. 'For the first time in my life I had someone who knew me. You were here when I learnt that my dreams were changing reality. See after I dream of a death my head goes into problem-solving mode. I figure out an alternative and dream it up. I dreamt of those kids and their grandma again, and now if you *Google* any news stories from the last week of a family drowning, you won't find any. I saved their lives.'

'Is that what you did with my dad?' he asked slowly, trying to grasp the concept of the question. 'Did you save his life?'

I pressed my lips together and nodded just as firmly. 'And three hundred and twenty-six other people on the plane.'

'That's what you meant in the dream on the lake. You were crying and I was telling you I'd make my way back to you. We knew it was going to happen, didn't we?'

'All signs were pointing that way, so yeah, we kind of saw it coming.'

His fingers massaged his forehead. 'That's why I left you the message in the book? Because all trace of me would be gone.'

'Everything except my memory of you.'

'Cal, Sean, the girls...I've known them before?'

'You've known all of this before.' I shifted my gaze over his shoulder to capture the expanse of school grounds around us. 'But neither you nor they remember any of it.'

'I can't believe my dad died. Shit. It feels weird. Like I feel kinda sad, you know, the thought of it.'

'Yeah.' I plucked up a blade of grass, letting the weight of the idea settle around us.

He gulped and took in our surroundings, as if it would somehow become familiar to him. 'How long was I here?'

'About four months. From April until early August.'

His eyes lit up, erasing his sombre expression, and he shook a finger in front of my face. 'That's why you know I'll be able to snowboard.'

A full and enthusiastic grin flooded my face. 'You were very good.'

'And we were together?'

'Yes.' I lowered my eyes, fascinated by the edges of the M&M's packet.

'Did we?'

I shot my head up. 'What? Oh, no, we didn't.' My cheeks flamed with heat at his question, beet-red warm. 'Only kissing.'

'Good, I'd hate to forget that.' He chuckled. 'So, was it good?'

'The kissing? You should know, you've had those dreams.' Oh God, it was hot out today.

'Yeah, I know, I just wanted to hear you say it.'

'Oh my God!' I threw a handful of M&M'S at him, and he flinched away with a belly laugh.

The merriment faded and we sat in contemplative silence. My breathing had settled, my pulse not quite so ear-splitting. I'd done it, I'd said the words, told him everything. Now it was over to him. Would he believe it – believe me?

—26—

'Y OU'RE RIGHT,' HE SAID, plucking at a piece of grass. 'Your story sounds so much worse.'

'And you were worried about a few little dreams.'

'It was more than a dream. Like I said, it was the feelings. I don't think I'd believe half of what you said if I hadn't felt half of it myself. But there's no way I could've felt those things for you in my dreams for there not to have been more. That was the more, my unremembered life here with you. See, it happened again, I sound insane.'

'Get used to it.'

'So, this must be really weird for you. You had to pretend you didn't know me when I turned up.'

'Did I convince you?'

'Kind of, it's not the first thing you think when someone clues in to who you are. Oh this person must've shared another life with me. And you asked questions about me, why'd you do that if you already knew me?'

'If I didn't, you'd think I had no interest in you whatsoever. Plus, I did have questions about you. You're not the same person you were before.'

He peered down at himself and held his arms out. 'I'm not?'

'No. I mean mostly you are, but you were grieving last time. You'd lost your dad, your mum was a wreck, and you'd taken on a lot. Yet when I wasn't coping, *you* were the one who helped guide me through my issues. You were like everyone's hero.'

'Gee, you make it sound like you're talking about someone else.'

'I kind of am.'

'What else was different?'

'Oh.' I smacked my leg. 'You didn't have a driver's license.'

'Really? Why the hell not?'

'I dunno, I mean half of us don't, it didn't seem that unusual really. I guess the fact that you do this time round would suggest it had something to do with your dad dying.'

'Yeah, I suppose,' he said, his voice trailing off at the thought of how close he came to living an alternate life without his dad. 'So, is there anything about me that you like, other than my awesome driving skills, or am I competing with my other self?'

I raised my brow, my eyes brimming with satisfaction. 'Are you jealous?'

'Should I be?'

'Of yourself? Is that even possible?'

'Well, is there anything you like about me that isn't because of him?'

'Because of you, you mean?'

He shrugged.

'Even if it is, it's still you. Anything you did or said comes from who you are. Then, now, it doesn't matter.'

'Saturday when you said there was another guy, someone you were in love with, but didn't love you back...was that –'

'Yes...' I didn't shift my eyes from his, reserved, but hopeful. 'It's you. I'm sorry, that must be weird for you, and I don't expect things to go back to the way they were. It's not like you feel the same for me, you can't, I mean I've had months of knowing you, and –'

'Stop.' Tyler held up a hand and my shoulders slumped. 'Who

said it's weird for me? It's actually pretty amazing. I've been dreaming of you and feeling all sorts of things I shouldn't feel for someone I don't know. Would you think I was weird if I said I'm not far behind you?'

'Far behind me?' I said shakily from lack of air. My fingers twisted together, the pack of M&M's laying forgotten at their side.

'You're amazing, Lucy. I knew that before I even met you. I'm already feeling more than I should for someone who I've only known for a few weeks.' He covered my tense fingers with his hands, the stroke of his thumb on my skin, loosening them and sending a bolt of electricity up my arm. Happiness flowed through me and welled behind my eyes. This was too much, more than I could ever have hoped for.

His piercing gaze locked onto mine. 'I told you I'd make my way back to you.'

I gasped and a small tear escaped onto my cheek. He wiped it away with his thumb before sitting back, as if nervous all of a sudden.

'That was one of the worst dreams I had. It felt like the last one.' He questioned me with his eyes, and I confirmed with a small nod. 'I remember you being sucked from my arms, but more than that I remember this overwhelming sadness. And when I woke each time I had that dream I'd feel the loss all over again, all for someone I'd never met.' He barked out a nervous laugh. 'Gee, I hope there's no cameras hidden in this tree. We sound like a couple of whack jobs.'

'Maybe we should've had this conversation in a dream.'

'Can we do that? Can we really share dreams?'

'You know we can.'

'Yeah, but I don't remember anything either side of that. How did we do it?'

'The first ones were when we were near each other.'

• 204 •

'That's right, you were going to explain that,' he said with a smirk.

'I was, but it's not as exciting as it sounds.' I grinned at the eagerness seeping from him and told him how we'd been dragging mattresses onto the floor at Cal's since we were about eight. 'The first dream happened by accident. Then the next night we actually tried it on purpose, but we couldn't figure out how we could only do it when we were near each other. Until I started to meditate like you, then we were able to dream without being near each other. The snowboarding one was the first one.'

'Oh, yeah, that was fun. That was one of the reasons I secretly looked forward to moving here. I can't wait to try it for real.'

'Just a few more months.' I plucked a stem of grass, twiddling it in my fingers.

'Think we can try to share a dream again?'

'God yes!' Enthusiasm bubbled over and I grinned widely. 'Why do you think I've been meditating all these months?'

'What, so you've just been doing it in case I came back?'

'Kind of. But also hoping it'd help me gain some control in my dreams.'

'Has it?'

'I think so. I've been able to leave a dream when I wanted to. I'd never been able to do that before. Mind you, the other day when I dreamed the drowning, I got so panicked I forgot I could.' Tyler shook his head. 'What?'

'I'm just a bit in awe. You act so casual about all of this. I'd be going nuts if I had to live with all that – hell, I almost did with my own dreams.'

'That's only because you didn't know what it meant. It's easier to deal with when you have the whole picture. You were actually the one who helped me when, as you put it, I was going nuts. I haven't always dealt with it this easily.'

'Well, I'm glad I could be of assistance.' His cheeks rose with his lopsided smile, and once again I lost myself in the feelings it stirred within me.

The bell rang out across the school yard and we both jumped.

'Do the guys know?' Tyler asked.

'About you or the dreams?'

'Both.'

'They've known about my dreams to some extent for a while, but I told them everything last year. Max and Amber were actually in on the whole Sydney thing and coming to see you at the school.'

'And the boys, Sean...he's okay with it?'

'Seems to be. He's not the sort of guy to begrudge someone their happiness, and he wouldn't bother competing with someone if he had no chance of winning.' I lowered my gaze, fighting against the urge to bury myself in his scent and the feel of him again, but I had to remind myself he was miles from that point. He said he wasn't far behind me, but did he know how head-over-heels I was for him?

Tyler stood and flicked his head at the table over his shoulder. 'Should we?' He held out his hands.

'Yeah, probably.' I clutched his fingers as he helped me up. 'Thanks,' I said, not wanting to let go of his grasp, but I didn't need to worry, he wasn't loosening his grip.

'Hey, you two! No smoochin' behind the tree!' Cal called and we dropped our hands.

I expanded my chest, breathing steadily to lower the heat rising in my cheeks, and waltzed straight over to Cal and whacked his arm.

He slapped my hand away. 'Hey, what's that for?'

'For being an idiot.'

'You weren't smoochin' under the tree then?' He tried to hide his laughter, but once he started he was unstoppable.

'No, Cal, we were not.' I glared at him. 'Not everyone's like you.'

'Why were you hidin' over there then?' he said. 'It's the hiding part that makes it suss, you know.'

'Yeah, I do, but I don't care. We got kicked out of the library, so we had our free under the tree.' I dropped my bag to the ground.

'You got kicked out of the library?'

'Lucy went a bit loopy,' Tyler said. 'She wouldn't stop laughing.'

Cal's eyes widened in disbelief. 'The loopy bit I get.' I swiped at him but he jumped away. 'The laughing, though, really?'

'Really,' Tyler said, smiling.

I slid onto the bench beside Tyler and let the jostling of my friends whirl around me. I felt like I'd run a marathon and had no energy left to fill anyone in on what'd just happened. And so, I sat uninvolved, quietly listening to the chatter around the table as I tried to slow the beating of my erratic heart.

I'd been fine sitting under the tree talking with Tyler, but now, with his bare arms inches from mine, and buzzing from the closeness, I struggled to concentrate on anything other than my own breathing. Away from the tree and the intensity of that moment, I craved to know his thoughts? Had the impact of my words sunk in and freaked him out yet? Maybe he was trying to work out how to get away, un-noticeably, from the fruit loop. He stared straight ahead, seriousness obscuring his face and creasing his eyes. His silence near killing me.

My hands gripped the edge of the bench seat, my heart racing in anticipation of the unknown, and then his fingers brushed against mine. My eyes flicked down; it wasn't an accident. He moved his small finger over mine and held it there, as if he'd heard all my inner thoughts and wanted to reassure me he wasn't going anywhere.

I angled my head and fell into the beautiful depths of his gaze. His dark eyes peered into mine and the dimple on his chin deepened with his smile. Dizzy with ecstasy, I wanted to raise my arms and float to the clouds, but his little finger held onto mine with the weight of a lead balloon and kept me in the one place I wanted to be most of all – next to him.

—27—

THE BELL SOUNDED FOR the end of the day, and Max and I packed up our P.E. gear and wandered to the school exit.

'So, you told him everything and he's okay with it?' She guessed he knew something at lunch time and confronted me once we had a chance to talk, which as it turned out had been right before the bell went.

'I think so, I mean, he said he was, but who knows really. He's probably planning his escape as we speak.' I laughed, but inside desperately itched to be alone with him again.

'If he's anything like the Tyler you told us about and the one I've gotten to know, I highly doubt it, hon. And you said he felt things. He won't be going anywhere.' She bumped her shoulder into mine.

We reached the edge of the student car park as Tyler and Sean approached from the opposite direction. Tyler's eyes met mine immediately, and my steps faltered and quickened at the same time.

'Hey, you two,' Sean said, yanking my attention away. 'You ready for another ride of your lives?' He held up a set of keys and pointed it at his car halfway across the car park.

Max rolled her eyes. 'You've had your license for all of five days and already you think you're better than everyone else.'

'Confidence behind the wheel is a must,' he said, squaring his shoulders.

'In small doses, Sean,' I said.

'Whatever. So, you catchin' a lift with us?'

'Uh –'

'Actually,' Max butted in. 'I need you to take me past the shops on the way home, I need to pick up some, uh, razors. Sorry to be a pain, hon. Maybe you could catch a lift with Tyler?' She winked, and I coughed to contain my laughter. So subtle. 'You wouldn't mind, would you, Tyler?'

'No, no of course not,' he said, smiling, not in the least bit fooled.

'Great, thanks. See you tomorrow.' Max hugged me before jogging off.

Heavy footsteps barrelled over to us, and Sean paused mid-turn at Ollie's abrupt arrival.

'Hey, Sean,' he said panting. 'You guys cool if I ride with you today instead of walking?' The words rushed out. 'I need to get home so I can have a Skype session with Fletch. We've only got until four-thirty before his mum gets home and kicks him off the computer.'

Sean whacked a hand on Ollie's shoulder. 'You know I would, mate, but I've gotta run Max to the shops. Lucy's riding with Tyler, maybe he'll drop you home too?' He ignored my daggers and drew his brows up, questioning Tyler.

'Yeah, sure, no worries, man.'

'Cool thanks, I'm Ollie by the way. Lucy's younger, more handsomer brother.' Ollie grinned and bounced on the balls of his feet as if eager to get going.

'Handsomer?' I raised an eyebrow.

'You know it's true.'

We strolled toward Tyler's car, but before Sean left, he leaned in to whisper in my ear, 'You're welcome.'

I swatted at him like the annoying fly he was, but missed, and because Tyler would hear any obscenities leaving my mouth, I lifted my hand and delivered the finger over my shoulder. Sean's chuckle let me know he'd caught my salute.

'And I'm Tyler, Lucy's even handsomer neighbour,' Tyler said to Ollie as we strode across the car park. My lips rose but I inspected the dark grey bitumen.

'Really, where do you live?'

'He's not our neighbour, Ollie.' I didn't correct Tyler on the other detail. Ollie shrugged.

Jada leaned against the passenger door of Tyler's car, an opened book held in front of her face. She peered up when Tyler pressed the car remote.

'Lucy, Jada,' Tyler said, pointing between us. 'Jada, Lucy.'

'Hey, hi, you're our new neighbour.' She slapped the book closed and smiled warmly, opening the door. Ollie frowned in confusion and Tyler huffed out a laugh. 'I've heard lots about you.'

'Is that so?' I turned to Tyler who quickly jumped in behind the wheel. I hopped into the seat behind his and caught his eye in the rear-view mirror.

'All good, of course. He seems to have taken quite a liking to the girl on the hill.'

'You wanna walk home?' Tyler's eyes left mine and he directed a deathly glare at his sister.

'Nope, I'm good.' She suppressed a smile and opened her book.

Jada was completely different to the person I'd met all those months ago; in fact, I could've sworn it wasn't even the same girl. Her eyes, and even her skin, had a shine that'd been non-existent before. Maybe that could be bottled up as a skin treatment. *Grief reversal – transform your look with the resurrection of a loved one. Removes puffy eyes and droopy complexion with one life-altering dream.*

I giggled to myself, and Tyler's gaze returned to the mirror, his cheeks tinging with embarrassment. He thought I was laughing at him and not my stupid imagination. I mouthed the word 'Sorry', and he shook his head absolving me of my sins.

We arrived home a few minutes later, and Ollie jumped from the car, shouting a thanks over his shoulder as he rushed into the house. Not as eager for my imminent separation from Tyler, I climbed out a little more slowly.

'Thanks for the lift,' I said through Tyler's unwound window. 'Nice to meet you, Jada.'

She bent her head to catch my eye. 'You too.' She waved and returned to the book in her lap.

'What are you up to now?' Tyler asked, leaning his forearm against the window frame.

I shifted. 'Nothing much, probably work on my art project, go for a run later, and I think Mum's at work, so I'll probably have to make dinner.'

'You can cook?'

'I can follow the instructions she left for me. What about you?'

'Nothing much for me either. Might go for a trek up to the hill a bit later,' he said with a suggestive glimmer in his eye.

'Yeah? Might bump into you there then.'

'Mmm, I suppose if you were there, say around four-thirty, it could be likely.'

I checked the time on my watch – three-forty – I had fifty minutes. It'd take me fifteen minutes to get up the hill, so that left me with a little over half an hour to change and prepare dinner. 'I'd better get going then, my afternoon's looking busy all of a sudden.' His grin filled his face, and I took a couple steps back and turned to the house, trying desperately not to skip across the lawn.

I made it up the hill in record time. My pulse beat faster than normal after the steady climb up the steep road, and I slowed as I neared the end of the track, needing to even my breathing or I'd be a heaving mess when I met up with Tyler. Not a good look. As it was, I didn't think my heart rate would ever go back to normal, not when it held so much expectation.

I strolled along the last of the track and climbed through the fence as Tyler approached from the other side. He'd changed into black shorts and a grey T-shirt, and wow, the sight of him casually strolling up the hill made my breath hitch.

His smile crinkled around his eyes when he caught sight of me. 'We need to build you a stile,' he called.

'No way, and invite every Tom, Dick, and Harry over here?'

'You said yourself no one ever comes up here. Besides, I kinda hoped you'd be using it a bit more from now on.' His voice lowered as the distance between us closed and my traitorous heart picked up speed again.

'I've already been using it for years, but thanks for the thought.'

We came within a metre of each other and stopped, eyes locked. Our chests rose and fell in unison as we stood in awkward silence.

'Hi,' he said softly, his smooth voice melting my insides.

'Hi.' My cheeks warmed from the intensity in his gaze and the quiet that settled in with the breeze. Something about this moment shouted an intimacy I only ever had with the old Tyler, and I held back from flying into his arms. But I reminded myself that although all those feelings were incredibly real to me, they were more than likely not for the boy standing in front of me.

'What are you thinking?' Tyler asked.

'Nothing.'

'That's your thinking face. Definitely not a nothing face.'

I scrunched my brow with a little huff. 'A nothing face? What does that even look like?'

'This.' Tyler swiped a hand over his face revealing a dead pan expression as his eyes glazed over into the distance. I burst into laughter and any awkwardness between us floated away.

Without speaking we wandered to the shade of the trees further down the fence line and sat amongst the tall grass and dandelions.

'So, what were you thinking back there?'

I absently picked a flower and began plucking the petals off one by one. 'That it felt the same as old times, the way you were looking at me. All of this makes me wonder what bits are the guy I remember and what are you now, but that felt like old Tyler.'

'I really am competing,' he said, humour lightening his words.

'No, you're not. I just can't tell what you're thinking, and for a moment I felt like I did.'

'And what might that've been?'

That you wanted me as much as I wanted you. 'Can't say.'

He tipped his head, narrowing his eyes. 'Can't or won't?'

'Definitely won't.'

'All right then, I'll tell you.' He held my gaze, and my heart tripped up and fell into my guts. 'I was thinking about how long I'd waited for that moment. And I don't mean the fifty minutes since I dropped you at your place. I have dreamt of you so many times in the last year, I nearly had a heart attack when I stood face to face with you for real. To finally hear you tell me I wasn't insane, or at least, not the only one who –'

'Hey.' I nudged him with my elbow and he laughed.

'It felt like I could finally relax. Not having to hide what you mean to me.'

What I mean to him?

He exhaled with a shrug. 'That's what I was thinking. Is that the sort of thing old me would've been thinking if he looked at you like that?'

I brushed at the tendrils of hair whipping around my face in the gentle wind. 'Yeah, that sounds like something he'd think. But don't worry, you're not competing with anything. You are what's real and right in front of me, and the fact you believe the crazy words coming out of my mouth, well, that's what made you so special in the first place.'

'Well, I'm glad the reality hasn't disappointed the memory.'

'Not even in the slightest.' The reality was more than I could ever have hoped for. I couldn't have back what I had before, but I'd like to imagine what lay ahead might be even better.

'I still feel like I'm missing so much of the story though. Like, I've got the feelings right, at least I think I do,' he said with a half-smile. 'But the rest, it's a bit confusing. I've figured out some bits, the cupcakes, that's why I had a feeling they'd taste so good. When someone mentions them like you did in the dream, like my world would forever be a lie without knowing their taste.'

I shrugged. 'Was I right?'

'Spot on, they're amazing, and my life, one big lie.' I laughed at his straight face. 'Reckon you can help me make sense of the rest?'

'Sure. What else do you want to know?'

A spray of dry grass blew onto his thigh and he wiped it onto the ground. 'What the bracelet means, who Granny Tess is, and when did you pummel into me like a train wreck?'

I huffed out a laugh as I recalled the first time I'd seen Tyler, when I ran full pelt into him and landed in a heap at his feet. 'That was when we first met...the first time.'

'Obviously,' he said.

'It was pretty funny, and completely terrifying. Because I'd seen you in a dream first. When you dropped your dad to the airport and we both went to help an old lady who fell over.'

He frowned. 'I think I remember her. I ran and helped her up, yeah? That's why you remembered me, because of my gallantry?' He puffed out his chest in pride.

'No, actually.' I went on and told him how I'd been the one to help the lady and how he'd seen me in the dream even though I wasn't actually there.

'Impressive.' He ran his fingers back and forth over his bottom lip, the frown returning to his forehead. 'That was the day Dad made an emergency landing. That was the one. You did that, didn't you?'

I gave him a small nod.

'That was the catalyst for us moving here, you know.'

'Really?'

'It shook him up pretty bad, he blamed himself and couldn't stop thinking about the "what ifs."'

I knew the feeling.

'He was a little to blame,' I whispered, and Tyler quizzed me with his eyes. 'He spilt his coffee.' Without the man who failed to do his job in air traffic control, it all came down to his dad.

He shook his head. 'Blows my mind that you know stuff like that, I mean maybe you read it in the news, but I have a feeling you didn't. And the old lady, she wasn't in any news stories.'

A nervous 'have I gone too far' laugh broke free. With no idea what Tyler's breaking point might be, I asked the question with each new revelation. 'Freaked out?'

'Totally,' he said, and his laughter joined mine and rumbled down the hillside.

I answered his other questions and filled him in on some of the things that happened on either side of the dreams. What we'd been talking about in the dreams, what it all meant.

We didn't notice the minutes shifting away, drifting off in the breeze as the sun lowered on the horizon, our words were the only things around us that mattered. And when at last we ran out of them and the silence on the mountains and the trees and in the air caught up to us, so did all the words we'd exchanged. So much had passed between us now, there was no going back.

—28—

'Here, hold these.' I passed Tyler the small cake box and climbed through the fence.

'Man, you have the best job.'

I hadn't worked that afternoon, but Laurie had extras again, and after dropping a few bags to the shelter, I carried a couple of cakes up the hill to meet with Tyler.

We found a stretch of shade further down the tree line and lowered ourselves into the dry grass. 'So, what new flavours have you got today?'

'I think it's a raspberry cheesecake flavour and maybe choc orange?'

'I want them both,' he said.

I flipped the lid off and held up a small paring knife. 'I come prepared. Amber's taught me well.'

We shared the cakes and came to the monumental decision that the raspberry cheesecake flavour tasted the best.

'Tell me.' Tyler held the last of each flavour in each hand. 'Do you think we can have a dream any time soon?' The same question plagued me many times over the last week, but I didn't want to rush anything, rush him. We'd spent our days learning more about each other and filling in the gaps, and I spent my nights falling to sleep hoping.

'Good question. Maybe we could give it a try and see what

happens?'

'Yeah? I'm dying to have 'em again. I haven't had any dreams since I moved here. Not since I saw you in the flesh. I want that feeling again.' He paused, and my heart fluttered at the appreciation in his eyes.

'I haven't had any of those dreams since you left last year, so it's been even longer for me.'

He finished his choc orange and wiped at the crumbs on the edge of his lips. 'So you're keen to try it again too?'

I cocked my head. 'Do you even need to ask? Those dreams are some of my happiest memories of us together.'

'Glad I remember some of the better times.' His smile lit up the corners of his eyes and showcased the dimple on his chin, but then it disappeared, replaced by seriousness. 'Was it hard for you after I left?'

I peered straight into his eyes. 'Like a piece of my heart had been ripped out. And my lungs. Oh God, I remember whole days not being able to get a decent breath of air.'

'And no one else knew what'd happened?'

I tore off a piece of cake. 'Not at that point. I covered it up as a cold...and I came out here. This was my solitude.' I paused, taking in the abundance of grassy hills, fresh air, and silence. 'You know something, I really miss the cows. They were like a constant in my shifting sand, always listening, not judging.'

'How do you know? I mean, I've always thought cows were a little bit shifty myself. I prefer horses, at least their eyes aren't so conniving.'

'Conniving? You think cows are conniving?' I plopped a piece of cake in my mouth.

'Yeah, the way they chew the grass, giving you the side eye, judging. They were definitely judging.'

I laughed. 'What makes horses any better?'

'They don't give you the side eye, for one.'

'How is it you even know this?'

'I'm very observant and I like nice eyes,' he said, staring directly into mine. 'Horses have nice eyes.'

I brushed the crumbs off my legs. 'Do they? We should go for another drive one day. If we go to the other side of the mountains, we might be able to find some wild brumbies.'

'Really? We should so do that.' He leaned back, his hands splayed in the grass. A hot breeze flicked his hair across his brow, and I wanted to thread my fingers through the tendrils and brush them away. I steered my attention to the mountains and burning sun closing in on the horizon. 'Do your parents know, about the dreams and all that?'

'Actually, my dad's the same as me.' I lowered my voice. 'But I'm a little more powerful than he is.' Tyler laughed and my smile fell away. 'And we don't really talk about it with Mum. She doesn't like it and if she doesn't see it, it doesn't exist, so we don't mention it around her.'

'That must be tough.'

'Not really. I've kinda been doing it for years already. At least she's no longer trying to make the dreams go away.'

'Would they? Go away that is?'

I plucked at a thread of grass and twirled it between my fingers. 'They do when I'm on medication, but the side effects are horrible.'

'And you can't save lives like that either.'

'Exactly.' The one and only reason I could deal with my ailment.

Tyler tilted his head, his hair flopping to the side, his eyes twinkling. 'Or have dreams with me.'

'We don't know if I can yet. We might not be able to do it this time 'round.'

'If you think like that, we really won't be able to.'

'That's what *you* would have said.'

He frowned. 'I just did.'

'No, other you.'

'Damn him, he keeps stealing my lines.' We laughed at that, at our strange predicament. Could this odd new beginning be the start of a happy future for me, for us?

'All right then,' Tyler said, the remains of the laughter still on his lips. 'How do we do this?'

'Last time all we did was agree on a place and met there.'

'That's it? No special chant or dance or potion we need to prepare first?'

'Would that make it more or less weird if we did?'

'I don't think anything would make this any less weird. Okay, so I just think of our meeting place as I'm going to sleep?'

'With a bit of meditation as I drifted off, not sure if you ever did that though. You're a bit calmer than me to begin with, so I don't think you ever needed that.'

'Think I'll do whatever might help tonight. Should we meet back here then?'

I scanned the area around us, as if making a decision. 'Sounds like a plan.'

'Better get going, sun's going down.' Tyler closed the lid and collected up the cake box before standing.

I stood and brushed the back of my shorts. 'You just want to get on with the day so you can go to sleep and try it out.'

A smirk crept across his face and he lowered his eyes. 'Maybe.' And he thought the cows were conniving.

'Well, I hope it doesn't disappoint.'

'I don't think that's possible.'

'Hey, can I ask you something?' Tyler asked as we made our way back to my spot in the fence. 'I'm Batman, right?'

Not what I'd been expecting. 'What?'

'In our dream I said, "We're meant to be, Batman and Robin belong together". I'm assuming that I meant we're a team, right?' I nodded. 'And I'm Batman in this equation?' His eyes held so much hope, and I didn't want to ruin his fun, but my answer was a dead giveaway when I pressed my lips together and lowered my eyes. His shoulders slumped and he stopped walking. 'I'm only the lowly sidekick?'

'You're not lowly, you're a very necessary part of the team. You've shown me the light in all my Batman darkness. You're a superhero in your own right.'

His chest rose and fell. 'Let me get this straight. You're a super-hero to the world, but I'm *your* superhero?'

My lips rose in acknowledgement. 'Something like that.'

'Think I can live with that.'

I BOUNCED UP THE stairs, barely able to contain my excitement about the prospect of the night ahead. Tyler itched to do it again, experience it in real time, but I'd had eight months of missing it, pining for the loss; my itch had become raw with a burning need to ease. The thought of experiencing it again within hours filled me with tingling anticipation.

Mum noticed my distraction at dinner, her eyes flitting to me, scrunching as she examined my body language, and shifting to drill Jake about his week at uni – he loved the social life, hated the workload. But since our altercation and Dad's revelation, it wasn't something she asked about anymore, like she'd passed that baton to Dad. '*Here you take it, you wanted this, she's your responsibility now, you deal with it.*' Except he didn't ask for it, neither of us asked to be dealt these cards, to live with what we saw each night. But she'd admitted defeat, she couldn't fix me, and she'd finally stopped trying.

And almost on cue, as if there'd been a silent family memo, Dad arrived at my bedroom door later in the evening as I prepared for bed.

'Can I come in?' he asked, the deep tremor of his voice gliding in first. He waited until I nodded before he stepped in. 'Just coming to check in on my little girl. See how your dreams are treating you.'

I shoved my chair away from the round desk in the centre of my room, swivelling to face him. 'You don't have to do that, I'm okay.'

'I know that, but I told you I'd be here for you, this is me being here for you. You seemed a little...distracted at dinner. I wanted to check everything was...well, if there was anything I could do.'

'Nope, nothing you can do, Dad, we've already established that. The dreams are back, all the same as usual. I had a drowning last week. Saved two kids and their grandma. And there was some workplace accident where some guy got trapped in a vice thing, pretty gross.'

'You saved him then?'

'Yep.'

'Amazing.' He rubbed his jaw. 'Man, ours would make an amazing story. Shame I can't tell it.'

'The best stories are usually the ones we keep to ourselves, our deepest, darkest secrets.'

'Who's the wise girl all of a sudden?'

I tucked a foot under my knee. 'Not wise, just experienced.'

'And you got some deep, dark secrets you need to share?'

My hair flailed around my face with the shake of my head. 'No way. Not with you, anyway.'

His shoulders shook with laughter. 'No, that's probably a good idea.' He rested a hand on the bed frame, hesitating. 'So any reason why you've been distracted? Is it the dreams or something else?'

Yeah, a psychopath took a photo of me and my friends and sent it to me. 'Bit of both.' I faltered. No, the photo was a big deal, but not my current cause for distraction. 'There's also a boy.'

Dad's eyes widened, and then softened with relief at the normalcy of the news. 'Oh...well, that's new. Is he a nice lad? What's his name?'

'Tyler.'

'Can we meet him?'

'It's nothing serious yet, we're just good friends. Maybe I'll bring him around one day.'

'That'd be nice.' He pushed away from the bed. 'I'll leave you be then, but promise you'll let me know if you need your dad, okay?' He eased an arm over my shoulder and kissed the top of my head.

'I will. Thanks, Dad.'

Dad left and the house eased itself from the busyness of the day into the stillness of a quiet Friday evening. My shoulders relaxed. I climbed into bed, pillows propped behind me, and dragged my sketchbook onto my raised knees. My pencil glided across the page, and Tyler's eyes took shape. Followed by his nose, lips, and the slight dimple in his chin. I drew the creases around his eyes and the shadow of his high cheeks, raised in an adorable smile. My focus rested solely on him as I transcribed the image to mind as well as the paper, so when I laid my pencil and book down, and lowered my eyelids, he was all I saw. My breathing slowed as did my mind. All the thoughts and worries from the day disappeared, and I sank heavily into my pillow.

THE WIND WHISPERED THROUGH *the grass, back and forth, waving hello as I stepped into my dream. The cool breeze burst through the trees and rushed at me, blowing my hair around my face. I collected it from my* eyes, wishing for something to tie it back with. I shoved it into the neck of my jumper.

Tyler strode from the bottom of the hill, a large beam spread across his face.

'Hey!' I called into the air.

'This is incredible!' he shouted, lifting both arms and spinning to take in everything around us. The swaying trees, the mountains in the distance, the rich blue of the sky above us. 'Why's it so windy?'

'I don't know.' I raised my voice even though we were now only a metre or two apart. 'Crazy, isn't it. Let's go down the hill, it might be less windy down there.'

'This way?' He pointed and I nodded. Tyler stepped forward and clasped hold of my hand. I glanced at our entwined fingers, my heart picking up pace with the escalating wind. He peered into my eyes, a question: was this okay? I smiled: yes. We started down the hillside, but the wind whipped around us and pushed us into a jog. We ran down the slope, hands still joined and laughing all the way. We reached the bottom, into the seclusion of a gully, where the wind dropped away.

Gasping, we collapsed to the ground and propped ourselves against the trunk of a fallen tree, providing even more protection from the weather breezing above us.

'I can't believe this,' Tyler said. 'We actually did it. This is by far so much better than any of the other second-hand ones.'

'Second-hand ones?' I laughed.

'I don't remember the original real-time ones. Oh my God, this is happening, we're making this happen.' His happiness stretched to the edges of his eyes. Those eyes. 'Why didn't you tell me how good it felt?'

'How do you describe this?' I tucked wisps of loose hair behind my ear. 'I think you have to experience it.'

'Can say that again.' He stared off into the distance, taking in the sights around us. The mountains had fallen from view behind the hills we now sought shelter in. *Further down the hill a channel, lined with trees and brush, carved out a dry creek bed. Sunlight streamed from overhead, spilling through the leaves of the mighty gum, lighting the ground near our feet, and turning the grass a blush tinge. The wind settled into a gentle whisper, as if it had achieved what it set out to do, drive us down to this tranquil spot that until now had remained undiscovered by either of us.*

'Have you ever been out here?' Tyler asked.

'No, but now I'm wondering why.'

'We'll have to check it out properly some time, see if it's really like this.'

I broke off a piece of bark from the log, turning it over in my fingers. 'It is.'

'How can you be sure?'

'Because everything always is as I dream it.'

Tyler rested an ankle over the other. 'Well, aren't you a bit self-assured. And here I was thinking you were timid and bashful.'

'Bashful? Isn't he the dwarf who's always batting his eyelids? Think I'm more Grumpy or Sleepy.'

'When are you grumpy?'

'Ha, you don't know me very well, do you?'

'I guess not. But I'd like to.' *He tilted his head and peered at me through heated eyes.*

'I'd like that too.'

'All those puzzle pieces finally came together and yet...I get the feeling there's still so much to discover about you.'

I flicked the bark into the grass. 'I'm not sure if that's a good thing or a bad thing.'

'It's a great thing. You're fascinating, and everything I learn only adds to that. I just hope even though this is new for me, it doesn't bore you to death doing it all again.'

I closed my eyes, disbelief at his words. I opened them, shifted in the grass, and stared directly at him. 'Tyler, I didn't think I'd ever see you *again. I have cried more tears this last year than I have in my whole lifetime, because the best thing that ever happened to me vanished. I've never known such crippling loneliness. You knew me, and I mean, knew me.' Tears pooled behind my eyes, and I held my hands in my lap to clench the trembling. 'No one ever saw me the way you did and then you were gone. And I knew if I ever saw you again it wouldn't be anything like that because you'd have no memory of me. You won't believe what it meant to see you again, but to hear you say you remembered some of what we had... that was the most un-boring thing I've ever experienced in my life. This – being able to do this again with you – is more than I could have ever hoped for. So please, bore me to death, I think I can handle it.' I blinked back the tears. Had I shared too much too soon?*

Tyler's tender smile eased my doubt. 'Look at those eyes. Who says you're not Bashful?'

I pointed to my face. 'This is not bashful blinking, this is "don't cry in front of Tyler" blinking.' We laughed and I sniffed.

'You can cry in front of me, but I'd rather you didn't cry at all. I hate that I've caused you so much pain.'

'You're not to blame; I am. You didn't have any say in it, neither of us did really.'

'I know, but still, you've come to mean something to me, and I can't brush away my involvement however innocent I am, and I don't think I'd want to anyway.'

A lump formed in my throat, all the emotions stirring within me threatening to rise to the surface.

Tyler placed his hand on my cheek, wiping at a stray tear. My skin warmed beneath the touch of the fingers I'd once known so well. I placed my hand over his and he leaned closer, brushing his mouth tenderly against mine. He hovered, tentative then sure, as he placed his hand behind my neck and drew me in, crushing our lips together. My hands found their way to the nape of his neck, my fingers combing through his hair as our mouths moved as one. His lips were exactly as I remembered, soft and gentle, but earnest. He wanted this as much as I did, and my heart danced wildly in celebration. Our lips moved together in a song all their own, with a cadence and movement as if we'd never parted, and perhaps in a way we hadn't. All this time our minds had stayed connected. Tyler had found the link and followed it here, to me, to this.

Our rhythm slowed and lips parted. Tyler pressed his forehead to mine, and we breathed heavily sharing the same air.

His skin creased beneath mine as his mouth turned up. Pulling away, I gazed into his eyes and melted from the warmth they infused.

'Man, that was even better to do in real time. It's like it was diluted before.'

'Wait until the real thing.'

'We can do that? I mean that would be okay with you?'

I frowned. 'What do you mean?'

'You seem so much more reserved in real life.'

'Yeah, I am.'

'But you'd still like me to kiss you?' His words were rugged, unsure.

'Yes.' I nodded. 'I'd like you to kiss me.'

'I gather it's even better than this?'

My all-knowing lips rose in answer.

'Can we wake up now?' he said, and the rumble of our laughter floated through the gully.

—29—

THE MAIN STREET IN Antil heaved with locals and tourists, the end of summer bringing everyone out for Saturday brunch. We weren't brunch people; Slice of Heaven was more our style. We ordered and found a table on the edge of the road, empty but covered in the last patron's dirty dishes. It sat under a much-needed yellow umbrella, the sun blaring down and around its frayed edges.

I stacked the dirty cups and carried them in. Plodding back outside, I spotted Tyler strolling along the pavement toward us, heat and a flicker of trepidation in his eyes.

'Good morning.'

'Sure is.' He stepped up to my side, and his meltingly smooth voice almost had my knees buckling beneath me. I lowered my eyes from the intensity of his gaze and the reminder of the night gone. 'Especially now.'

'Were you lonely when you woke up?' I teased.

'You have no idea.'

I raised an eyebrow. 'I think I might have an inkling.'

'It's the pits, hey.'

'The worst. But we can't complain, we have an advantage over all these guys.' I nodded toward the group at the table.

'Advantage all right.'

'If only they knew.'

'They'll never know' – his voice lowered as he whispered the accented words into my ear – '*notre petit* secret.'

I crinkled my brow, trying to piece the unfamiliar yet familiar words together. 'Our little secret?' He confirmed with a nod. 'You think it's little? I'd have thought massive would be more appropriate.'

'*Oui. Massif,*' he said, accentuating the 'if' like it was a separate word in capital letters. I laughed at his effortless ability to speak something so foreign to me.

We settled onto the bench seat, the length of our legs touching as we bunched up to fit everyone in. Tingles rippled through me, but the fear and silent conversation brimming between Max and Sean dispersed it immediately.

'What is it?' I swallowed and straightened.

Sean's gaze flew from Max to me, his eyes flitting to Cal. 'You didn't hear then?'

'Hear what?'

His shoulders sagged as he exhaled. 'There was another abduction.'

'What?'

'Attempted, I mean.' Sean waved a hand as if he were trying to erase his words. 'She got away.'

'That's good, right?' Amber said, her voice barely louder than the hum of the cars and conversations nearby.

No one answered. It might be good that the girl got away, but this signified something far greater to us.

'Was she blonde?' Cal asked through clenched teeth.

Sean nodded, and Cal's fist landed on the tabletop.

My head swam with the news that Benjamin Webb had tried to kill another innocent girl. I rested my elbows on the table and dropped my head into my hands, my fingers tangling through the dark hair falling around my face.

'I need to make him stop.'

'Lucy, you can't.' Max rested her hand on the table before yanking it away as a waiter arrived with a tray of drinks.

I ignored her and gripped the drink placed in front of me, relishing in the ice-cold glass under my fingers. 'I could have a dream. I might not see it because she didn't die, but if I could, I might be able to find more evidence.'

'And what are you going to do with it?' Cal's horror-filled eyes pleaded with me. 'Call the police and put him on your tail again? You can't, we need to keep Amber safe.'

I cast my eyes down. He was right; she was more important than some random stranger I couldn't help anyway. I lifted my head and nodded.

I startled when Tyler spoke. 'Is this the same guy who sent you the photo?' Our silence answered his question. 'Why are you involved in this, what does it have to do with you?' He turned to me, waiting for my words to fill in the holes of his knowledge.

'Last year I tried to save Megan Sanders, the girl who was abducted and killed in Sydney. Well, I did save her, but the guy came after her again. There was nothing I could do, nothing I tried would've worked. That's why I came to Sydney.'

'Not to see me?'

'You were just on the side.'

'Nice to know where I stand.' His smile eased some of the nerves roaring through my veins.

'Hang on, back up.' Sean leaned forward, eyes shifting between me and Tyler. 'He knows, doesn't he?'

''Course he does,' Max said. 'Seriously, where have you been all week?'

'And he's still here?' Sean said with a huff.

'So far.' I let out a short laugh too.

'So far?' Tyler leaned his forearm on the table. 'Haven't you heard anything I've been saying?' He spoke gently, and my heart fluttered. His eyes found mine, reassuring me and ignoring the undeniable gapes around the table. 'How much do they know?'

'Everything.'

'So, do you think they'll be freaked out if I tell them I dreamt about you before we met?'

'I'm not sure...probably?'

'We're far past freaked out.' Cal shrugged. 'This is our new norm.'

'Hang on. You dreamt of Lucy before you moved here?' Sean's eyes narrowed. 'How is that possible?'

'How is any of this possible?' I said.

'I'm just...' Sean threw his arms in the air and shook his head. 'I give up trying to understand any of this. It's insane. I mean you're not insane.' He put his hand up to stop my train of thought. 'Not you, but this whole thing, you know?'

My shoulders shook with laughter, enjoying Sean's discomfort. 'It's all right, I know what you mean. I couldn't agree more.'

'So, no guys,' Tyler started up again. 'I'm not going anywhere. Which means I need the rest of this story. If it wasn't to see me, why'd you go to Sydney?'

'I figured if I couldn't save her in my dream, maybe I could save the next girl by getting him arrested. I went to Sydney to get his number plate. He covered it up when he took her, so I didn't see it in my dream.'

He shifted and faced me. 'So, you got the number plate and what, called the cops?'

'Yeah. But they couldn't hold him with the evidence I gave. And now he's warned me not to get involved, so there's nothing else I can do. But I feel so guilty, like her life, and anyone else he kills, is because of me.'

Tyler frowned. 'How could it be because of you? You're not to blame.'

'That's what I said, but she wouldn't listen to me,' Amber said, picking up a slice of the pizza that'd arrived.

I swallowed the knot in my throat that formed each time my responsibility in the mess got shoved in my face. I blinked back the tears glistening my eyes.

'What is it?' Tyler asked.

'I saved him. He was on the plane.'

Confusion creased his brow, and then understanding straightened it out again. 'How do you know?'

'Because I sat across from him.'

'Hang on, what? You were actually *on* the plane? Only in the dream, yeah? I'm so confused.' He shook his head.

'Yeah, in my dream. And when I saw him in the dream after he kidnapped Megan, I recognised him straight away.'

'Woah, okay, I get where this is going now.'

'And now I'm crippled with the guilt with no way to get rid of it.'

'But there were what, over three-hundred people on that plane? Not everyone was a psycho. I'm sure you saved some pretty decent people too, my dad being one of them.'

'Yeah, he's pretty decent.' I rubbed my fingers along the tabletop. 'Don't worry, I don't regret it, but my part in Megan's death hurts if I think too hard about it.'

'Then don't. Think about the other people instead.'

'Like your dad?'

'Yeah.'

I tried, I really did. Tyler's dad was a good man. But so were the girls Webb kept killing, and as much as I tried to keep my mind from thinking on them too much, it was useless. I wouldn't do anything to put Amber in harm's way, but it didn't mean I wouldn't think about the potential danger that put others in.

AFTER LUNCH, WHEN THE sun had ducked behind the clouds, Tyler and I said our goodbyes and wandered back to his property. We trekked up the steep incline at the edge of town where I pointed out the house he'd once called home.

'That?' He shook his head. 'Mum must've been severely depressed or desperate to leave Sydney if that's what she chose.'

'I think it might've been a bit of both, she was seriously bad the last time I saw her.'

'You mean in the last life?'

I nodded. 'She was a mess. Barely able to keep going.'

'How did we end up here then, how did she manage the move on her own?'

'She didn't. She had you.' Even through his own grief, he'd been so strong, for them, for me.

At the top of the hill we climbed through the fence, and without even noticing it happen, our hands were entwined, at home, at last. My heart content from that one small but significant moment, that in time would lead to so much more. We strolled down the grassy slope, the breeze less demanding than it'd been in our dream.

'If we find a gully over there, I say we leave town and start up a gypsy wagon.'

I put my hand to my heart, mocking. 'You'd exploit me like that?'

'All the way. Think of the money we could make.'

'I knew you were too good to be true.'

His eyes twinkled. 'The good ones usually are.'

Was it possible to combust from too much happiness? I'd almost reached boiling point, at imminent risk of bubbling over.

My hand in Tyler's, the ease of our conversations, no secrets; it all added up to a moment of pure joy. I struggled to remember not feeling like this as the hugeness of it surrounded me. It was hard to recall the pain of the months before he arrived and slid back into my life. He was the same, he was different, yet still so perfect for me.

Tyler's hand jerked on mine, two steps behind me. I glanced back at him, his eyes wide, staring over my shoulder.

'Holy shit.'

What? I spun around, my gaze drifting down the hill to the tree-lined gully he'd fully expected to stay in our dreams. I laughed at his obvious shock.

We strolled over to the fallen log, this time climbing on instead of sheltering below it. Our legs dangled inches off the ground, and our hands rested by our sides, entwining in each other's fingers again, drawn together by an invisible force.

'It feels like I've entered some kind of magical world, with you, with this. Will anything feel normal again?'

'Do you want it to?'

'No, I like my new normal.'

'Don't get too used to it. If there's one thing I've learnt it's that things can change quite quickly.' My mind drifted to Cal's accident and all the discoveries leading up to Tyler leaving.

'Oh, I'm getting used to it all right.' He rubbed his thumb over the back of my fingers.

'So, did you like your first real-time shared dream?'

'You have to ask?' He smirked. 'But do you ever feel empty when you wake up?'

'I wouldn't say empty. Maybe lost? Depends on the dream, really. But anyway, I thought you wanted to wake up?' I turned my head on the side, quizzing him with my eyes.

'I did, but when I woke up you were gone.'

'I'm here now.'

'Yes, you are.'

I lowered my eyes, shielding myself from the intensity in his. Tyler placed a finger below my chin and returned my focus to him. His eyes pinched at the outer edges, a question. I held his gaze, reassuring and answering at the same time.

His finger grazed my jaw, shivering at the touch. My pulse ran with wild abandon, and he closed the gap between us. His mouth pressed to mine before easing away. He stared into my eyes, and I immersed myself in their deep-blue depths, full of an adoration I wanted to drown in. We both smiled, a full rise of our cheeks that made the crow's feet at the edges of our eyes multiply in acknowledgement of the mutual ecstasy sizzling between us. His mouth found mine again, and his fingers slid into my hair, drawing me close. I brought my hands to the back of his neck and revelled in the touch of his skin beneath my fingertips. With my eyes closed I focused solely on the feel and smell of him. The tenderness of his lips as they moved with mine, the scent of coffee and coconut soap and a little bit of spice. How I'd missed this, missed him.

Our lips parted, our chests heaved, but as Tyler inched away, I grabbed hold of his face and kissed him again, quick and hard. We laughed when I let him go.

'Wow,' he said. 'You were right – way better.'

'Like magic.' I brushed my thumb against the top of his knuckles. 'I've waited so long for that.'

'So have I.'

'Not the same.' I shook my head. 'There's no way you could have missed that as much as I have.'

Tyler's gaze simmered with awareness. 'Not missed, but anticipated. That might be worse.'

'How?'

'Because you build it up in your head until you're about to explode.'

Contented bliss radiated over me at his admission, and even though the heat of the sun didn't reach the shelter of the trees in the gully, my cheeks warmed.

'And did it live up to your expectations?'

'Ha, my expectations were as high as the clouds. You took me to the moon.'

'The moon. Really? Not the stars?' I needled, unsure how I could sound out anything after he spoke words like that.

'Something to aim for.' The glint in his eyes teased, tempted.

I drew in a breath, a little extra air to keep me from drowning completely as I became lost in the vastness of his eyes. But I'd been here before and already knew it wouldn't matter how much I had, I'd still end up drowning.

'You know, when I was having those dreams, I thought I might be going crazy. If I'd told anyone that I'd fallen for this girl in my dreams they'd have had me detained for sure. That was well before we moved here...it's why I had to break up with Chloe. Hard to be genuine when you're kind of in love with someone else.'

My heart jumped into my throat.

'It's embarrassing really, being in love with your imagination, but it wasn't, it was you. And now I'm here, and I'm finding out everything was *not* a figment of my imagination, but also nothing in comparison to the real thing, to the real you. And now I'm falling even harder than I thought it possible to fall for someone.'

Happiness tugged on my heart. He'd said he wasn't far behind me, and he hadn't been lying. He was falling for me, and I fell right along with him.

Tyler ignored my gaping smile and leaned in again to capture my mouth.

—30—

CHOKING BACK ON THE *shock as I landed in my dream, I stepped forward, toward the pale blonde, the girl who got away, as she strode across the car park. Behind her, a large cream building stood proud and old, on her left, edging the bitumen, an expanse of green grass faded into the distance.*

She hunched over, reached into the bag slung over her shoulder, and plucked out a set of keys.

The white van appeared on the other side of the car park, the crunch of the old bitumen under its tyres growing as it neared. I spun toward it, and my fear ignited with the pulse in my neck. The man I had saved, who I'd come to know more in my dreams than anywhere else, sat behind the wheel. My eyes darted back to her, imploring her to get to her car faster, away from the looming danger closing in.

She reached her car and climbed in the front seat. But the van drew to a stop at her car's rear, blocking her exit; my throat clogged with dread again. She opened her door and I lurched forward.

'Stay in your car. It's a trap.' I held my arms out as if I could stop her, as if she could hear me.

He climbed out the van, pretending to be completely oblivious to his blockade, and proceeded to slide the side door open.

'Excuse me,' she said, faltering in her step as the opening in the van exposed its dark interior. 'I need to back my car out. Do you think you could move?'

Benjamin Webb raised his head and flashed her a shockingly friendly smile and took a step closer to her, resting a hand on the boot of her car. 'Oh dear, pardon me, I didn't notice you there. Sorry to trouble you. Just a jiffy, got something in my shoe.' He leaned against the car, raised a booted foot and instead of plucking out a pebble, whipped a cloth from the bottom of his pants. He lunged forward and grabbed the girl's arm. Two seconds ahead of him, she whipped away from his grasp and in the same swift move, bolted onto the lawn and sprinted away without looking back.

He tumbled a few steps behind her onto the grass, stopped, started again, and dropped his arms to his side. With a grunt he shuffled back to the van. He slammed the back door shut, hauled himself into his seat and spun the tyres to get away from the scene.

My body landed in the van, in the passenger's seat beside him. He concentrated on the road ahead, his clenched fingers gripping the steering wheel, and a pulsing vein protruded from the side of his forehead. My chest tightened, the air constricting in my throat. Every ounce of my body reacted in repulsion to him, repelling against his nearness as if I were in real danger.

I closed my eyes and muttered, 'You're fine, you're safe, he can't hurt you.' I exhaled and lifted my gaze.

I twisted to peer into the rear of the van. A black curtain hung between our seats and blocked the claustrophobic space in the back. I straightened, trying to take in everything I could find, anything that might offer insight into where he headed, what he had planned, what I could use against him if needed.

Like a work desk, his dash held a mess of papers and an assortment of junk mail, except he ran a business so it couldn't be anything too important. I ran my eyes down to the console between the two seats and spotted an old GPS, the sort people used before everyone had them on their phones.

A circle flashed on and off as it moved along the road we currently travelled. A right arrow trailed across the top of the screen, but he made *a left, followed by a few more turns, and pulled up in front of a modest suburban home.*

He burst out of the van and through the front door. My entire body thrummed with adrenalin as I shuffled into step behind him. Not wanting to be near, but not wanting to miss a single thing.

'You're back early. I thought you were out all night.' An elderly, feminine voice drifted from the rear of the home.

He stomped the length of the house and threw open the fridge. 'Change of plans.' He yanked out a long brown bottle and twisted off the lid.

'Do you want some dinner then? Now you're home?' Home? Who was she? Did he still live with his parents? He was like forty years old.

My head grew foggy, the whisper of realisation landing in my guts. He lived here. *Not at the house attached to the computer repair business. I rubbed my jaw, glancing around the homely kitchen. I gave the police the number plate. But if it was registered to this address, it's no wonder they found no connection.*

'Thanks, Aunt Dora, you're a gem.' He kissed the side of her head, his charm returning in full force. 'Could you bring it to my room?'

*****

TYLER STROLLED THROUGH THE library, a wide beam spread across his face. He slid a manila folder across the table and sat opposite me.

I glanced from him to the folder and back again. 'What's this?'

'You know how bad you feel about doing a Lazarus on that man.'

'A Lazarus?'

'You brought him back to life.'

'Oh right, from the Bible.'

'Yeah. So he's alive, but so are the rest of them, and I have names.' He flipped the folder open, a list of about twenty names printed down the side. 'They're the people you sat near on the plane.'

I slammed my hands on the pages, my eyes widening. 'How did you get this?'

'My dad had it on file, would you believe? He kept it to remind himself how lucky he got that day. Talking about it yesterday reminded me.'

'And your dad, he just gave you the names?' I cocked an eyebrow.

'Well...not really, but it's not hurting anyone, so I figured –'

'Tyler.'

'I can take them back if you'd like?' He reached his hand out for the folder.

'No, no that's okay.' I dragged the folder closer. Names, dates of birth, seat numbers, and any special requirements for the flight ran down the page. I gaped at the information in front of me, at the names of the people I'd sat beside on that plane, the lives I'd saved. 'How did you know I sat in this section?'

'I knew you sat across from Benjamin Webb.' He pointed to his name on the page. 'This was the only empty seat, 41H. I figured you must've seen some or all of these people.'

'Wow. Not a bad detective, are you?'

'Gotta hold up my end of the bargain.'

I tilted my head with a frown. 'Which is?'

'Being your Robin.'

I ran my hands over the pages, gazing at the expectant hope in Tyler's eyes. 'I don't know what to say.'

'You don't have to say anything. I just hope this helps.'

'What do I do now?'

'That's up to you, Batman. Nothing if you want, or you could try to locate them, give 'em a call, ask about the accident, might help you come to terms with the goodness you've achieved.'

'I *have* come to terms with it. It's coming to terms with the negative impact that I'm having more difficulty with.'

'Then I hope this helps you let that go.' He placed his hand over mine, the care in his caress, and his gesture, pressing equally against the edges of my heart.

I wished it were that easy. I closed my eyes, seeing her blonde hair fly around her face as she wrestled out of his grasp and bolted safely away. But what about the next time?

'Can I ask you something?' I grabbed hold of the assurance in his eyes. 'If you thought you could save them, would you do it?'

He frowned. 'Are you talking about the girls?'

I nodded. 'If you knew a way, but it came with risks, would you still do it? Like if you knew you had a ninety-percent chance of winning the lotto, would you buy a ticket?'

'Does the other ten put your friend in danger?'

'That's the risk, yeah.'

'Then no, I wouldn't buy the ticket. If it was to win money, absolutely not, but if it might save lives, maybe, I'm not sure.' He grabbed hold of my fingers and gripped them as forcefully as his gaze fixed on me, willing me to understand his next words. 'But if Amber gets hurt, if it goes badly, you will never forgive yourself.'

My eyes welled up. 'Not only would I never forgive myself, I don't think I'd be able to *live* with myself.' I blinked back the tears and shook off the fear. 'No. It's not worth it. There's too much at stake if it goes wrong, even if that is only ten percent. I need to let it rest. Live with what's happened.'

Tyler placed his palms on the folder. 'Call someone. It might help. Because there's gotta be some good stories in here. Focus on that.'

*****

TYLER AND I COLLAPSED onto the benches on either side of the table. Max and Amber had already settled under the shady branches of the maple tree. I dropped my bag to the ground, and sensing a flicker of white, shot my head up, my heart accelerating with adrenalin. A white hatchback flew along the road outside the school, no van in sight. *Calm down, Lucy.* I'd been on edge all morning, every spot of white had me visualising that horrid van.

And every swish of Amber's blonde hair had me seeing the billowing mass behind the girl as she ran away from her would-be attacker. Amber was the heart of this group; she was everything that was sweet and pure and good. My eyes glistened as I stared at her profile, the light shining from her eyes for no reason other than simply being happy, which she always was.

She turned to me. 'You okay?'

'Huh? Yeah, perfectly fine.' I dragged my lips up into a smile, disguising where my mind had been. Fingers curled around mine on my leg, the delicate pink fingers of my friend. She had no idea what I battled with, yet she still offered her silent support, as always. Yes, this girl was totally not worth the risk.

She nudged my shoulder, jostling for my attention again. 'Has Mum called you yet?'

''Bout what?'

'Friday. She needs us to work now.'

Cal and Sean came barrelling across the lawn, shoulders locked as if in a contest for a seat, and thumped onto the bench.

'What'd we miss?' Cal blinked, his gaze darting to each of us.

'I was telling Luce the bad news; we need to work Friday night.'

'You gonna drive up after your shift or come on Saturday?' Sean asked.

The long weekend loomed at the end of the week. I couldn't wait for three perfect days at the lake house with Cal and his parents, but more than that, the prospect of being back there with Tyler. To show him some of where our previous life and dreams had taken place thrilled me with anticipation.

'I'll drive us up after. Dad said I can use his car.'

'No rush, we've got, what, three days. Come whenever you're ready.' Cal scanned the bright sky. 'Damn this weather's got me pumped. The water's gonna be awesome.'

'I could take you both,' Tyler said.

'You don't mind waiting around all night for us?' I asked.

'Nah, not at all. Like Cal said, no rush. Although, tell me, I'm keen to know, am I as good at water skiing as you say I am at snowboarding?' He pressed his palms onto the table, shoulders hunched forward in eagerness, his face full of hope.

'Well...' I screwed my nose up.

He dropped his shoulders. 'Really?'

'You were all right...once you got up, that is.' Laughter erupted around the table.

'Dude, I so can't wait for the weekend now.' Cal slapped Tyler on the back with another chuckle.

*****

MY PULSE TREMBLED IN the thumb hovering over the green telephone icon. All I had to do was touch the screen and I could talk to her. The old lady from the plane now had a name – Daphne Marie Jacobs – and after some online investigations, I also had her phone number. Her words had plagued me for nearly two years. What had they meant? Who needed her that day? Shoving aside any remaining uncertainty, I tapped the phone and hitched myself onto my bed.

'Hello?' Her timid voice, the same gentle one I remembered from the airport, filtered through the line.

'Hello. My name's Lucy. Lucy Piper. Am I speaking with Daphne Jacobs?'

'Yes, this is she.'

'Hi. I got your number from a friend of mine, Susan Mathers.' Stalking Facebook had its perks. Of course Susan wasn't a friend of mine, but she could've been with one click. For now, I'd pretend we were on more familiar terms to get where I needed with this conversation. 'I'm a student studying the after-effects of trauma. I wondered if I could ask you about the incident last year on flight S108?'

'The emergency landing? My trauma had nothing to do with that flight.'

'Oh, I'm sorry. I hope everything's okay now.'

'It really depends on the day.' Her breathy sigh trembled down the phone line.

'So you didn't suffer any trauma from the flight then?' I asked tentatively, squeezing the covers on my bed to prevent the urgency from sounding in my voice.

'Yes and no. That flight was taking me to see my daughter.' The daughter must've been one of the 'they' in 'they need me'. 'You've no idea how important it was to get to her that day. I try not to imagine what may have been if the plane did crash and I let her down.' How could dying let someone down?

'What would've happened if you didn't get there?' Who else made up part of 'they'?

'She'd have been alone when she turned the switch off her daughter's life support.'

I swallowed, the sadness creeping up the back of my throat. 'I'm so sorry. Was she waiting for you to arrive?'

'In more ways than one. You see my granddaughter, Mia, had given me power of attorney to be her medical decision maker some years ago. My son-in-law was fighting my decision to turn the life support off.'

'That's terrible. Can I ask what happened to her, why she ended up on life support?'

'Mia was sick. Had been for a very long time. She had a very rare degenerative disease; she was near the end.' Her voice quieted, the defeat of the ordeal returning to her as she rehashed the story. 'But she'd developed pneumonia, and then complications from that. She wasn't going to get better even if she did wake up. Her dad held onto an unrealistic hope that she'd miraculously be cured when she woke up. But even if that were remotely possible, Mia never wanted to lie there waiting, she never wanted to end up comatose. And that's why she needed my help to begin with. Her father hadn't wanted her to write up an advance care directive, didn't want to imagine it ever getting to that point. But she was an adult; she was able to make those decisions for herself.'

'Why didn't he respect that?'

'He claimed she'd been incapable of reason when she made the decision.'

'Had she?'

'Oh no. Not at all. He just didn't want to lose his baby girl. None of us did.'

'And you being there on that day meant something in this fight?'

'Because they were in the U.S., but the paperwork had been done in Australia, I needed to get the original signed paperwork to them. I had it with me on the plane. The doctors, Mark, they couldn't do anything to stop it with that.'

'So your granddaughter dying was dependent on you getting there?'

'Very. Who knows where my girls would be now if we hadn't sorted it out that day.'

'Wow. That's a terribly sad story. I'm so sorry for your loss.'

'Thank you, dear. So as I said, the trauma after the plane landed far outweighed anything that happened during the flight. Hospital fights are the worst. Everyone's already in a world of pain. But nothing in my long and eventful life could ever prepare me for the pain of holding my daughter's hand while she let go of her own.'

Maybe Tyler was right. Hearing these stories would help me live with the burden of responsibility over Megan's life. Mia had been able to leave hers as she'd wished, and her mum had her mother beside her as she let her go. Neither of those things would have been possible if the plane had gone down, if I hadn't saved Daphne's life. It never ceased to amaze me how intricately we weave our lives with others and how a simple change for one person can cause destruction in another's. Daphne's death, had the plane gone down, would have resulted in more pain for this family than her loss alone.

I'd never know the full effects of my intervention, how great the ripple might spread, what the eventual impact would be. Would the butterfly effect be a subtle one or a far-reaching cyclonic shift for many? Still, saving a person's life had to be worth it, even if the waves caused a tsunami, because for that person's loved ones, that one single life meant everything.

But what about the rest of the population drowning in the waves? I wanted to save them all, but it seemed impossible; an endless, expanding race with no end in sight. The overwhelming guilt seized hold of me once again, even through the genuine relief Daphne provided, because she was proof that the repercussions could be a good thing, beyond the saving of a life.

Had I been given fresh evidence for that reason? To ensure a positive flow-on in the lives of the girls Webb planned to kill, just like there'd been when Daphne's life had been saved?

Yes, this had to be my chance to rectify things. Make it right and whole again. Do what I do best – save the people caught up in the tsunami.

—31—

I slid my feet into a pair of sneakers, my phone secured firmly in my armband and my earphones securely in my ears. I thumped down the stairs and out the door in search of a pay phone. I didn't want the police to trace the call. They'd have questions I wouldn't be able to answer without them flipping their investigation onto me, and I did *not* need a spotlight shone in my direction.

I found the strange glass box, almost as ancient as the Colosseum, sitting outside the council offices in town. I grabbed some coins from my backpack and with clammy hands inserted them into the slot. I shared my suspicion with the policewoman on the end of the line, that something seemed weird when I used the private toilet at a business recently. Sometimes I loved lying. I told her I'd seen into a back room where pictures of women were tacked to the wall, and it wasn't until I got home that I realised why one of the faces looked familiar, it was that Megan girl who'd been killed last year.

The cop lady on the end of the phone spoke calmly. 'Can you tell me the name of this business, Miss?'

'Yes, of course,' I replied with an air of calm being betrayed by my thumping heartbeat. 'Salander Computer Repairs.'

'And do you know the name of the person working that day?'

I gripped the handset. 'Pretty sure it was the man who owns the business. His name is Benjamin Webb, that's what his business card says anyway.'

'All right, we'll have a look into it, see what we can find. Thanks for the call, we appreciate any new information the public can give us.'

She hung up, and my pounding heart echoed in the tiny glass cubicle. My hands trembled as I opened the door and stepped outside. Nerves rushed through me, and I darted my eyes up the street and back down again, half expecting a white van to approach from behind and drag me inside.

My thoughts drifted to Amber, but there was no way he'd know anything about my interference, not until the moment the police stood on his doorstep. Which meant she'd be protected in the same moment he thought about following through with his threat.

I still vibrated with adrenalin as I typed a quick text to Tyler.

Me: *I need to see you. Are you home?*

I hit send, swiped at the music choices, and hit play.

A current favourite, Bishop Briggs's 'Wild Horses', belted into my ears, the thrum of the music drowning out the thud of my feet on the road and the cars driving past. I paid no attention to anything around me. It was just me and my music. The chorus started up – Bishop Briggs calling on the wild horses to run faster – I increased the volume.

My feet transitioned from the bitumen to the dirt, and I welcomed the relief of the trees from the intensity of the afternoon sun, right as my phone beeped. I stopped and ran the back of my hand across my forehead.

Tyler: *I'm home, but Dad's cracking the whip. He's building a pizza oven for Mum. Everything alright?*

Disappointment flooded through me.

Me: *Yeah. Guess I'm running solo then.*
Tyler: *At least you're not making mud bricks. What is this life? :/ Bring on the weekend!*
Me: *The weekend is days away.*
Me: *Hey maybe we can meet later, in a dream?*

How lucky were we to have more than the hours of the day to see one another.

Tyler: *Hell yeah. Where?*

His infectious enthusiasm caught on, and happiness spread across my face.

Me: *Tree?*
Tyler: *School tree or gully tree?*
Me: *Gully?*
Tyler: *I'll be there. Looking forward to it x*

He wasn't the only one, and the rest of the day dragged as I waited for the shift in the breeze as it carried the sounds of the day away to the rising light of the moon.

'HELLO, YOU,' TYLER SAID, *welcoming me into our dream. He held an arm out, and I stepped into it and into him. My eyes met his and he pressed his lips to mine softly before leading me to the fallen log by the creek. We climbed onto the top, our fingers entwined between us, feet dangling over the side.*
  'So, what did you need to see me for...other than the obvious?' He

bumped shoulders with mine and awarded me a sideways smirk, that adorable smirk that'd come back into my life and sent my stomach soaring.

'I called the old lady. Her name's Daphne.' My eyes sparked with the joy from all I'd learned as I relayed her story to Tyler.

'Damn, that's awful. I mean awful good...I dunno, seems weird to think of a person dying as good, but I guess sometimes it really is.'

'I know, right?'

'So you gonna call anyone else?'

'I called the police.' The words rushed out.

'You did? You feel okay?'

Lips pressed tight, I nodded. 'I'm certain everything will be fine. He'll be caught, and Amber and the girls will be safe. It's all going to be perfect. And now I want to forget about all of it and focus on everything else, all the other good changes I can make, on us.'

Tyler twirled a strand of my hair in his fingers and tucked it behind my ear. 'I like that there's an "us."'

I leaned into his hand. 'Me too.'

Our words quieted. The air grew still. The gentle rustle of the leaves and chirping of the birds in the branches above us intermingled with our thoughts as we bumped the heels of our feet on the log.

'Have you ever tried to change anything in your dreams while you're in the dream?'

I frowned. 'You mean like what I do in my repeat dreams?'

'Dunno. Don't you already have an idea before you go into those dreams, have it already planned out?'

I nodded, still a bit lost as to what Tyler might be implying.

'I mean, have you ever tried to diverge from that plan?' he asked. 'Make something else happen, make things appear, or do things you hadn't planned?'

'I'm not sure. No, I do. I did. I made you appear once, in a dream. Before I came to Sydney. I meditated and made you appear, but it wasn't really you, just my memory. I think most of what I see is like that, made out of what I know or what's already there. I'm not sure how I could make a flying car appear.'

'A flying car?'

'I don't know.' I shrugged with a small laugh. 'A flying car, a cow, whatever.'

'Now there's an idea. A cow.'

'You want me to make a cow appear?'

'It's a dream, anything's possible, right?'

'I like your thinking.' I closed my eyes and brought to mind an alternative within my imagination. I had no idea if it would work, but hey, it was worth a try. I conjured the image of the cows I'd grown to love up where the trees met the fence and the grassy hills.

My eyelids fluttered open. 'There. Done.'

'Just like that?'

'How else?' I jumped onto the ground. 'C'mon, let's go find our cow.'

Tyler landed with a thud beside me and gestured up the hill with his arm. 'Lead the way.'

I grabbed his hand and snaked out of the woody shade into the full light of the dream. We waded through the tall grass as we climbed the steep slope. By the time we reached the summit we were panting. We scanned the area, turning slowly. The image of the cow appeared in my mind, but he hadn't shown up here.

My shoulders slumped. 'Oh well.' We turned our attention to the mountains in the distance and the shadow of the gully between the hills.

Tyler squeezed my hand, sharing my disappointment. One side of his mouth slanted, his own form of 'oh well.' 'Next time, maybe?'

Behind us, the low vibration of a moo drifted up the hill and we both spun. A cow stood ten metres away, staring directly at us with her large round eyes. She opened her mouth and let out another deep moo.

'Holy crap,' Tyler said, echoing my own sentiment. We gaped at one *another before taking in the cow again. Her long droopy eyelashes lowered with her head as she took a large bite of the grass at her feet. She peered up with the blades between her teeth, turning to give us a side eye, and our bubble of wonder burst into laughter.*

Tyler tipped his head back. 'See!' He pointed at the cow. 'She's giving us the side eye.'

'No, she's giving you the side eye.' My laughter roared from deep in my chest, and I collapsed in the grass. I lay on the warm earth, my chest heaving out the last of my laughter as I regained an even breath. 'She's thinking, who's this strange guy?'

Tyler sat beside me. 'No, she's thinking, who's that lucky guy?' His gaze rested on my face, heat pooling in his eyes. 'So beautiful.' His fingers brushed the side of my jaw, sending a shiver right to my core. His eyes locked with mine, and he lowered his head to meet my lips, his hand resting on my hip. His body hovered over mine, a tingling heat between the length of us. My arms reached behind his neck, bringing him closer still, and our mouths melted into one another.

*****

I ZIPPED UP MY bag and heaved it down the stairs. I wasn't due to start work for another half an hour. I itched to get on the road to the lake house, but with no choice but to wait until the end of my shift, I had time to kill. Mum stood at the opened fridge hauling vegetable after vegetable onto the kitchen bench. *Here she goes, dinner for fifty.*

I stepped forward. 'Need a hand with anything?

'Could you top and tail the beans?'

She passed me a bag, and I tipped the contents onto the chopping board. My phone chimed from my backside. I slid it out of my back pocket and turned to lean against the kitchen bench.

Laurie: *Change of plans. I won't need you tonight after all.*
Me: *Awesome. What about Amber?*
Laurie: *I still need her. She'll come up after her shift.*
Me: *Okay. Thanks*

'I don't have to work anymore. Might head off soon if that's all right?'

'Of course. I wasn't expecting you for dinner anyway.'

I arched my brow, taking in the massive chicken and prepped vegetables piled high.

'What? Jake's arriving later. He'll be hungry.'

I rolled my eyes, a slight smile twitching my lips. Whatever. I tapped out a quick message to Amber and munched on a raw bean.

Me: *You right if Tyler and I go without you? Can you borrow your dad's car?*

Amber: *Yeah, that's fine. See you there later.*

—32—

WE WERE FIVE MINUTES away from the lake house. Tall gums whirled past outside the windows, and Tyler slowed the car down to turn off the main road as we drew closer.

I shifted to face Tyler, to take in the perfect profile of his face, not quite sure how I got so lucky. 'You excited?' I asked.

'Are you kidding?' He reached across the console and claimed my fingers with his, the corners of his eyes crinkling with his smile. 'I get a whole weekend with you. And if my dream memories of this place are anything to go by, we're in for a fun few days.'

My heart skipped with giddy excitement, but added with the anticipation in his eyes, turned it into a somersault.

My phone vibrated at my feet, the ringtone urging me to pick up. I grabbed it from my bag, Laurie's name flashing across the screen with green and red lights.

Tyler frowned with a question. God, I hoped I didn't need to turn around and go to work after all.

I shrugged and put the phone to my ear. 'Hey, Laurie.'

'Lucy. Where are you?' Clanging silverware sounded in the background. Her frantic voice grilled me as if I were standing in her kitchen.

I pressed the phone into my cheek. 'I'm almost at the lake house. You didn't need me.'

'What're you talking about? I needed you and Amber like ten

• 256 •

minutes ago.'

'Amber's not there?'

'No. And I can't get hold of her, I think her phone's off.'

Her words were like lead. 'Hang on. You sent me a text telling me not to come in.'

'If you got a text, it wasn't from me. You should see the food I have to get out tonight. I need more than the two of you.'

I gripped the phone, my head buzzing. How did I receive texts saying they were from Laurie if she didn't send them? Where was Amber?

Tyler's piercing eyes flashed between the road and me. Road. Me.

A thousand thoughts crammed for attention: my phone, Amber, missing. The deluge roared louder than the deafening pulse raging behind my ears. My eyes flew open.

'He took her.'

'Who? What are you talking about?'

'I'll explain later. Laurie, you need to go home. See if she's there. Look for a white van and don't let it get away if you see one. Call Rick and –'

'He's in Sydney.'

Crap.

'Okay, you might still want to call him. I have a really bad feeling.'

'Lucy. You're scaring me.'

'I know. I'm scared too. I'm calling the police. I'm so sorry.'

I fumbled with the end button, and the phone fell from my fingers.

'The house is right up there on the left. You'll see a light green letterbox.'

Tyler gripped the steering wheel. I picked the phone up, hands shaking, and dialled triple zero.

'What?!' Cal knotted both hands into his hair. 'How do you know? Are you sure?' He slid his phone out his back pocket and dialled Amber's number. Pacing the floor with it to his ear, he rubbed the back of his neck.

My hands twisted at my sides, and tears sprang to my eyes. I jumped at the sound of my phone ringing.

Cal hurled his phone onto the couch, and Marie put her arm around his shoulder. He shrugged her off.

'Laurie?' Everyone stood still and silent.

'She's not here. The car's here. Her school bag is gone, but I found the car keys on the front lawn.' I gasped and rested my trembling fingers to my lips. 'You need to get back here. The cops are going to have questions about what you know, and so am I.'

'I'll be there as soon as I can.'

I collapsed onto a dining chair and relayed the latest. Max held her hands on the back of her head and paced the floor. Sean's nostrils flared as he bit into his thumbnail. I couldn't bear to look at Cal and risk catching his wrath.

'I'm so sorry.' I shook my head.

'What did you do?' Cal's words were a spear through my chest.

'I thought I had enough to arrest him, and she'd be okay 'cause he'd be behind bars.'

'You called the cops? Why would you do that? You knew he'd been watching you.'

My lip wobbled. 'I needed to protect the girls.'

'What about Amber?' Cal threw his head back and cried out like he'd been punched. The pain emanated from him, sending tears trailing down my face. 'You have to fix this. You need to fall asleep and find her.'

I nodded and bit the inside of my lip. 'I will.' I needed to. Because if Webb was as good as he'd always been, there wouldn't be any crumbs to find, and she'd be well and truly dead before anyone got a whiff of her whereabouts. The clamp around my chest tightened, and I fought for air as I remembered my attempt to locate Megan. All I got was the destination, not the address.

My head fell into my hands.

*****

TYLER AND I ARRIVED back at Laurie's with Cal, where the police were just finishing up with her. The sadness in Laurie's eyes, worn and piercing, landed like a boot to my chest. The two male police officers, with their broad shoulders and air of authority, were much more intimidating. They took my information, and even though they appeared doubtful as to why my story might be legit, they still wrote down notes.

I didn't have much to back up my story though. My dreams weren't really a solid form of evidence when it came to the law. So, I did what I did best – I lied. Tyler stilled my jiggling leg with his hand.

'I visited a friend in Sydney last year and saw this man across the road to her house. He got in his van and followed my bus. I thought I lost him, but...' I slid the photograph across the table, and the officers sat up a little straighter, suddenly interested in what I had to say.

'Why didn't you say anything?' Laurie asked, her voice catching in her throat.

Cal's hands gripped the side of his head, and I could only imagine he asked himself the same thing.

'He stole my backpack and put this in it. It was months later before I found it. And I had no proof it was him.'

The officer with the pen and pad paused his writing. 'He returned your bag?'

'Yes.'

'With everything in it?'

I shook my head. 'Not my wallet or sketchbook. He made it look like a robbery, and I didn't think it was any more than that until I found that.' I nodded to the photo.

'Was your phone in your bag?'

'I got that back.'

'That might explain the texts. If he tapped into your phone while he had it, then he's probably been tracking your texts ever since.'

'He can do that?'

'Afraid so. And it's possible he was able to replicate incoming messages too.' My stomach roiled, nauseated that I'd been tricked so easily. I gave them the number plate and the name of the details of the business where I 'saw him'.

'So, you believe me?'

'It's more a case of some of your specifics matching other evidence we've already received about our suspect, thereby leading us to proceed with every precaution as if we are dealing with this man now.'

'You are.' I pressed my hands into the table and used my eyes to convey the desperation I wished they would summon.

'We've got patrols searching the surrounding areas, but we're also patrolling the highway for the van you described.'

When they left, Laurie clutched my hands and demanded I tell her what I hadn't told the police. 'You didn't go there to visit a friend. Why were you near his place?'

And I knew in that moment I had no choice but to tell her the truth. She listened intently to the entire thing, barely shifting her focus from me. 'And when I wake tomorrow, I'll know how Amber was taken and maybe even where he's taken her.'

'Oh God.' Laurie covered her mouth with a shaking hand.

'I promise I'll find her. She's going to be okay.' I wanted to believe my own words, but the tremble in my chin and the suffocating terror wrapping around me made it hard to swallow my weak assurances.

TYLER DROVE ME AND Cal back to his place where Max and Sean had returned with Marie and Harry. She'd shoved us away from the lake house saying, 'You're all staying at our place in Antil tonight. You'll want to be together, I imagine. Off you go, we'll be right behind you.'

'What were you thinking?' Cal said, pacing his room.

'You know what I was thinking.'

'What I can't understand is why you'd put her life at risk like this. She could die.'

I clenched my teeth. 'You think I haven't thought that?'

He spun and faced me. 'Yeah, I do. If you did there's no way you would have done this.'

'How could you say that? I love her as much –'

'As much as me?' He spat the words out, as if there was no way I possibly could. 'She's the first thing I think of when I wake up. She's who I think of when I go to sleep. She's the reason for everything I do. Everything!' His shoulders shook, and I moved toward his pain, but I stopped when I caught his eyes, a mix of anger, fear, and love. Tears ran down my face, and he stepped forward, wrapping his arms around me, his sobs tangling with mine.

'Can you find her?' His voice trembled into my shoulder.

I pushed back and placed a hand on his red, tear-stained face. 'I'll try to do more than that, I promise.'

Cal nodded. 'Can you wake us when you've seen something?'

It was my turn to nod.

'What do you need?'

Slightly less pressure would be nice. 'A comfortable bed and maybe some silence?'

SETTLING INTO THE LAST bedroom down the corridor, I sat and crossed my legs under the covers and closed my eyes. But I failed to find stillness as thoughts of Amber, and the distance stretching between us, flashed in my vision and curled around in my stomach. My desperation usually aided my sleep – tonight it prevented it.

I concluded it might be for the best, tossed the covers off, and paced the length of the passageway. I turned and marched to the other end. I needed a deep sleep to dream, and for that I'd need complete and utter exhaustion. My feet slapped the wooden floorboards, my eyes fixed straight ahead, ignoring the light under Cal's door.

The door cracked open and Tyler stepped in front of my path.

'What're you doing?' he whispered.

'Exhausting myself. I can't sleep.'

'I don't think you're the only one.' He rested his hand on my elbow and steered me back to the bedroom. 'I've got an idea.'

He sat on the bed and lowered me down with him. 'If you're trying to help me relax, I'm not sure this is going to help.'

He kissed me quickly. 'That's it, you get one kiss. And now I *am* going to help you relax.'

His arms wrapped around me and we lay together facing the wall, our bodies moulding into one. My stomach fluttered at the feel of him so close, and his fingers laced with mine, but within moments, the same thing – his being there – offered comfort and a calm to my storm.

My laboured breathing slowed to match the cool breeze of his own on my neck. Weariness grew behind my eyes, and even with the fear raging through me, I succumbed to the strengthening fatigue and drifted into the void.

AMBER BUMPED UP THE *curb, steering her car into the driveway. The white van was parked out the front. Pretty ballsy move, being that obvious. How did she not turn around and leave? She knew a white van took Megan. Didn't she? I climbed out the car along with her. She grabbed her school bag from the back seat and slid it over both shoulders.*

A man wearing a high-vis vest, gloves, and a blue baseball cap lurched from the rear of the house – Webb. Amber startled and hopped back a step. My pulse gathered speed. Amber had seen my drawings of Webb, but the hat obscured any identifying features. Added to the name badge clipped to the orange vest and he appeared perfectly legit.

'Can I help you?' she asked, a questioning frown creasing her eyes.

He raised an arm. 'Sorry, I'm trying to find the meter box.' He glanced to the rear of the house, a clipboard in his hand.

'Um, maybe it's on the other side of the house?' She turned around as if to show him the way, and Webb lunged forward, grabbing around her body.

'No!' I charged, intending to attack, but was as useless as Amber's pinned-down arms. She kicked her legs and shook her head, failing to shake free. His free gloved hand slammed over her mouth, holding it there until Amber's body grew limp.

He hurried across the front lawn and lowered her into the back of the van. Like a practiced surgeon at work, he swiftly and efficiently bound her hands and feet and knotted a gag around her face. Her beautiful, perfect face. I closed my eyes, a tear escaping free. I did this.

I stood paralysed as he slammed the door and ran to retrieve the clipboard he'd dropped. Something glistened in the grass, and I shifted my attention to Amber's set of car keys nestled near my feet.

The van roared to life, and my dream threw me into the back of the cabin with Amber. I scrambled to get closer to her unconscious body but couldn't move. I was as restrained as she was.

I struggled against the bindings, the panic coming out in rapid bursts. My eyes watered, the cloth tied around my mouth, and digging into the back of my head, ripped into my hair. Wriggling my hands behind me did nothing but send my panic into overdrive.

Amber's eyes fluttered open, and I clamped my back teeth into the gag at the sight of her complete and utter terror. Tears trailed down her cheeks as she absorbed her surroundings and the fate I'd so carelessly thrown at her. She didn't deserve this – no one did – but Amber was one of the sweetest, kindest people in the world – in my world. What made me think her life was worth risking? I could save a thousand people's lives, and it would never be worth the loss of hers.

Tears slid onto my cheeks. Like knives sliding down my face, I deserved every one of them.

—33—

SUCKING IN THE STIFLING air around me, I shot up in bed. Tyler sat a little slower. I rubbed at my wrists, free from the bindings, but the tears came with me, falling to my lap.

I wiped at my eyes. 'What's the time?'

Tyler grabbed one of the phones by the bed. 'Two thirty-eight.'

'Good.'

'What did you see?' Tyler whispered into the blackened night.

'Pretty much what I expected. He was waiting for her when she got home. He pretended to be a meter reader.'

'Should we go wake the others?'

I shook my head. 'It won't help. If I tell them what I saw it'll only upset them more. Besides, by the time they wake they won't remember it anyway.'

'What do you mean?'

'I'm going back to sleep and saving her tonight.'

'Already?'

'I normally need to think a story over, to come up with an alternative. I don't need time; I know what I need to do.' Groaning, I lowered my head, letting my hair cascade around me. 'God, I'm so scared.'

Tyler twisted on the mattress and brushed my hair away from my face. 'That it won't work?'

'There's so much at stake this time. I mean there always is, but if it doesn't work, she could die. And if he kills me, it's not like the other dreams where I'm just a bystander. I'm going back and altering our lives, *my* life. If I die, that's it. I don't wake up. There's no do-over for me. There's no do-over for anyone.'

'What the hell are you planning to do?' Tyler laughed nervously, terror behind the humour.

'He wants Amber...because of me. If I save her, he'll just try again, like he did with Megan. I have to stop him, and I have to keep him around until the police arrive.'

'And how do you plan on doing that?'

'I'm going to slash his tyres.' My words were sure, certain. I shook my head, blinked back the moisture in the edges of my eyes, feeling no amount of certainty. 'But it could all go horribly wrong. I could die. He could turn that knife on me, Tyler.'

He brushed his fingers across my cheek and stared intently into my eyes. 'Don't think it. You know what happens when you think it. Remember the cow. You can make it exactly how you want it.'

What he didn't realise was it'd be different this time. I'd be acting out my thoughts instead of simply watching it appear. I'd have complete control, and with that came the unknown.

'Please don't die on me.' He pressed his forehead to mine. 'I'm only Robin, I can't bring you back.' I laughed at that, a solemn huff of a laugh and leaned in for a quick kiss.

'I'll try,' I said when our lips parted.

'Good.' He placed both palms against my cheeks and stared into my eyes. 'Because I love you.'

My heart hitched, and I paused to let it sink in. Tyler loved me again. It was never a question, but I said the words anyway, I might never have another chance. 'I love you too.'

His eyes overflowed with adoration, his momentary happiness rising to the corners of his mouth before falling away and shifting to fear. 'You are not allowed to die today.' He fixed his eyes on me with a desperation that pierced directly into my own aching heart. 'I only just found you, I can't lose you. Stay alive for Amber, for me, for everyone who loves you.' He leaned forward and kissed me, sending the tears sliding down my cheeks.

He squeezed my fingers, ran his hands up my arms, and gathered me into his warmth. I clung to him for dear life, because this might be it for us, this might be the last time we held each other. But this time it'd be Tyler who remembered me. That thought alone crammed me with more dread than the fear of dying myself, because I knew that pain, I knew what he'd potentially be facing, and I did not want to do that to him, or Cal.

Tyler tilted his face and his lips found mine again, desperate and seeking. They pressed into me, and I surrendered myself to him as he gave himself to me. His hands caressed me, memorising me, and my fingers traced the lines of his neck, his jaw, him. We became one, all our fear, love and desire melding together. Our warm tears ran into my mouth.

Agony furled itself around my heart, lacerating and tearing it into shreds. How could I leave him like this? I couldn't do it – I couldn't let go. But this moment was only a segue into what I really needed to do. From the depths of my torn body, and with one final taste, I summoned the will to break away.

Tears fell over his cheeks. I wiped at a stray one while ignoring my own, the anguish in his eyes shattering my already broken heart. He brushed the hair from my face, and my body leaned into the delicate stroke of his fingers.

He lowered us down to the mattress and tugged the blanket over us. I leaned into his embrace.

'See you on the other side,' I said, failing to keep the tremor from my voice.

'Yes you will.' He pressed his lips into my shoulder. 'Now let's see you do your thing, Batman.'

I SUCKED IN A *lung full of fresh autumn air from the middle of the school oval. My sleeping body remained with Tyler, and I was now striding from the school oval with Max. I had rewound the hand of time to the day before, a day I'd already lived, which meant I knew we were heading in for the end of the day; the bell was about to sound.*

I'd arrived too late.

Crap.

I clutched Max's arm and jerked her to a stop. She shot wide, confused eyes at my abrupt assault.

'I need you to go to the car park and find Amber. Don't let her leave the school.'

'What's going on?' She glared at my hand on her arm.

'I'll explain everything when I see you both. Please. Can you do it?' She nodded mutely, and I dropped my hand, sidestepped away and took off in a run. 'Go!' I yelled over my shoulder at the same instant the bell sounded. The shrill travelled over my skin and propelled my feet forward.

I needed a knife, something to slash his tyres. Anything sharp would do at this point. I was running out of time. I bolted to the art room, hoping for a small miracle when I turned the door handle. It opened and I dashed straight to the jars of tools on the back bench. Spotting a large pair of black handled scissors, I barely stopped to yank them out before leaving the room.

I jogged around to the front of the school, breaking into a run when I caught sight of Max, Cal, Tyler, and Sean at the end of Cal's car. Tearing across the bitumen park, I scanned the area for Amber.

Max scrunched her hands into her hair, and I aimed my question at her. 'Where is she?' I leaned my hand on the back of the car. My breathing grew rapid, my sudden desperation to save her swallowing me whole. 'Where's Amber?'

Max opened her mouth to speak, but Cal beat her to it. 'She's already gone home. Just left so she could pack before work.'

'Shit.' I squeezed my hands into tight balls and clenched my teeth, shaking my head. Think, Lucy, think. 'Okay, this is going to sound nuts, but I'm in a dream right now. I'm lying on a bed, in your house actually, and I've come back to save Amber.' My eyes bored into Cal's, hoping he, as well as the rest of them would understand the meaning and urgency of my words.

Confusion and shock spread across his face, followed by a dawning realisation. Only one reason would make me come back.

'Where is she? What happened?' His voice trembled, his eyes pleading with mine.

Tears stung the back of my throat. 'He's taken her, or he's about to. We don't have much time. I need you to call the police. But not until I'm there and I've stalled him.'

'I'm coming with you.' Cal stepped toward the front door of his car.

'You can't. It'll scare him off. We can't let him get away because he'll try again. You know he will. Give me ten minutes, then send the cops round.'

Cal pressed a hand to the back of his neck. 'I should've gone with her. I should've kept her safe. If anything happens to her, I'll never forgive myself.'

'Stop. This is all on me.' I turned to Tyler. 'Can you drive me?'

The air clung thick in the car on the two-minute drive to Amber's house. I tapped my fingers on my thigh, the scissors nestled securely in my lap, my pulse raging with adrenalin. Tyler reached over and entwined his calm, sure fingers with mine.

'I don't know what you're planning, but whatever you do, make sure you wake up from this.'

My heart tugged at the trace of fear behind his words, a fear I couldn't think about in this moment, because Amber's house waited right around the bend. 'Pull over here.' I pointed up the road.

Tyler skidded to a stop at the curb. I plucked up the scissors, and before leaving, I placed a palm against his cheek, wanting to somehow ease his worry. 'I will.' I kissed him and opened the door.

Running like I'd never run before, I barrelled around the bend and ducked behind a tree as the van and Amber's house came into view. He already had hold of her, marching with her in his arm across the lawn.

I was too late.

But I couldn't let him get away. No need for stealth anymore, I left the footpath and sprinted down the middle of the road, my arm raised, the scissors poised for impact.

Webb hesitated, glanced down at Amber and back to me, hurtling for his vehicle. His calm façade swiftly shifted to anger, and he dropped Amber onto the lawn.

I lunged for the tyre and rammed the scissors into the black rubber. I wrenched my arm back.

Whack!

The scissors clattered to the ground, and I slammed onto my side on the bitumen.

A shadow blurred over my right shoulder, a black flicker of a shape sensed more than seen, and an urgency to move, to get up and do more damage to the tyres forced its way through me. I pushed up on my arm, screaming in agony and collapsing again.

The scissors, I need the scissors.

A burning fire tore from my shoulder to my head, and I fought against the pain as I sat myself up with my other arm.

My body lurched forward from a force against my back, an arm circling around my waist, pinching my skin, hauling me off the ground.

A hand clasped over my mouth, muffling the sound of my scream. I kicked my legs, smashed my heel into his shin, shoved my head back into his face, but his strength overpowered my determination.

'You're always two steps ahead of me, aren't you?' He carried me to the side of the van and threw me onto my back, towering over me, pinning me down with his knees. His temple pulsated with anger, his warm breath odourless, thanks to my dream. 'Something to do with your creepy accurate drawings, I think. I have no idea how the fuck you did that.'

My legs hung out of the van and I kicked at the air, flailing my forearms as much as I could beneath the overpowering strength trapping them. I shook my head, my eyes watering from the gagging sensation as he tied a cloth around my mouth.

'I'm meticulous with my planning. It's how I've gotten away with this for so long.' Oh my God, Megan really hadn't been his only one. My eyes widened as I stared into the dark recesses in the centre of his ugly face. He yanked the cloth into a knot behind my head. 'Five. I was planning a sixth when you sent the pigs on me again.

'You keep opening your big mouth and calling the fucking cops! Such an unwise move, particularly for your friend.' His crooked sneer, only inches from my face, filled my hazy vision.

He held a cloth to my nose. I had no sense of smell in the dream, but I refused to inhale whatever was on that rag. I held my breath, letting my body go limp and clinging fiercely to my desperation so I wouldn't black out.

The faint but piercing sound of sirens started up. Webb tilted his head, questioning if he'd heard right. My vision blurred, and I could swear I heard Tyler's voice calling my name in the distance.

The dagger of Webb's gaze landed squarely on my chest, and satisfaction crept into my eyes.

'You little bitch!' He curled his left hand into a fist and slammed it into my face.

MY BODY JERKED AS the van sped around a corner, and I landed on my side, a searing pain slicing through the shoulder that'd hit the road. I cracked open my eyes, and pain engulfed me, searing behind my temple.

I placed my hand to my head. Moisture trickled under my fingers and seeped into my eye.

I hefted myself into a sitting position against the wall of the van, muffling out a groan from the fresh agony in my shoulder. I sucked in a stodgy breath around the gag at the sight of Amber sprawled on the floor, eyes closed, backpack still attached to one arm. Her body rolled around the padded floor each time the van jerked sideways.

Panic seized me, tightening around me with the pain. My pulse thudded an erratic rhythm of fear behind my temple.

Breathe, Lucy.

I slumped my head forward, wincing as I failed to lift my left arm to untie the gag on the back of my head. I couldn't do it. Instead, I hooked my fingers where it covered my mouth and yanked it over my chin to hang around my neck.

My ears pricked up at the sound of sirens, but I couldn't tell if it was real or only an echo of the hope raging through me.

Amber stirred, and I scrambled forward on my knees, pressing a finger to my lips and brushing a clump of loose hair off her face. Her eyes widened with horror as she took in our surroundings and sat up, shrugging the backpack off her shoulder.

A black make-shift curtain flapped at the front of the van, shifting enough for us to view Webb behind the wheel, eyes focused on the road, unaware we'd both woken up. The fact neither of us were any more restrained than when he knocked me out, meant he was still trying to outrun the cops. I tilted my head. No sirens. If he'd already outrun them, we were in big trouble.

Lowering myself beside Amber, I clutched her hand and she gripped firm. I had no other way of reassuring her we'd be okay...I didn't know if we would. But I assessed our options all the same. I eyed the back of the van. We could push the door open from the inside and jump. But at the speed we travelled? I shuddered at the thought of broken bones. We could wait it out, hope the cops caught up.

No. I didn't come into this dream to sit around and hope. I came here to stop him and that's what I planned to do.

Amber's school bag caught my eye. I squeezed her fingers and leaned forward, dragging it to me. The van made an abrupt turn, and I flew sideways onto my bad shoulder, biting my lip to stifle my scream.

The burning sensation drove tears to the surface, but I ignored it all, and focused on the backpack. If Amber was as predictable as I hoped, it could literally hold the secret weapon. I held the bag and silently questioned her with my eyes. She frowned, compiling the fragments of everything happening and piecing it together with how that could possibly connect with her bag. She shot her eyes to me, and I didn't flinch, just raised my brows. Is it in there? She closed her eyes with a nod.

Stilling my breath, I slid the zip one notch at a time. If he heard me, we were screwed. It opened enough for me to stick my hand in and feel around.

Bingo.

I gripped my clammy fingers around the handle of Amber's cupcake knife and slid it out. Holding Amber's stare for a moment, I nodded and bolted from my place on the floor. Moving quickly, I had no time to acknowledge the pain in my shoulder as I swept the black curtain aside, but enough time for me to get into position and aim.

I shoved the blade into the side of Webb's right arm, a furious cry bellowing from my throat as I rammed it in deep. Webb spun his deathly glare on me, crimson blood spurting onto my fingers as I clenched the knife to tug it free. Webb's arm twisted and he slammed his hand into the side of my eye. My head lurched sideways and I yelled out, releasing my hold on the knife still wedged in his arm. He grabbed my wrist, latching himself to me and digging his thumb in. Shooting pain ran up my arm and forced out another agonising scream, cut short when my body flew across the van.

Upside down, tumbling. I smashed into the roof, the floor, the walls. Everything collapsed, turned in on itself, my body being destroyed like an ice cube in a cocktail. The spinning lasted for an eternity – over and over and over – an explosion of pain tearing through every limb with each blow, until the van jerked to a sudden and deafening stop.

SIRENS. LIGHTS FLASHING. BLACK, red, black, blue.

Pain. Blunt and excruciating torture.

Blood. My forehead warmed with the wet sensation of it trickling across my skin.

Amber. Where is she?

'Amber?' Slowly, I moved my head to search her out. 'Amber.'

A bright light from outside lit up the space around me and Amber's unmoving form a few feet away. I raised my arm, reaching for her, but not close enough.

'Amber, please wake up.' I kept my hand outstretched for hers, a numbing ache hovering over me at her lifeless body. 'Don't you dare die on me.'

Reality tugged at me, my life prodding me awake.

My life, but what about Amber's! No, I couldn't leave yet.

I fought to stay in my dream, my heart rate escalating to a speed of gut-wrenching fear and expectation. I'd never altered my own life. What came next? The fear of the unknown tightened around my throat. This wasn't how it was supposed to turn out.

'Amber, wake up.'

The blinding light streamed in through the front window, my vision narrowed – my dream right along with it.

—34—

'Lucy?'

Mum?

'Lucy, honey, are you awake?' Soft fingers tightened around mine. No strength to squeeze, I settled for a wriggle. 'I'm here, sweetie.'

My eyelids fluttered open, and Mum's face filled my entire view. Artificial light from above penetrated my eyes, and I squeezed them closed as tears brimmed at the corners and pain seared behind my temple.

'Mum?' I croaked, opening my eyes to take in the tiny hospital cubicle. Pale green curtains hung on either side of me, machines beeped behind me. Mum sat on the side of the bed, and I shuffled to prop myself up. Pain ricocheted from my right ankle, and I collapsed onto my pillow with a cry.

'You're in pain.' I don't think I'd ever understood the meaning of the word until now. Mum pressed the call button behind the bed. 'You're due some more meds.'

Along with the pain in my leg, a persistent throb drove into my temple. My face felt five times its usual size. My fingers trembled as I raised them to my forehead where a small bandage fit snugly at my hairline. Lowering them to the hollow below my eye where Webb's fist had connected with my skin, I sucked in a hiss through my teeth. That bruise would be a rich shade of purple by now.

'What happened?' I struggled to grasp at the reality surrounding me. The lines in my brow deepened, my confusion only making my head hurt more. My left arm, encased in thick bandages, ached in a way that almost didn't feel like it was part of me anymore.

'Oh, honey.' She wiped at my tears with her thumb. 'You were in an accident.'

Accident? My eyes flung open, searching hers. 'Where's Amber?' My chest tightened. I killed her. 'Please tell me she's okay?'

Mum rested a hand on my good cheek. 'She's okay. She fared better than you, a couple of broken ribs and a sprained wrist, she'll be fine. You on the other hand.'

'I'm worse than that?'

'Much. You've got a broken collarbone, you had ten stiches to the laceration on your forehead, and you've been unconscious since they pulled you out of the wreck. We've been so worried. I've never been more scared in my life.'

'When?' I croaked the word out.

'It's three pm. The accident was yesterday afternoon.'

'And Webb...I mean...the man, what happened to him?'

Mum's lids closed for a moment. 'He died at the scene.'

My heart didn't miss a beat, not a shred of sadness for the man who'd destroyed so many lives. 'Good.'

A nurse stepped into the small space at the end of the bed. 'So good to see you awake, Lucy.' I groaned. 'How about we get you another dose of meds for the pain?'

Time shifted by in a fog. Dad rushed in with Jake and Ollie as soon as Mum called him, the nurses monitored my vitals, and once the doctor checked on me, he was confident to have me moved from the ICU to a regular room.

I gasped when they wheeled me into a room where Amber sat somewhat comfortably propped up on her own bed, holding hands with Cal. The benefits of staying in the hospital where your mum and friend's mum worked – sharing a room with your friend.

'Lucy,' Cal said, jumping to his feet to stand beside my bed. His eyes scanned my bruised face. 'I'd hug you, but I don't want to hurt you.'

'I'd hug you too, but I don't want to move.' I lifted my lips instead.

'You scared the crap out of us,' he said.

An overwhelming sadness settled over me at the events I'd put in motion and all I'd put my friends through. 'I'm sorry.'

'Don't be sorry.' Cal's eyes speared me with a warning, serious, yet still kind. 'But don't ever do that again. Any of it.'

'I'll try to remember that next time,' I said, with a reassuring slant in my lips that said, 'there won't be a next time'.

It grew late. The pain medication became my friend, I ate half the food brought in for me, and visiting hours ended. Cal left, as did any hope I'd been holding that I might see Tyler before the day ended.

The light in the room dimmed, and I eased my head to face Amber. 'I'm sorry.'

Tears shone in her eyes and she shook her head, but there was no way I couldn't give her this apology.

'I'm sorry, I've never been more sorry for anything in my life. I thought I could save you all. The girls *and* you. I thought it would be okay.' My lip quivered, the fullness of my words and how much I meant them pouring through me. 'You're one of my best friends. I never should've valued their lives above yours.'

'You didn't. Just because you wanted to save them doesn't mean you wanted this for me. One doesn't counter out your care for the other. You cared for us all, and that's okay. You're one of the kindest, selfless people I know, I'm not sure you know of any other way.'

'If I hadn't been able to save you, if you had died, or things had turned out differently, I'm not sure it would've been worth the risk.' I closed my eyes, contemplating it. 'No, I know it wouldn't have been.'

'I'm just so glad we're both okay.'

'Me too. And even though it worked out this time, I think it's time for me to accept I can't save everyone.'

My empathy might roar louder than others, and my imaginings of a better world gave me the ability to save lives, but I would never place the kind of expectations I shouldered onto anyone else. It was time to loosen the binding pressure I'd tightened around myself.

*****

MAX'S LAUGHTER TRICKLED DOWN the hospital corridor, and tears clouded my eyes as my friends spilled into our small hospital room – Max, Sean, Cal. The faces of those I loved crowded my view, making it difficult to locate the one face I desperately needed to see – Tyler's.

My chest tightened with the wanting, my heart pounding from within, shouting 'where is he, where is he'. My eyes darted around the faces, and then he stepped from behind them. He stopped when he saw me, as did my heart. The room quieted; sounds slipped away, but maybe that was just me.

Tyler's gaze held mine, locked together in the strongest hold they'd ever been in, incapable and refusing to let go. Max shifted to the direction of my attention and seeing Tyler, moved aside to allow him through. I wanted to run to him, but incapacitated as I was, I settled for watching the boy of my dreams stride across the room and ease himself onto the side of my bed. He brushed his fingers against the good side of my face, wiped the tears under my eyes and closed his mouth delicately over mine. I inhaled his scent, grounding me to the here and now, to my safety, and reminding me how close I came to a death there was no coming back from.

'Am I dreaming?' he asked, peering into my glistening eyes. I shook my head as much as I could. 'Are you?'

'Not anymore.'

'When did it stop?'

Casting my mind back, recalling reality and dream, distinguishing one from the other. And this time, for me at least, the dream became the reality, and the part before, only a nightmare that'd now never happened. 'Just after the crash. Before they pulled us from the wreckage.'

'I thought I'd lost you. When I heard you scream, saw him throw you into the van, I've never run so hard in my life.'

I *had* heard his voice.

'It didn't turn out quite how I planned.'

'You think?' He laughed and I started, only to stop for the pain in my head.

*****

GRANNY TESS DRAGGED HER chair closer to the bed. Mum had stepped from the room with Pop, and we were alone. 'I think you're kind of incredible,' she said, leaning forward.

I twisted my fingers together in my lap. 'I just did what any friend would do.'

'You know that's not true. It takes a special person to know something's about to happen before it does.' Granny Tess searched my eyes. How did she know? 'Your dad told me.'

I gulped. 'Dad?'

'The one and only.' The curtain swung away, and Dad strode in with a coffee in each hand, his face bursting into a grin. 'You're sitting up.' He handed me a cup.

I lifted it to my lips, the strong scent of coffee making my stomach churn, or maybe the fact it felt like they knew more than they were letting on. I passed it to Granny Tess to put on the table.

Dad settled onto the edge of a seat, the tenderness in his eyes reassuring me, telling me I could trust them. 'How?' I whispered out on a breath.

'I dreamt it too.' Dad dragged his seat up alongside Granny Tess. 'But unlike you, I can't go back as easily to change things, no matter how hard I try sometimes. But I dreamt what happened to Amber the night she was taken, and when I woke, I had two memories; that one and this one. There's only one way that could have happened.'

'He would have killed her, I'm sure of it. I had to do something.'

'And thank God you did.' Granny Tess raised her eyes to the ceiling.

I grasped hold of her trembling fingers. 'But do you? Do you thank God?' She'd admitted many times that her belief didn't quite fit into the traditional God mould.

'I thank whatever helped bring you back, dear. Be that God, the universe, goodness, divine intervention, fate, it doesn't matter, so long as I'm thankful. And I am...We all are.'

Tears prickled behind my eyes. 'So am I. I don't know who or what to, but I'm thankful as well.' I turned to Dad. 'Does Mum know?'

'I've been acting strange, so she knows something unusual has happened, but she doesn't know what. She doesn't want or need to know more than that.' Dad paused, coming to terms yet again with the realisation he'd never have more than that himself. 'All that matters to her now is that you're okay.'

When it came time for her to leave, Granny Tess held me for a fraction longer than normal.

'I'm so proud of you,' she whispered in my hair. 'I can't take any of the credit, but –'

I cut her off, shaking my head. 'Yes, you can. You've only ever shown me love. This' – I placed a hand on my heart – 'all comes down to that.'

* * * * *

'M AN, I CAN'T BELIEVE how lucky I am,' Tyler said as we lay together on my bed after being discharged two days later. With his head propped in one hand, he traced his fingers delicately across my face, avoiding the cuts and bruises.

'You and me both.' I diverted my eyes away, the harrowing memory of how close I came to death smashing into me once again.

'You're amazing, you know that?' Tyler gazed down at me before adding, 'And beautiful.'

I huffed out a laugh. 'That comes as an afterthought?'

'At the moment, yes. I mean you're always beautiful.' His grin took over his entire face, lifting his cheeks, lighting his dark eyes. 'But I can't get the image of you, the serial killer slayer, out of my head.'

'Way to ruin a moment, Tyler.' I shoved his arm and he fell against me. I hissed from the pain in my shoulder and Tyler muttered an apology. 'That's an image I can't get out of my head either!'

'Ah bugger, yeah, sorry.' He laughed. 'Would you like me to go back to the part about you being beautiful?'

'That would be better, yes.'

'Well, these, right here.' His fingertips skimmed the creases beside my mouth. 'Are beautiful when you smile. And your eyes... stunning. They were the first thing I loved about you when I saw you in my dreams.' My cheeks warmed beneath his unhidden adoration as he lowered to meet my lips. Hot, sweet and tender. And like our subconsciousness's had done – they became one – two pieces of a puzzle that belonged together. His taste ignited a fire deep in my core I feared might never stop burning, but then I never wanted it to either. His hand drifted around my neck and, avoiding my bandaged arm, down to my lower back, gathering me close. I raised my good arm and ran my fingers onto the back of his neck. I was his and he was mine.

Our lips parted, and Tyler pressed his forehead against mine with a contented sigh. '*Je t'aime*. I love you.'

My forehead crinkled beneath his, recalling the words we'd exchanged in the reality I'd erased. 'I know. You told me already.'

Tyler drew back. 'What? When?'

'Before I went into the dream and saved Amber.'

'And what did you say when I said that to you?'

'I said I loved you too.'

His mouth turned up in a broad smile, the lines at the edges of his eyes rising, making their depth more visible.

'Good. And did you mean it, or was it only 'cause you thought you might die?'

'I meant it.' I huffed out a laugh. 'Did you?'

Pressing his brow into a deep furrow, he tilted his head. 'That's hard to say...considering I can't remember it, but I'm going to say yes.'

My heart did a somersault. 'When did you know?'

'I think it started in my dreams, those little tastes of something that felt so real.' He paused, his eyes closing for a moment. 'Then when I saw you and found out you actually were real, it knocked the breath right out of me. But I think it was our first dream. That's when I knew you meant more to me than...well...more than anything else.'

—35—

I SAT ON MY bed, back against the wall, feet dangling off the side, my usual comforts of pencil and paper in hand. No fresh faces to draw, so I indulged in the opportunity to sketch some that I didn't normally make time to draw – my friends.

A week after returning from the hospital I still hadn't had any dreams. I wasn't sure if it was coincidence, or because everyone seemed determined to keep me away from the news and the news away from me. Part of me wanted to jump back on the bike, see if I could still keep my balance, but another part of me quite liked the relief from the pressure of anything more than my own recovery.

Dad stuck his head around the door and offered a couple of taps to ask if he could come in. I'd talked endlessly with him when I first came home from the hospital; about the plane, Webb, and my actions that'd spiralled into that life-changing event ten days ago.

The mattress bounced as he sat on the edge of the bed. 'How you doing, love?'

'I'm fine.' The reality of all I'd been through still settled over me, still gripped me with tortuous visions at times, but I was alive. I'd nearly died. Nothing on this side of that knife edge would ever be anything other than perfectly fine.

Dad's brow arched, unconvinced.

'Really, I am.' I chuckled at his doubt. 'You know this has actually been good for me.'

He laughed with me. 'In what way, shape or form is getting abducted and being in a high-speed car accident good for you?'

'In the way that it's helped me realise the consequences aren't my responsibility. Like, everything we do has some kind of ripple effect right, you give the homeless man a burger to eat thinking it helps him out, but what if it gives him food poisoning. Would you still give him the burger? Of course. Without knowing the repercussions, good or bad, you can only act on what you know. He's hungry and *you* have the power to help him. If we're acting out of kindness, there shouldn't ever be guilt for what comes after.

'I saved that plane full of people. If I'd known it would cause the death of those girls, would I still do it? No question, because at the time, that was the right choice. Calling the police was the wrong one, I know that now. I tried to control too much; I thought it was my responsibility.'

'Hindsight is a wonderful thing.'

'Or not. It's just lucky Amber's alive, or the hindsight would've eaten me alive.'

'So, you're relinquishing some of the control?'

'Only the bits that are out of my hands, yes. Like what happens after I do my good deed.'

'And the dreams you have?'

I flashed him a look that said 'you're kidding?'

'Dad, I've never been able to control that. I gave up a long time ago.'

'Have you had any dreams since the accident?'

My shoulders sagged. 'No. I'm parts relieved and parts anxious. The news always had a way of finding me before, so it's a bit weird. But I'm relinquishing control. It'll happen when it needs to.'

Dad shifted on the bed, sliding his phone from the back pocket of his jeans. He hesitated. 'I think it needs to.' Uncertainty hinged on his voice, and I nodded, conveying the permission he needed. He tapped on the screen and read. A news story of a woman, who'd been killed while chasing her frightened dog after it ran onto the road during a storm. A mum to three small children whose life had ended prematurely on a dark and wet night on a quiet road, doing something instinctively natural to get her beloved dog back.

'Give that here.' I snatched the phone from Dad's fingers and re-read the words from the news article.

She didn't need to die – she wouldn't have to.

That night my dreams came back. My desire to save the frizzy-haired lady, with the adorable but frightened little mate, added fuel to the simmering coals waiting dormant since my ordeal. They returned with full force over the coming weeks, saving first, Jane with the dog, a builder on a treacherous ladder, and close second on my most proud of silent achievements, a dozen teens from a suicide bomber on an inner-city street in Perth.

*****

THE SOUND OF BEEPING stirred me from my empty sleep. I reached blindly for my phone on the bedside table.

Tyler: *Happy Birthday! Are you up?*

I rubbed at my eyes and wiped at the hair in my face.

Me: *Am now*
Tyler: *Good. Meet me on the hill? I have a surprise*
Me: *What? Now?? It's Monday*

I shoved the covers back and sat.

Tyler: *It's your birthday. You're not up, are you?*
Me: *Feet on the floor*

With a wide yawn, I swivelled until my toes touched the carpet.

Tyler: *Feet up the hill in an hour. Don't eat breakfast. Love you!*

A smile spread all the way to my eyes, and I climbed into the shallow bath. I still couldn't have a shower, thanks to the sling for my broken collarbone restricting any movement in my shoulder. But still, I revelled at how quickly life had returned to normal. Two weeks ago I'd been in hospital, and now I barely noticed the pain in my ankle, the bruise by my eye was a light shade of yellow, and the stitches had been removed from my forehead. I ran my hand over the nasty-looking scar that remained.

There hadn't been enough time to ease the feeling of being watched or settle my nerves whenever I left the house though. But I made myself get out, to do everything I'd always done despite the fear resonating in my guts.

I dressed and hobbled down the stairs. Mum stood at the stove flipping pancakes.

'Happy birthday, honey.'

'Thanks,' I said with a smile that came as easy as my love for Tyler. I plonked into a seat at the table. 'Can you please do my laces?' I hated needing help for the simplest tasks, but the way Mum rushed from the kitchen to assist told me she didn't mind at all.

Mum knelt in front of me and tied my shoes. 'Where are you going?' she asked, her brow furrowing in concern as she returned to the kitchen.

'Tyler wants to meet me on the hill. He said not to eat. You don't mind, do you?'

'No, that's lovely. Ollie will be happy. More for him.' She smiled, glancing down at the pan, before her good spirits fell away and her concern returned. 'You're not worried going out on your own?' It hadn't slipped her notice that the only time I'd gone out since the accident had been with Tyler by my side. But I didn't have him there because I was scared; I had him there because I could.

Did it mean I didn't feel afraid? Hell no. You don't confront death like that without thoughts of it creeping into every part of your day.

But there are moments in our life when the things we were once afraid of don't exist anymore. Like the realisation that the frightening monsters under the bed were never there all along, that they only lived in our head. I think most of our fears are like that. The odds of the plane going down are next to nothing, the white van isn't likely to have a serial killer lurking behind its doors, but we fear these things and they're the stronger of the forces when we battle the rationality in our minds. I fought with the force stronger than anyone, I'd seen it all, had borne witness to the realities of these fears. Come face to face with it when I'd been thrown in the back of that van. But it hadn't beaten me then, and I wouldn't let it now.

'No. I'm perfectly fine, Mum.'

She sighed and kissed me on the head as I hugged her on my way out.

It was a struggle not to run, but with my ankle only just healed and my shoulder still a way to go, I needed to refrain from the urge. Tyler stood waiting for me at the bottom of the path before the road turned into dirt track. He paced the ground as I strolled up the hill toward him.

'Hello?' It was more a question than a greeting, a 'why are you here'? I wasn't used to him waiting for me on this side of the bush.

He pressed a quick kiss on my cheek. 'I have a surprise.'

I smiled. 'You said that already.'

'So, I need your eyes and ears closed for this.'

'Really?' I scrunched up my face and he laughed.

'Yep. Earphones in and music right up, please. And...the surprise will be even surprisier –'

'Surprisier?' I cocked my neck and laughed.

'Yes, it will be *surprisier* if your eyes are closed. But only right at the end. I'll tell you when.'

I placed my headphones in and reached into my pocket to turn up the volume. The sweet harmony of Sleeping at Last's version of 'Never Tear Us Apart', seeped through me. Hooking my good arm through Tyler's, we ambled slowly up the path until we were almost there, and he turned to me with a nod. I closed my eyes and angled into his side as he led me along. My heart accelerated, partly from the anticipated excitement of the surprise, but also the sensory block-out. I pressed harder into him.

He stopped and tugged on my hand, my eyes still closed, the music filling my mind through the mini speakers in my ears. I had no time to process anything before his mouth was on mine, his hands on my cheeks, and everything but that moment vanished. He stepped back and the wind whipped past my face making the heat on my lips prickle under the breeze. Tyler's face remained close to mine, his fingers sliding to my ears and removing my earphones before he whispered, 'Open your eyes.'

I fluttered my lids open and saw him, only him. Then he steered me to the fence and the familiar view, and –

'Oh.' I clasped a hand to my mouth – the cows were back. I spun and faced him, his proud smile deepening the dimple on his chin. 'What? How?' I glanced back at the paddock, at the six cows grazing on the hill.

'Let's just say Dad's easily persuaded. Plus, he's always been a big romantic, so once I told him my reasons, he couldn't say no.'

'I was your reason?'

'You'll always be my reason.' He twined his fingers through mine. 'C'mon.' We climbed through the wire and wandered down the slope where a picnic blanket laid in the grass.

'You brought breakfast up here?' I couldn't wipe the euphoria off my face.

We settled onto the blanket across from one another with the length of our legs touching. Tyler reached into a bag and revealed a thermos. 'And coffee.'

'You really are the boy of my dreams.'

His shoulders shook with laughter as he poured the steaming brown liquid into a plastic cup. 'If I'd known all it'd take was cows and coffee, I'd have done this way sooner.' He handed me the cup.

Holding it snugly in my fingers, I gazed out at the cows, their heads bent low eating the thick green stalks of grass, and back up to Tyler as he reached into the picnic basket for strawberries, a couple tubs of yoghurt and – our *favourite* – peanut butter chocolate cupcakes.

'Happy birthday,' he said, passing me a cake.

My heart soared, because no matter what I'd gone through, in that moment I felt like the luckiest girl in the world.

*****

3 WEEKS LATER:

I PULLED THE CAR to the rear of the lake house, turned off the ignition, and shifted toward Tyler with a large grin spread across my face.

'Ready?' he asked.

'Yep.' I reached for his hand. 'You?'

Tyler's face softened. 'More than you know.' He leaned over the middle console and closed his lips over mine.

Climbing from the car, I allowed myself to absorb the beauty around me. The scent of eucalyptus from the gum trees filled the air, a honeyeater hopped from branch to branch in a tree by the side of the house, and the brilliance of the blue sky framing our home away from home made my shoulders relax and insides calm instantly. I startled at the slam of the boot, and Tyler stepped alongside me with our bags, taking hold of my hand.

I heaved open the large door, and we shuffled into the warmth of the lake house. The smell of the roast pork we enjoyed each year for Richie's birthday, drifted from the oven, welcoming us into the home. Marie hurried across the room, an apron tied around her waist, smiling with a mouth full of food and hands covered in what looked like some kind of dough, gesturing for us to 'Come in'.

'Hey, you made it!' Max called from the kitchen, and Amber poked her head out from behind the cake she was working on, a grin radiating on her face.

I returned her smile. 'It's Richie's birthday – have I missed one yet?' He'd have been nineteen tomorrow.

'Not one, and we're glad about it.' Cal landed on the couch.

Tyler dropped our bags in the corner as I scanned the room. 'Where's Sean?'

'He's helping Dad bring up wood for the fire.'

'And what are you doing, lazy bones?'

'Getting my shoes on.' His face screwed up and he stuck out his tongue before bending to tie his laces.

'I'll come too.' Tyler planted a kiss on my cheek and followed Cal out the large glass doors and down toward the shed. Warmth radiated where the feel of his lips remained.

'You guys are so cute,' Amber said.

'So are you two.' I stepped up to her and wound my arms around her stomach, laying my head on her back. Max did the same behind me until we must've looked like a family of koalas. 'I love you, girls. Have I told you that lately?'

'Only every day since the accident, hon,' Max said, her half-groan rumbling onto my back.

'But we're not complaining,' Amber cut in. 'We love you too.' And she spun with her spatula full of dark chocolate ganache and smeared it across my cheek.

'Hey!' I swiped at the blob and stuck my finger in my mouth. 'Ooh, yum.'

THE SUN HUNG LOW in the bronze skyline, its rays shimmering on the surface of the water like crystal glass. I stood on the deck, the grassy bank and lake below me. A magpie flew overhead, taking refuge in a gumtree at the water's edge. Its familiar gargled song filled the air with the sound of home.

'Hey, you.' I jumped at Tyler's approach, but his tender embrace from behind eased me back down to earth. 'What you lookin' at?' he asked, resting his chin on my shoulder.

I pointed to the tree. 'The maggie. I love the sound they make, I'm gonna miss that when we're gone.'

'Yes, but you'll get to hear...hang on, what sort of birds do they have in Canada?'

I laughed. 'I have no idea.'

'Well, you will soon.'

'Seven months does not feel like soon,' I said.

'Tell me about it, but I really would like to learn to snowboard on the less intimidating slopes here first.'

'How many times do I have to tell you, you're going to be great. I know this, remember?'

'So you keep saying.' He kissed the side of my neck and the strap of my little black bikini. I twisted to catch his lips with mine and relished in the taste and feel of him that I could never get enough of. This was home.

'You two quite ready?' Cal called from the grass. Tyler's mouth lingered before we separated and laughed. He grabbed my hand and we dashed down the steps to meet the rest of our crew. The people who I'd never forget stepped up to the demanding challenge of being my friends this last year. They'd believed me when it would've been easier to keep their heads in the sand. I'd needed them when I'd been drowning, and not only did they stand beside me, they picked me up and carried me to higher ground. Tears welled in my eyes as I took my place and scanned the row of them all, dressed in their swimming attire, ready for our mid-autumn plunge.

'Ready now,' I said, my heart calm and content.

'Thank God for that,' Sean joked, humour in his eyes.

'You two are worse than Amber and I were when we first got together.' He wrapped his fingers around hers.

Max fake-heaved. 'That is so not possible.' Our laughter echoed across the wide expanse of water: calm, expectant...a place of dreams.

'All right, everyone ready?' I shouted, locking eyes with Tyler. He answered with a firm squeeze around my fingers. I stepped my foot forward, poised to take flight. 'Set...Fly!'

And fly I would. Because one of the most powerful realisations for me as I'd surrendered my control and returned to my night-time vigilante escapades, was that even if I didn't know how the wings worked, or where the flight would take me, I wanted that wind in my hair, no matter how many tangles might turn up later.

This understanding turned my outlook into one of exquisite clarity, and I came to view the possibility of how great things could be instead of fearing how bad it might become. I'd always believed Queen Victoria wore black because she was so focused on the death, but maybe she wore it to be reminded of how good it had been – how good it *could* be.

For too many years I'd been blinded by the constant shadow of death – and more recently the darker shadow of the consequences of life; and although it showed no sign of leaving, I chose to lift my eyes to the flicker of light just beyond the edge of the darkness. And ever-so-softly, like the sunrise over the sea, my world turned into a luminous reflection of hope.

Acknowledgements

People say writing a second book is hard, and whilst that is true, this one rode on the back of *Lucid* and was so much fun to get back into and revisit characters I'd grown to love. It has evolved over the course of its life and that's thanks to my editors and many of the early readers who helped shape it into the story it's become. I don't have quite so many people to thank this time round, bit like a second child, it all just comes together a little bit easier, with a bit less help from those around you.

The writing of this book feels like it has two sides to it. It was written pre contract, when I was blissfully unaware of the mistakes I was making, just enjoying the writing of the story. And the other side, post *Lucid*, when I had readers and I'd become a part of the local writing community. And although this book was written while I only had myself to push me forward, it has come into the finish with a lot of support and cheering from both my readers and some newly dear writers.

I'm so thankful for the friendship I have made with local writers Poppy Nwosu and Sue Morgan. It was a friendship formed while we were all releasing our debut books, and in the lonely world of writing it's pretty special to find people who understand what that feels like. And when they're as lovely as this lot, even better. It's a crazy and emotional ride and they helped get me through it with wine, arancini balls and the occasional fervent email.

This book is dedicated to my husband Joe; my reason. He was my first love and he'll be my last. Our family is what it is because of the tireless work he does to provide for us, and because of that, he's also the reason this book was possible. Thank you for everything.

To my daughter, Ajah, *Luminous*'s very first reader. Thank you for your encouragement and never failing to tell me when you didn't like something. I hope you enjoy the second read, which is only a little bit {cough} different from the first version. Please don't hate me for what I did to a couple of your favourite characters.

To my boys, Marley & Oskar. I don't know when you'll get around to reading this book, maybe when you finish reading *Lucid* {wink, wink}. And when you do, you'll be able to see some of the conversations my characters were having in my head all the times you spoke to me and I didn't listen. Thanks for sharing me with my world of make believe.

Lyn Steele, my mum, is one of my biggest supporters, always keen to read my new stories, but that's what a mum is for right. She is the absolute best cheerleader, always thrilled with each piece of exciting news, big or small. Her positivity and belief in my ability to see this out has never wavered and for that I'm always grateful. Thanks Mum.

To my mother-in-law Judith, and her critical eye and knowledge. For reading *Luminous* and helping with some important specifics of one scene, which although minor, means I have faith that the details are correct. If they're not, it's my fault. Thank you for your constant encouragement, and for your son.

I didn't have as many early or along the way readers for this book, but I'm thankful and appreciate the few I did have. Jessica Cassada; emails from overseas to tell me I kept you past your bedtime are the best to wake up to. Kate Bradley; better late than never, and with an excuse like Erica, you'll always be forgiven. Stephanie Childs; I'm so happy you laughed at the Batman bit. My sister, Naomi Buick; I keep making you read books, and the fact you got through this one when you were so unwell means a lot.

Huge thanks must also go to my editors, Kate Foster and

Rebecca Carpenter. Kate, you are truly incredible at seeing what's not quite right in my stories. Thanks for waving your magic wand over my story and being a wonderful support and sounding board. Rebecca, thank you for polishing my sentences and adding sparkle to my words. I'll forever be grateful that my books and I found you both.

A special thanks and big love to my dearest friends, Amanda, Rachael, and Amy, who remind me that there's more to life than just writing, and who regularly drag me out of my isolation for movies and binge watching T.V. series. Your support and friendship mean the world.

To everyone who has read *Lucid* and left a review somewhere online, or shared my book with a friend, thank you a thousand times. Reviews and word of mouth are the best form of advertising for a small writer like me, and I appreciate them all. If the sequel was all you hoped for, maybe you'll consider leaving a review for this one too.

About the Author

Kristy Fairlamb is an Australian author of young adult novels with high stakes and heart. She enjoys spending her days drinking coffee and torturing her characters with loads of tension – both love related and the nail biting kind.

Long before her days of writing began, she spent half her childhood in a make believe world, daydreaming about growing up, falling in love, and travelling the world.

She's worked as a nanny in country England, a junior matron in a boy's boarding school south of London, a governess in East Timor, and made coffees and cleared tables in the New South Wales snow fields.

She lives with her husband, teenage daughter, and two sons in the beautiful Adelaide Hills where they're lucky enough to get occasional visits from the local koalas.

She's terrible at gardening, likes her bookshelves sorted by colour, and recently checked off a lifelong dream of jumping from a plane.

When she's not writing or daydreaming about her stories you'll find her reading, cooking for her family, or doing anything to avoid the housework.

To keep up to date with Kristy's author news visit her website:
kristyfairlamb.com
On Facebook: KristyFairlambAuthor
On Instagram: kristyfairlambwriter
On Twitter: @kristy_fairlamb

Lightning Source UK Ltd.
Milton Keynes UK
UKHW031509260520
363905UK00003B/414

9 780648 7